Murder Most Fowl

Books by Edith Maxwell

A TINE TO LIVE, A TINE TO DIE

'TIL DIRT DO US PART

FARMED AND DANGEROUS

MURDER MOST FOWL

Published by Kensington Publishing Corporation

Murder
Most Fowl

EDITH
MAXWELL

KENSINGTON BOOKS
www.kensingtonbooks.com

KENSINGTON BOOKS are published by

Kensington Publishing Corp.
119 West 40th Street
New York, NY 10018

All Kensington titles, imprints and distributed lines are available at special quantity discounts for bulk purchases for sales promotion, premiums,
fund-raising, educational or institutional use. Special book excerpts or
customized printings can also be created to fit specific needs. For details, write or phone the office of the Kensington Special Sales Man-
ager: Kensington Publishing Corp., 119 West 40th Street, New York,
NY, 10018. Attn. Special Sales Department. Phone: 1-800-221-2647.

Kensington and the K logo Reg. U.S. Pat. & TM Off.

Library of Congress Card Catalogue Number: 2015958946

ISBN-13: 978-1-4967-0025-4
ISBN-10: 1-4967-0025-2
First Kensington Hardcover Edition: June 2016

eISBN-13: 978-1-4967-0026-1
eISBN-10: 1-4967-0026-0
First Kensington Electronic Edition: June 2016

10 9 8 7 6 5 4 3 2 1

Printed in the United States of America

To small organic farmers everywhere, for working incredibly hard to provide us with delicious healthy food.

Acknowledgments

Once again I am grateful to so many for helping me get this book into the hands of readers. My Wicked Cozy partners in crime—Jessie Crockett/Jessica Estevao, Sherry Harris, Julie Hennrikus/Julianne Holmes, Liz Mugavero/Kate Conte, and Barb Ross—you're the best, and I couldn't imagine traveling this path without you. My agent, John Talbot, my editor at Kensington, John Scognamiglio, and the entire Kensington team who make it happen: thank you. The Monday Night Salem Writers' Group heard some of this book and much improved it with their spot-on critiques, with special thanks to Sam Sherman for the idea of giving Greta more depth via Harry Potter. Sheila Connolly helped with the Irish dialect, and I totally stole the name of her Irish pub in her County Cork mystery series. Sherry Harris once again expertly edited the manuscript before I turned it in, and helped me get the last suspense scene up to snuff (in several iterations).

Sisters in Crime both locally and nationally, Guppies, the New England chapter of Mystery Writers of America, locavores, farmers, and faithful readers everywhere: I'm living my dream and it's thanks to you. Particular thanks to fellow Guppy E. R. Dillon, who came up with the fabulous title! I also thank Amesbury Police Detective Kevin Donovan for ongoing consultations about police procedure.

Several decades ago I used to attend West Newbury town meeting, and I used those memories for scenes in this book. I particularly want to acknowledge inspiration from Deborah Hamilton and KC Swallow. You'll recognize yourselves, I think.

Acknowledgments

As ever, I thank my two wonderful sons, Allan and John David, for help with details about people their age (including Postmodern Jukebox), information about chickens and farming, and most of all, for their love and unfailing enthusiasm for my work. To Hugh—who doesn't even read fiction—thanks and love, always.

And if you like the story, posting a positive review somewhere is a great way to help authors.

Chapter 1

"*Beware the ides of March.*" Shakespeare might have been onto something, Cam Flaherty mused. She and half the registered voters of Westbury had been sitting in the March fifteenth town meeting for seven hours on the first warmish Saturday since October. Instead of perching on a hard wooden chair listening to desperate townies and intransigent newcomers slug it out over priorities for the small semirural town, Cam could have been on her organic farm pruning the grapevines, blueberry bushes, and her one apple tree.

But she was trying to be a good citizen, and these were important issues, particularly the questions of open space and affordable housing. The newbies, almost all highly educated men and women with families, commuted the hour into Boston or Burlington to earn the kind of income that enabled them not only to buy expensive McMansions near the Merrimack River but also to live on one salary while the children were young. The locals were almost all hardworking folks holding down at least one job apiece. Their families had lived in town for generations but now could barely afford to pay the property taxes on their homes, and there was little affordable rental property available, either.

The current topic to be voted on had been under discussion for two hours, and it was now past three o'clock. The question on the table was what to do with a newly acquired parcel of land: preserve it as open space for walkers and wildlife, build soccer and baseball fields, or erect low-cost apartments. The air inside the hall was way too warm, and smelled of wood over a century old. The gray-haired woman next to Cam snoozed quietly in her seat, head on her chest, hands folded neatly on her ample midsection.

Wayne Laitinen stood patiently in line for the public microphone, his plaid flannel shirt tucked neatly into clean blue jeans, his thin blond hair combed straight back from his forehead. The slender woman in front of him, who'd expressed her view that an extreme injustice would be done to the children of the town if new state-of-the art soccer fields were not created, finally sat down.

"Wayne Laitinen, eighty-five Stone Mill Road. Madam Moderator, Selectmen, my Westbury neighbors." He turned and waved behind him to the right, and did it again to the left. He returned his face toward the stage and the tables full of selectmen, school committee members, the town clerk and town counsel, and the petite moderator standing at the podium. "Most of you know I'm a farmer. My wife, Greta, and me own thirty-six acres for ourselves and our chickens. Lots of it is wooded, and the rest grows a new crop of rocks every spring."

Spots of laughter broke out throughout the audience, although a young couple in front of Cam turned to each other with quizzical looks. Cam knew the effect the winter frost heaves produced. In about a month her land would appear very much as though the soil she'd carefully cleared of any stone bigger than her fingertip the summer before suddenly sprouted a new harvest of rocks, golf-ball sized and up. Cam glanced around for Greta Laitinen and spied her across the hall, plump arms folded, frizzy strawberry blond hair barely tamed, mouth clamped in a grim line.

Wayne went on. "We work hard for our livin'. Haven't had a vacation away since our honeymoon twenty-eight years ago. We love Westbury. Our family's been here a few generations. But my son can't afford to buy a house for his wife and his family. My daughter's a teacher at the Page School, and she can't rent in town, because there ain't no decent rental properties. Me and Greta barely make our taxes, neither. I ain't complainin,' but if we have the chance to help our long-time residents stay right here in town, I think we should do it. Let's build housin' stock our kids can afford. Hell, that we can afford. Thank you." He turned and made his way back to his seat amid a roar of applause. Not everyone clapped.

Why didn't Wayne offer a parcel of his own land to his son for building a house on? Cam assumed he had his reasons. Or maybe the son didn't want to live that close. Families were complicated.

The woman in line behind Wayne, a tall congenial real estate agent in her fifties, took the mike and identified herself. "Madam Moderator, I applaud Wayne's sentiment. But I feel strongly that open space should be left as just that. Our farmlands are being paved over and built on. Ball fields will require drainage work, constant lawn maintenance probably including herbicides and definitely power equipment, and will involve parking lots, trash removal, lights at night, and who knows what else? The natural habitat would be destroyed. Our bird population, our wild foxes and deer, all of it would be displaced. We need undeveloped open space so we can walk through it, ride along it, ski it in the winter, and appreciate what God gave us. I vote to keep the Danson parcel exactly as it is."

A different portion of audience clapped this time. Cam had seen the woman riding her horse on the trails behind Mill Pond. Cam herself loved to cross-country ski on fresh snow but was lucky enough to be able to head out behind her farm on her own land. She took a second glance when she saw who the next speaker was, a man she'd debated in the winter at a forum on the topic of using pesticides and herbicides in farming. She'd taken the position of organic farming, obviously, and he had staunchly defended his employer, an agro-chemical giant. As he had during the debate, he wore an expensive-looking suit and a neatly knotted tie.

"I'm Paul Underwood, two Riverview Circle. Wayne knows me." He glanced over at Wayne with an uneasy look, and then back to the front of the hall. He cleared his throat. "Most of you know me, since I also grew up right here in Westbury. I stayed here to raise my three sons, who are now four, six, and eight, and I work hard at what I do. I say our children need those ball fields."

A man behind Cam muttered, "Yeah, and he'll be sure they get sprayed with every chemical around."

"The few playing fields we have are in terrible condition and aren't anywhere near big enough," Paul continued. "You all know the high school has the best fields, but it's way down Main Street on the Groveland line. Our children should be able to ride their bikes to Little League practice or a Saturday morning soccer game. My vote is with ball fields." He garnered his own modicum of applause, almost all from folks in their twenties and thirties who likely were itching to get home, pay the babysitter, and use the rest of the sunny day to take their kids on a bike ride or start the spring yard cleanup.

Cam could see his side of the argument, but didn't think it had as much merit as the other two choices. She shifted on her

4

seat. It could be hours before feeling returned to her butt. Checking the booklet, called a warrant, that included all the topics to be voted on, she groaned. This was only the eighteenth article. Nine more remained. They couldn't possibly try to finish it all today. Could they? The long-time moderator was a dean at a local college and knew how to control this group. She leaned over to speak with the lawyer who provided counsel to the town, and the murmur of conversation in the hall rose. The moderator straightened and rapped the gavel.

"Quiet, please. Does anyone have something *new* to offer? If not, I will entertain a motion to put this to a vote." She shaded her eyes with her hand and scanned the crowd, then audibly sighed when she saw who stood at the public mike. She addressed the woman. "Do you have something that hasn't already been said in the last two hours?"

Being tall, Cam easily saw over the heads of those in front of her that the speaker was an older woman. Albert had told her she was not known for being either short-winded or particularly articulate.

"I just wanted to say that I support the public housing idea. We'll always have birds, we'll always have children who want to play sports. But we won't always have our long-time families." Walking with a slow, painful-looking gait, the stocky woman returned to her seat. Cries and hoots of approval filled the hall until Cam expected the flaking paint on the arched ceiling to loosen and fall on their heads.

The moderator's eyebrows ascended nearly into her hairline. She opened her mouth to speak, but it took a couple of seconds before she smiled broadly. "Thank you for that brief message. Now, do I hear a motion?"

In short order, the move to vote was seconded and approved. The moderator took time to explain the mechanics of the unusual three-way vote, saying that voters would be approving or disapproving each option. "I'm quite sure we'll need a direct count."

Her appointed monitors handed voting cards to each person seated in the hall. Cam thought each argument had merit, but she'd decided to vote for the affordable housing option. The woman who'd spoken last had a good point.

After the vote resulted in a near three-way tie, a motion was made to continue the article and the meeting until the following Wednesday at seven o'clock in the evening. Cam groaned inwardly at the thought of a long, drawn-out evening meeting, but she knew she'd go. The ayes had it when the motion to continue was seconded and put to a vote, and everyone trooped out. Greta Laitinen strolled out with a younger man who resembled her. Several dozen people stayed in small clutches conferring with like-looking friends, although Cam knew the lines between the groups were not clearly drawn. Townies and parents alike loved to hike the fields with their dogs. Woodsie types had grandchildren playing sports. Justice-minded bankers approved of public housing.

Cam stretched her arms to the sky after she reached her old Ford truck near the far end of the parking lot behind Old Town Hall. The sunny day continued, rapidly melting the few remaining patches of snow and ice. Woods bordered the far edge of the lot, and white clumps remained on the north side of the larger trees. The relentless progress toward spring wouldn't leave them there for long.

She was about to open the creaky door of the Ford when she heard voices from beyond the enormous Escalade to her left. She paused to listen. One was definitely Wayne Laitinen. The other voice was of a forthright woman, but Cam couldn't place whose it was. Which was no surprise, really, since she'd only lived in town for a year and a half.

"I'm making you a good offer, Wayne. You and Greta would never want for money again."

"Ms. Patterson, how many times do I have to tell you? I'm not interested. It's my land. My family's land, my children's land. We'll figure out a way to pay for it. But I ain't sellin'."

"Look, we're neighbors, Wayne. Our land abuts. My daughter wants to stable her horse at home, but we need more room. I simply want the portion of your property that abuts mine."

"Nope. No deal." A car door slammed and a moment later a dusty station wagon rattled away from the other side of the Escalade in a spray of gravel. Cam was pretty sure that was Wayne. Anybody with enough money to buy a few dozen acres would own a Cadillac SUV, not an old Subaru.

Cam eased her truck's door open and slid onto the seat, not keen to be spotted eavesdropping on such a touchy topic. She breathed out her relief when the Escalade backed out behind her and drove away in the opposite direction. So Ms. Patterson was Wayne's neighbor, and she wanted horse land for her daughter. Cam had never met this Patterson woman, but she knew and liked Wayne. Tough that he was having trouble making ends meet. She thought most of his cash came from his egg and meat-bird business, which must not have that big of a profit margin.

She had her own collection of hens, plus now the troublesome rooster named Ruffles some anonymous city dweller had dropped off at her farm in January. But Cam's niche was smaller and even less profitable. She gave the birds organic feed and sold their eggs to the members of her CSA, a community supported agriculture farm-share program. She was amazed that anyone would pay seven dollars a dozen for fresh eggs even though a number of the local food enthusiasts calling themselves locavores did exactly that. She didn't feel quite the pull to eat exclusively local foods that they did, but she was happy to grow the produce so they could. With the local eggs, though, even though she charged a high price, she lost money because of the expensive organic feed. And speaking of birds, she'd better get back to check on her new batch of chicks, which had come in the mail only a few days before. The little puff balls lived together in a box under a heating bulb for the time being and made her smile every time she saw them.

Pete Pappas made her smile, too, and she had a date with him this very night. Time to get out of here.

As Cam pulled into the driveway of her farm, she spied Preston lounging in a sunny spot of the herb garden. Her Norwegian Forest cat, a constant in her life, loved to nestle on the mulch among the sage, thyme, and rosemary. He raised his head, regarded her with his Arctic eyes, and then laid his cheek on his front paws and returned to his catnap. Cam turned off the ignition and sat for a moment. Longer days and warmer temperatures were on their way. She'd been sprung from her civic responsibility, for today, at least. Life was good.

And she was most of all blessed by owning Attic Hill Farm, where she'd grown up spending summers with Great-Uncle Albert and Great-Aunt Marie. Albert was now happily ensconced in a nearby assisted living residence. While he missed Marie since her death several years earlier, he'd recently taken up with Marilyn, a smart and caring senior at the place, also in her eighties. He'd offered the farm to Cam when she was laid off her job as a software engineer almost two years ago, and she'd decided to move to the countryside north of Boston and take the plunge. She'd converted the farm to organic practices and was two years into the three-year certification process. The local foods fanatics were members of a Locavore Club, and were some of her regular customers. Ellie, a high school Girl Scout, was a regular volunteer. She'd gotten started helping on the farm while she earned her Locavore badge, and now she and Cam were friends.

The life of an introverted solo farmer wasn't a smooth one. Cam hadn't realized how much time she'd need to spend schmoozing with customers, but had gotten marginally better at it since she sold her first harvest almost a year ago. It was hard to be the person in charge of all the myriad responsibilities of the farm. Seeding, weeding, harvesting. Promoting, selling, collecting. Cleaning, packaging, planning. And so much more. The rewards were myriad, too, though. She spent time alone outdoors in all seasons, with no company but the crops, the birds, the wind, and her buddy Preston. She had loads of fresh organic produce to eat, even if as the farmer she got only the second-quality stuff. And she was doing work that stretched her abilities. She knew she was a pro at putting her head down in a cubicle and churning out high-quality software. But farming and schmoozing—they widened her horizons, and she'd come to realize this was good for her.

Ruffles' crowing pierced her quiet bubble. Oh, yeah. Life. Chicks. And all the other chores of a farmer. Cam laughed and climbed out of the truck. She started to head for the barn, then looked down at her good jeans, sweater, and black leather boots, fit more for public company than for interacting with her clutch of fowl.

"No, Flaherty. Change your clothes first." She headed for Albert and Marie's antique saltbox, now hers.

A few minutes later she reemerged, in suitably worn work pants, an old sweater, and work boots. A cloud scudded over the slanting sun and when the temperature dropped ten degrees in an instant, she shoved her hands in her pockets. Sure enough, this was March in New England. Striding toward the barn, she stopped and gazed up at a bald eagle circling high above, its white head contrasting with the dark, wide wingspan. Every year the eagles nested in several places along the broad Merrimack River, a major comeback from their former status as an endangered species. After the bird soared off toward the river a couple of miles away, Cam resumed walking.

Preston popped up and stretched, then trotted over to keep her company.

"Don't get any big ideas about those chicks, Mr. P. You've been excellent about leaving the ladies alone. I want to see you do the same with the little girls." At least she hoped they were all females. One overaggressive rooster was entirely too much as it was.

But when she reached the warming box in the barn office where she'd left forty yellow puff balls, she saw that two lay motionless in the corner. The office door had been securely closed, so it hadn't been Preston who'd done them in. She reached in and stroked the closer chick. The warmth of its down must have come from the light because it was clearly dead. The other chicks scampered around and gave her hand fairy pecks. Cam scooped up the two dead chicks. She'd ordered them inoculated against Marek disease before they were mailed, so it wasn't that. These were her first baby hens and she had no idea what had caused their deaths.

As she stood examining them in her hand, a voice hailed her from the main part of the barn.

"Cam, you in there?" Alexandra's voice called. "Thought I'd see if you need some help today."

"I'm in the office. And so glad you're here," Cam called out in return.

Alexandra appeared in the doorway. "Always like to hear

that." She glanced at the chicks. "Too bad. Looks like you lost a couple."

Cam nodded. "And I'm clueless as to why."

"Me, too. DJ's my expert, and . . ." She opened her hands. "Can we call him?"

"Didn't I tell you? He left a few weeks ago."

Cam studied the younger woman, almost as tall as her own five foot eleven. The two idealistic twenty-somethings were a perfect match, and had both been active volunteers on the farm for months. DJ had taught Cam about her rescue hens' care and feeding. "I hope you guys didn't break up."

"No way." Alexandra laughed. "He's off at IMS on a three-month Buddhist retreat." At Cam's questioning look, Alexandra continued. "Insight Meditation Society. Out in western Mass. They teach Vipassana meditation, which comes from Tibet. He's been maintaining a daily practice and said he wanted to deepen it. Three months without talking? Not my deal, but, hey, he's cool. Shaved his head and everything."

"Cool, he is. And how have you been?" Cam asked.

"Good." She beamed. "Got a job doing freelance Web and marketing consulting with an environmental group, which could lead to other gigs. I've been out of college two years— about time I moved out of my parents' house and got my own place, don't you think?"

"Absolutely."

Alexandra frowned.

"What's the frown for?" Cam asked. She laid the dead chicks on a piece of paper on her desk and scanned the others. The rest seemed healthy enough.

"My sister. You met her. Katie?"

"The one who escaped to New York, and then came back almost immediately?"

"Yeah." Alexandra kept frowning as she reached into the

box and stroked an extra-small chick. "She's really into animal rights now."

"You are too, aren't you?"

"Not like Katie is. She wants to throw fake blood around and try to set farm animals loose. She hangs around with those radical PETA folks. Or whatever they call themselves."

"Setting farm animals loose? How stupid can you get? They don't know how to fend for themselves. They'd either get eaten by a predator or hit by a car," Cam said. "Anyway, I thought Katie was back in school."

"She is, at Northern Essex Community College. That's where she met these nuts. Hey, I got a postcard from Ellie in Florida where's she on that school service trip. Can you believe a fourteen-year-old would write a postcard?" Alexandra laughed.

"You know Ellie. She's cool. She doesn't mind being out of the mainstream, otherwise she wouldn't be a Girl Scout in high school. I got a card, too. Florida sure sounds a lot warmer than here, even if she is helping to clean up from a hurricane."

"Wearing shorts in the sunshine instead of all this?" Alexandra gestured to her down jacket and wool hat. "No brainer."

Chapter 2

After Alexandra left, Cam drove over to Stone Mill Road and down the bumpy dirt way to Wayne and Greta's farm. She had to figure out what happened to those chicks before she lost the rest of them, and Wayne was her closest expert now that DJ was off on retreat. The chicks lay in a shoe box on the truck's bench seat next to her.

The clouds no longer scudded but now obliterated the sun, and the air had the sharp, damp smell of impending snow. Not unheard of for mid-March, but not a bit welcome. She'd been so busy all day, what with town meeting, she hadn't taken time to check the weather forecast. She was already experienced enough at paying attention to the sight, smell, and feel of the air that she knew it would be snowing before midnight. What she didn't know was how heavy it would be and how long it would last.

A black sedan approached her on the narrow road. Cam pulled as far to the right as she could and glimpsed a frowning Paul Underwood at the sedan's wheel as it passed. He glowered at her, then sped up once he was clear. He must have been visiting Wayne and his wife, since theirs was the only house on this road. But why the mad face?

Cam drove by a sign that read LAITINEN POULTRY FARM and pulled up next to the tidy old Colonial on the rise. Mounds of mulch and several latticework trellises stuck up in the large fenced-in kitchen garden near the house. A barn with a sagging roofline and a long-ago paint job sat twenty yards away, and beyond it stretched the long narrow building that housed Wayne's hens. It was a pretty spot despite the pungency of several hundred hens living together, with fields rolling down the slope in front and woods behind the house.

As Cam climbed out holding the shoe box, Wayne appeared from the hen house, a bucket in his hand. He hailed her as he strode in her direction. An old black dog trailed behind him.

"What brings you out here, Cam?"

"Two of my new chicks died and I don't know why. Wondered if you could help me out."

"Bring 'em on in the house," he said as he reached her. "I'll take a look. Need any eggs?" He gestured with the hand holding the bucket, which was full of eggs of all sizes and hues.

"Thanks, but I have plenty at my farm."

When the dog, whose muzzle had turned to gray, gave a soft bark in Cam's direction, Wayne patted him on the head. "This is Pluto. Pluto, meet Cam."

"Hey, Pluto." Cam extended her fist for Pluto to sniff, and stroked his head when he pushed it into her hand.

"Right this way," Wayne said. He beckoned to Pluto. "Come on, boy."

"You sure have a pretty place out here, Wayne." Cam gestured at the fields. "Was there a stone mill on this road at one time?"

Wayne laughed softly. "Still is, down by the creek. But the name used to be Pig Turd Road. Can you believe it?"

"You're kidding." Cam looked at him with astonishment.

"Nope, I am not. Sure was glad when the town decided to change it to Stone Mill. Heck of a lot nicer."

A minute later she sat at a plank table in a kitchen that looked a lot like hers—unrenovated but functional and clean, with fifties-era linoleum on the floor and white painted wooden cabinets on the walls.

Wayne ran water into the bucket of eggs and let it stand in the sink. "Coffee?" he asked, pot in hand.

"Sure. After that all-day meeting, I could use some. With a little milk if you have it."

"The meeting was an endurance test." He shook his head as he poured them each a mug, then set them on the table along with spoons. He took a glass bottle of milk out of the re-frigerator and set it in front of Cam. "Hope you don't mind un-pasteurized. It's clean—don't worry—and straight from Betsy, the milk cow. Sugar's in the dish there, too."

"Not worried." Cam poured a bit of the creamy stuff into her coffee.

"An all-day town meetin'," Wayne said. "And nothing got re-solved, neither. I couldn't believe they continued the article."

"Kathleen said they needed more than a certain number of votes on any one choice for it to win out."

"I can't remember how many they needed. What this town needs is housin', but you already heard me say that."

"I agree with you," Cam said.

Wayne took a mouthful of coffee. "Ah. Good and strong, just like I like it."

Gazing around the room, Cam spied a key holder exactly like the one at her house. It featured a split-rail fence with the carved smiling heads and upper bodies of a man and a woman peering over it. The heads on the one at Cam's house turned a hundred and eighty degrees, so the couple could look like they were either friendly, not speaking, or both looking off in the distance in the same direction. On Wayne's hung several bunches of keys, including one that appeared to have a small magic wand attached to it.

"I have the same key rack," Cam said with a smile.

"It was my folks'. Came with the house."

Greta's voice called out from another room. "Wayne? Who's that you're talking to?"

"Cam Flaherty, hon." Wayne gazed at the doorway until Greta, dressed in jeans and a blue fleece top, appeared. "She's got some dead chicks she wants me to look at." He gave her a gentle smile, which she didn't return.

Greta greeted Cam and sank into a chair. She blinked several times and drummed sensibly trimmed nails on the table. The set to her mouth looked like she'd eaten a rotten egg.

"But you weren't talking about chicks," Greta said. "I heard you hashing over the town meeting again. Nothing's ever going to get done there. Nothing right, anyhow, with all those new bankers and whatnot telling us what to do with our land."

"Greta, they've been here for years," Wayne said. "The land belongs to all of us. You know that. Democracy means we get to have our say and then vote on it. If the vote doesn't go the way we want it to, well, we just have to accept it."

"I was surprised that Judith"—Greta said the name as if it were an obscenity—"didn't add her ever-so-valuable opinion."

"Now, hon, Ms. Patterson's our neighbor. We can't help it that she has some opinions we don't approve of."

"That *you* don't approve of, you mean. I don't know why you aren't willing to sell off a portion of the back woodlot to her. It'd get us out of the financial hole we're in." She looked at Cam. "I don't know where all our money goes. Seems like it vanishes into thin air, like some magician swooped his wand around, said '*Evanesco*,' and whoosh, it's gone."

"*Evanesco?*" Cam asked.

"You know, Harry Potter's vanishing spell. If I didn't work as an aide at the Newburyport Library, we'd be in sorry shape," Greta added. "Chicken farmers don't exactly rake in the big bucks."

Cam didn't quite squirm in her chair, but wished she didn't have to witness this domestic argument. She sipped the coffee, which was strong enough to stand a stick in, and set the mug down.

"We'll talk about that later," Wayne said, reaching out to pat Greta's hand until she snatched it away. "Cam don't want to hear our problems."

Whew.

"Show me those chicks now." He pointed at the box.

Cam pushed the box toward him and watched as he lifted one little body out and examined it, turning it every which way in his long-fingered hands.

"How old are they?" he asked, picking up the other chick.

"I got them in the mail on Thursday, so only a few days."

"Afraid they both got pasty butt." He glanced up with a half smile.

Greta snickered, but when Cam looked at her, she raised her eyebrows and said, "It's a thing."

"Ick. What in the world is that?" Cam asked.

"Their vents got clogged up by loose droppings that stuck to the down," Wayne said. "When the feces builds up and forms a blockage, little chicks can up and die from it. Like these two did."

"What causes it?" Cam asked. "I mean, the other chicks seem fine. Do I have to watch for it and wipe their little rear ends for them?"

"Nah. Could be these were too hot or too cold." Wayne laid both chicks back in the box. "Or something they ate. But since the rest are fine it might have been the stress of getting shipped. You know?"

"Totally," Cam said. "I can believe going through the postal service in a straw-lined box is stressful to the newborns' systems." She nodded.

"And maybe these girls were runts from the start and just couldn't take it. Anyhow, they're gone now. May their souls rest in peace." He bowed his head.

Surely he saw—no, caused—plenty of chicken death right here on his farm, since he sold meat birds. But this gentle man still grieved the demise of two newborns.

Chapter 3

Cam lifted her glass of an Oregon Pinot Noir and clinked it with Pete's beer glass. He'd driven her to a small bistro across the river in Amesbury, telling her it was one of his favorite restaurants. The air was full of tantalizing smells. What looked like neighborhood regulars lined the bar, and a petite woman in a pink chef's shirt and toque never stopped moving.

"Here's to you, kid." He gazed at Cam from under his heavy, dark eyebrows, then took a long drink and set the glass on the table.

"You must be glad you're off duty," she said after sipping her own drink. Pete Pappas's long hours and often irregular schedule as a state police detective made maintaining a relationship difficult.

"You bet. A whole weekend free. Had a relaxing day just hanging with Dasha. I think we walked every trail in Maudslay State Park. You should come sometime."

"I'd like that. It's one of my favorite places to walk. Did you finally get custody of Dasha from Alicia?" Cam had met Pete's intelligent husky in the winter, and Dasha had helped to bring down a murderer, but Pete's ex-wife had gotten the dog in the divorce.

"Didn't I tell you? Alicia never liked him, anyway. It was simply a power trip to claim custody. She finally realized she was a lot freer without him. Freedom is real big with her these days." He laughed softly. "Fine with me."

"I'm glad you got him and I'm sure he is, too." Cam twisted in her chair to read the specials written on a chalkboard behind her. The restaurant was in an old building that featured a stamped tin ceiling and brick walls, but the owners had added colorful sound-absorbing panels to cut down on noise, and the atmosphere was warm and bustling.

A ponytailed waiter in a white shirt, black jeans, and a black half apron approached them. "Ready to order?"

Cam looked at him. "What's in the lamb ragout on the specials menu?"

"Thyme, rosemary, roasted garlic, and a roasted heirloom tomato sauce, served over tiny new potatoes. It comes with grilled herbed asparagus."

"Perfect. I'll have that."

Pete ordered the Creole stew.

"Anything to start?" the waiter asked.

"Want to split a Fallen Caesar?" Pete looked at Cam.

"Sure."

The waiter gathered up their menus and turned away.

"How's your new partner working out?" Cam asked. "Detective Hobbs."

"Ivan? I was happy to have a break from him today. He's conscientious to a fault. Everything has to be by the book. I preferred working solo, but the new commander brought Ivan with him. Hard to relax around somebody so regimented."

"I didn't have a relaxing day, myself," Cam said, then told

him about the highlights of the town meeting. "All day long, it took. At the end, the question everybody had come for wasn't even resolved." She shook her head. "Albert warned me about New England town meetings. Speaking of a fallen Caesar, 'Beware the ides of March' kept running through my head. Not that I thought anybody was going to get assassinated, but Shakespeare—"

"You know that was a real thing, don't you? Shakespeare knew his Plutarch."

Cam wrinkled her nose. "Remind me about Plutarch? I didn't have much of a humanities education, being in computer science."

"He was a Greek biographer and historian who became a Roman citizen. He wrote about how a seer had warned Julius Caesar that he would be killed no later than the ides of March. And a different biographer and historian, Suetonius, said it was a haruspex named Spurinna who warned Caesar."

"A haruspex?"

"Someone who did divination by reading the lives of sacrificial sheep and chickens."

Cam stared at him and then laughed. "How in the world do you know all this?"

"I like reading Shakespeare, and that led to reading about Caesar." He grinned. "It's a break from crime, at least from crime in our own time period. They also had their share of small-town politics then, of course."

"We certainly have ours in Westbury."

"We don't get as much of that in Newburyport, since we have a mayor and a city council," Pete said. "But we have plenty of petty-minded conflicts, for sure."

"I heard a bit more conflict up close and personal after the meeting." She told him about overhearing the conversation between Wayne and Judith Patterson. "And then when I went over to Wayne's farm to get some chicken advice, he and his wife were arguing. Sounds like they have money problems. Greta wants to sell the parcel of land to the Patterson woman, but he's refusing."

"Can't blame him for wanting to hang on to the farm."

"I agree." Cam stood. "Excuse me a minute. Just want to wash my hands before the food comes."

"Come back soon. I'll miss you." Pete's wicked grin lit up his face, which in fact did look more relaxed than Cam had ever seen him.

"I promise." She reached out and ruffled his thick hair as she passed. Spying the RESTROOMS sign at the back of the restaurant, she headed in that direction, but slowed when she heard the same voice she'd heard earlier from behind the Escalade. The woman speaking, who had to be Judith Patterson, had her back to Cam. She shared a table with three other women, all with well-cut and expertly colored hair, Judith's a cap of streaked ash blond. Cam continued past the table, noticing expensive rings and manicured hands holding martini glasses. Cam glanced at her own unmanicured hands, with short-cut nails, calluses, and reddened skin from constantly scrubbing out ground-in dirt.

On her way back from the ladies' room, Cam paused at the open doorway to the small kitchen where two men and the pink-clad chef moved in what looked like an orchestrated dance. Steam curled off a wide pot and something sizzled in a sauté pan. It smelled like heaven. As she approached the table of well-groomed women, Cam saw Judith put a long cylinder to her mouth. It had to be an e-cigarette, which Cam had never seen anyone smoke before, if that was even the right verb. Judith blew out a puff of a smoky substance as Cam tried to get a good look at her face while she passed. When Judith glanced up with piercing dark eyes, Cam resisted the temptation to throw her own gaze elsewhere, and instead gave her a stranger's smile: not beaming, but not unfriendly, either.

Cam slid into her seat as the waiter brought two plates of romaine spears topped with anchovies, Parmesan cheese, and a creamy dressing, with a slab of cheesy toast at the side.

"Where do you get the lettuce?" she asked him.

The waiter frowned. "Our local source went under last fall. We'd like to get it from another farm around here but haven't found a reliable purveyor."

"I'm a farmer, over in Westbury. Maybe I should talk to the owner about supplying organic romaine."

His face lit up. "I think she'd love that. She tries to use local as much as possible. I'll get her out here before you leave."

Cam thanked him. "Here, give her my card." She dug a farm business card out of her bag and handed it to the waiter.

"This would be a good gig for me," she said to Pete. "Close by, steady business. And romaine is easy to grow." She cut a piece and savored the mix of the tangy dressing, the salty fish, and the fresh crunch of the greens.

"If I know you, you're going to go home tonight and plant lettuce seeds in the greenhouse."

"On a date night? Guess you don't know me too well. Yet." She set her chin on her hand, gazing at Pete. They'd met less than a year ago after the terrible murder on her farm last June, and Pete had been called in to help solve it. Their dealings were adversarial at first. But he'd asked for her help with a second case in the fall, and when it was over they'd begun going out. That had gotten complicated this winter when Cam was an initial suspect in a murder at Great-Uncle Albert's assisted living residence, but now their relationship seemed to be settling into an easy pattern of weekend dates, long conversations, and satisfying doses of passion.

She frowned as she spied the back of Judith's head beyond Pete.

"What's the frown for?" he asked.

"The woman who wants to buy Wayne's farm is right over there. Judith Patterson. I heard her voice when I went to wash my hands. Looks pretty well off, like she can afford to buy another few acres."

"Thank goodness she can't make him sell, no matter how much money she has."

Cam stretched in her robe and slippers the next morning. Through the window she watched fat, lazy flakes float out of the sky. The drip of the coffeepot was accompanied by an increasingly rich aroma. She hugged herself, smiling at the extremely enjoyable night Pete and she had enjoyed. She'd left him asleep in her bed when her farmer's internal alarm said her own rest was all done, even though the clock read only six. When the small coffee machine finally quieted, she poured herself a mug of the deep roast she loved, added a splash of milk, and curled her feet up on the couch, clicking on the local television news with the volume low.

The station showed footage of an accident on Route 495 due to the snow. The weather woman said the storm, which had left only three inches of light snow, would be letting up within the hour with warming temperatures. Preston jumped up and joined Cam, and she stroked him, barely listening to the TV. Until she caught the word *Laitinen*. Her gaze went straight to the screen and she jacked up the volume a couple of notches.

"Animal rights activists claimed responsibility for vandalism at the Laitinen Poultry Farm during the night, specifically on the chicken house, that long structure you see." The reporter gestured behind himself. "Before dawn, farmer Wayne Laitinen discovered that the structure had been sprayed with red paint and all the doors were left open to the storm. Police seek any information about the members of this group, the Animal Rights Front, which apparently is a split-off from PETA, People for the Ethical Treatment of Animals." The camera zoomed in on the chicken house, which indeed was splashed with red, with the letters ARF scrawled large. A good deal of paint also lay on the ground near the now-closed door, paint showing crimson under the light layer of fresh snow that had fallen since. "Farmer Laitinen reports that his hens fortunately had the good sense to stay indoors."

The camera panned to Wayne, who looked hastily dressed in an old work jacket and muck boots over his jeans. He also looked exhausted. "I don't know who done this. I'm good to my girls. I'd never hurt any of my animals. Any animal. All these people did was scare my hens and make them cold. Is that ethical treatment? I don't think so." He turned away and stomped toward the house with bent shoulders.

When the program cut to a commercial, Cam switched off the television. That was enough bad news for the day. Wayne was good to his hens, Cam had seen that. They weren't completely free range, and they didn't get organic feed, but they had a large netted-in run and plenty of space in the chicken house in the winter. He kept them clean and healthy, and he seemed an unfair target for this group, whoever they were. A group that likely included Katie Magnusson, Alexandra's sister. Why didn't they target one of the big commercial growers out there? With any luck they'd leave Wayne alone after this. She was sure any additional financial hit would only add to his woes.

Cam drained her coffee. Maybe Pete would be interested in a wake-up call before she headed out to feed her own chickens.

It was nearly ten and the snow had stopped by the time Cam and Pete got around to breakfast. After a pleasant interlude and a shower, she'd fed and watered the hens, gathered eggs, and cooked up a fresh cheese-mushroom omelet, fried potatoes, and toast for the two of them. While she prepared the food, she told him about the vandalism at Wayne's farm. After breakfast was ready, he brought two mugs of fresh coffee to the table, then sat across from her.

She gazed at him. His dark hair, already silvering, was still damp from the shower, and the pink Oxford shirt he'd worn to dinner he now wore untucked over his jeans. His left ring finger still showed a pale ring where his wedding band had been.

"What are you looking at?" he said around a mouthful of omelet, but his dark eyes smiled.

"You. Did I ever tell you I like you?"

"I like you, too." He grinned and pointed at her plate. "Now eat."

She complied, following the forkful with a sip of coffee. "You wouldn't believe how strong Wayne makes his coffee." She shuddered, remembering. "And he drinks it, too."

"Good thing the world is a big place with room for lots of different types."

After several more bites, Cam said, "Speaking of different types, any idea who's in this Animal Rights Front, this PETA splinter group?"

"We've heard a few threads of information. No real intelligence, though."

Cam fell silent as she ate. What if Katie had been part of the action at Wayne's?

"Looks like your brain is working overtime," Pete said, nudging her plate with his fork.

She glanced up. "I hate to say this, but I might know someone who was involved."

Pete glanced up from his plate. "Oh?"

"Alexandra said her sister Katie's getting kind of way out there for animal rights."

"Alexandra, your farm volunteer? The tall one?"

Cam nodded.

"What's the sister's full name?" He wiped a string of cheese off his chin.

Cam blew a breath out. "I don't want to get her in trouble. But maybe it's better if she gets in a little trouble now before things go too far."

It was Pete's turn to nod.

"Her name is Katie Magnusson."

"I'll let the team who handles that kind of thing know."

"Maybe a quick brush with the law will keep her from becoming more radical. I hope the group wouldn't resort to violence against people."

"Sometimes they do." He swiped the last of his omelet up with a piece of toast. "Breakfast was outstanding, thank you. Those fresh eggs make all the difference."

"I'll say."

A buzzing sound came from Pete's coat on the rack by the door and he groaned.

"Aren't you off duty?" Cam asked, stroking his hand.

"Yes. But, you know . . ." He rose and hustled to his coat, extracting his phone.

"When duty calls?"

Pete pressed his lips together before saying, "Pappas." As

he listened, his face darkened. He glanced at Cam and then turned away.

"Who made the discovery?" After a few moments, he said, "Okay. I'll be there as soon as I can. Have to let my dog out first." He disconnected. Picking up his shoes where he'd left them next to the door, he padded back to the table. He bent to kiss Cam's forehead, then sat.

She opened her mouth to ask what the news was. She shut it again. He'd tell her if he could, and when he was ready.

When both shoes were on and tied, Pete straightened. He laid his hand atop hers.

"Wayne Laitinen is dead." He watched her.

"Oh, no! The poor man." She brought her other hand to her mouth. "Did he . . . was it . . . wait." She watched him back. "If they called you, that means it's murder."

"We don't know. The local force's preliminary inspection doesn't show a wound of any kind. He could have had a heart attack. But with this PETA action, the Westbury police asked us to step in."

"He's such a gentle soul. I hope it was a natural death. Was his wife there? Greta?"

"He seems to have been alone. I've got to go let Dasha do his stuff and get over to the death scene."

"Let me handle Dasha. I haven't seen him in a while. I'll bring him over here, like I did before. How's that?"

"That's the offer of an angel. Thanks." He stood. Pulling her up with him, he encased her in one of his signature bear hugs.

"Hey, I can't breathe!" Cam laughed and pulled away enough to plant a big kiss on him, one that lasted longer than she'd intended.

He broke it off. "I'll call you when I can. Please keep this information to yourself for now." He pulled on his coat.

"Of course. Now go," Cam said, shutting the door firmly behind him. After he pulled his old Saab out of the drive, she gazed out the window at the sun glistening on his footprints in the snow. Wayne Laitinen wouldn't be leaving any more footprints on this earth.

Chapter 4

The sun was melting the snow fast as Cam drove back from Newburyport with Pete's husky, Dasha, in the cab of the truck with her. He perched on the bench seat and gazed out the window as the road dipped down next to the Artichoke Reservoir and then rose steadily again at Westbury's eastern border. A sign quietly announcing the Saint John the Evangelist monastery and Emery retreat house was on the right. Cam had never driven down the lane that led to the monastery, but she pictured robed monks walking the grounds in silence.

She came up to All Saints Episcopal Church on the left and slowed. The service must have recently ended. A dark-skinned white-robed priest stood on the front steps greeting parishioners as they emerged from the brick building, and families were loading into cars parked along both sides of the busy state route. Cam spied Greta walking away from the church with a woman a little taller than Greta's five foot five. Cam pulled over on the far side of the road. If Greta had been in church for an hour or more, she couldn't have heard the news yet.

Cam watched for a moment. It would be horrible for Greta to arrive home not knowing that Wayne was dead. The police should tell her, but she imagined they were looking for her and couldn't find her. If Cam told her, surely Pete wouldn't count Cam performing this terrible act of kindness as violating his request to keep the information of Wayne's death confidential. This was Wayne's wife, after all. She had a right to know. Or maybe Cam should call Pete and have him come and tell Greta. Cam had never delivered news of a death before and she wasn't close friends with Greta. Her thoughts pulled back and forth like a tug-of-war.

Across the road, Greta opened the passenger door of a small sedan in the church parking lot. The younger woman climbed into the driver's seat and a minute later they were headed toward town, making Cam's decision for her. She pulled onto the road after them. If they went straight home, then that was that, although they were driving away from the poultry farm. If they went out for breakfast or something, she could call Pete and tell him where they were.

Sure enough, less than five minutes later, the car pulled into Daisy's Donuts, the traditional donut shop that also made surprisingly good coffee. Cam pulled in, too, but parked at the far end of the lot. She watched them walk into the donut shop as she pressed Pete's number.

"Pappas," he answered tersely.

"Pete, I just saw Greta Laitinen come out of church with somebody who looked like her daughter. I thought of telling them about Wayne's death, but decided you should do that."

"Thank you, Cam. Where are they now?"

"I followed them to Daisy's Donuts and they went inside."

"If they come out before I get there, can you find a way to stall them?"

"Sure. You know where it is?"

"I do. And then stick around, will you. They'll need a friendly face."

He disconnected and Cam kept her eyes on the door. The front windows were large and clean, and she could see the two women at the counter. When they headed for the exit, white cups in their hands, Cam slid out of her seat. Pete hadn't yet arrived. She told Dasha to stay and then rushed over to the door of the shop, slowing to a normal pace as Greta and the younger woman emerged. The full aroma of coffee mixed with the tantalizing scent of fresh donuts escaping before the door closed behind them.

"Morning, Greta," Cam said.

"Hey, Cam. How's it going?" The buttons of Greta's black coat strained over her full figure.

"Not too bad." With raised eyebrows Cam glanced toward Greta's companion as she tried to block the women's path toward their car. Looking like a female and younger version of Wayne, the younger woman was clearly the couple's daughter and appeared to be in her late twenties. Her light hair was pulled back in a ponytail and she had Wayne's slender, wiry build.

"Have you met my daughter, Megan?"

"No." Cam held out her hand. "Cam Flaherty. Nice to meet you, Megan."

"Good to meet you, too." Megan smiled as she shook Cam's hand.

"Getting your morning coffee?" Cam asked. Which sounded trite, but she needed to keep them here.

Megan laughed. "After that sermon? We both need it."

"Absolutely," Greta said, with a fond smile for her daughter.

"I thought he would never stop talking," Megan continued. "Forgiveness instead of revenge was the topic of the day."

Cam tried to scan the lot while she nodded and smiled at Megan. Still no Pete.

"I haven't been to church since high school," Cam said, grasping at a topic, any topic, to make sure they didn't leave. "I used to go to Saint Ann's with my uncle and aunt." She pointed down Main Street in the direction of the Catholic Church a couple of miles away.

"How is Albert these days?" Greta asked. "He was real nice to us when Wayne started up the poultry business. Gave him a few tips on how to raise hens and on how to keep the books."

"Albert's doing very well, thanks."

Megan gently elbowed her mother. "I wanted to show you my new kitten, Mom, remember? At my apartment?"

"I remember," Greta said. She looked at Cam. "We need to get going."

At a crunch of gravel, Cam glanced over to see Pete pull into a parking space in a dark unmarked car. Just in time. Thank goodness he hadn't brought a cruiser. Pete, in gray slacks and a navy blazer, walked up to the three of them.

Greta cocked her head at him. "Friend of yours?" she asked Cam.

"Yes," Cam said, her gaze on Pete. She could hear Dasha barking from the truck across the parking lot. He must have spied his human.

"Excuse me, Ms. Laitinen. I'm State Police Detective Peter Pappas. I'm afraid I have some very bad news." He stood with his hands clasped in front of him, and his dark eyes were more somber than Cam had ever seen them.

"A detective? What news?" Greta barked out a laugh. "Is this more about those fool vandals? I told Wayne he ought to just shoot them next time."

The younger woman watched Pete with worried eyes. "Mom, I don't think he's talking about the vandals."

"If we could step over here." He ushered them to an outdoor seating area at the side of the building where four round cement tables were surrounded by curved benches. Since it was in the shade on the north side, soft mounds of snow still topped the tables. Cam followed slowly. Pete had asked her to stick around, but this wasn't going to be an easy conversation.

"No, I'm not talking about the vandals," Pete said. "I'm afraid Wayne has—"

"What's that idiot done now? I'll bet he ran his foot over with the manure spreader, or got knocked down by the cow." Greta folded her arms.

Megan winced, but Greta didn't seem to notice. Cam winced, too, inwardly, at Greta's insensitivity to her daughter. Cam took a step back. Maybe she shouldn't even be here. Pete glanced at her and made a little stop motion, so she stayed.

"Or did he find one of those stupid protesters and slug them in the mouth?" Greta asked. "It's what they deserve."

A well-dressed older couple strolling past the seating area glanced at Greta with an alarmed look and then walked briskly toward their car. Megan shivered and hugged herself.

Pete didn't speak until the couple was out of earshot. "Ma'am, I'm very sorry. Your husband was found dead this morning." He reached out and touched Greta's arm.

Greta's eyes widened and her daughter gasped.

"Dead?" the daughter asked. "Daddy's dead?" She looked from Pete to Cam and back to Pete.

"That can't be." Greta drew out her words. "I left him eating the breakfast I cooked him. He was fine. He was alive. Fine." She shook her head, looking into the distance as if she could conjure him up. A spot under her eye twitched with a fast beat.

"Was it a heart attack?" the daughter asked in an anguished tone. "I kept telling him to stop eating bacon, but he never listened to me."

"We don't know," Pete said. "I'm so very sorry to have to

tell you. We've been trying to reach you, and your son, as well."

Pete did look sorry. What a hard thing to have to do, to notify a family someone had died. Cam was glad she'd decided not to tell them herself.

"My phone was off because we were in church." Megan scrabbled in her purse and drew out her phone, then pressed the On button.

"My son's away. Took my grandchildren to Florida this morning. Disney. We were out to breakfast and then at church. Anyway, maybe it's a mistake." Greta shook her head with a quick move. "Maybe he just fainted or something."

"It's not a mistake," Pete said softly.

Greta swayed. She reached back and grasped the edge of the closest table, her knuckles turning white. Megan embraced her mother, arms clasped tight. A sob burst out of Megan and she buried her head in Greta's shoulder. Several customers gazed at the scene through the shop windows. Cam reached over and lightly rubbed Greta's back.

"I need to see him. I need to see Wayne," Greta said fiercely. "Did he die at home? Who found him?"

"He died at home. I'll drive you both to the house." He gestured to his car.

Who did find him? Pete clearly didn't want to tell them.

"What about my car?" Megan asked.

Greta looked at Cam. "Will you bring her car, Cam?"

Cam glanced at Pete, and after he nodded, she said, "Of course."

Megan handed Cam the keys.

"Come on, honey." Greta gently guided Megan into the backseat of Pete's car, then climbed into the back after her.

Cam headed for the truck to get Dasha, and glanced back

over her shoulder before Pete drove out. The sun silhouetted the figures of the two women, heads together in grief.

Even before she arrived at the Laitinen farm, Cam saw the blue lights flashing at the end of the drive. An unoccupied Westbury police car was parked sideways, with just enough room for Pete to drive around it and for Cam to squeeze Megan's car past it, too.

A darkened, quiet ambulance was parked in front of the house, along with a half dozen other marked and unmarked cars. Cam's childhood friend Ruth Dodge, a Westbury police officer, stood near the cruiser facing the house, hands clasped behind her back. Dasha barked at the sight of Pete exiting his car.

"It's okay, Dasha." When Cam reached out a hand and patted his head, he quieted.

Pete had just walked over to Ruth when Megan's car crunched on the gravel as Cam braked. Ruth whirled. She held a hand up, palm out, and waved it in a *no* gesture. She hurried toward Cam, slowing when she saw her at the wheel. Cam opened her door and unfolded herself from the driver's seat.

The back door on Pete's car opened. Cam peered past Ruth to watch Megan ease out and then extend a hand to her mother. Ruth went to them, and Cam leaned her head back into the car.

"You stay here, boy," she told Dasha before shutting the door. The poor dog was doing a lot of waiting in vehicles this morning.

"I am so sorry for your loss, Ms. Laitinen," Ruth said.

"Thank you," Greta said.

"You must be Megan Laitinen," Ruth addressed Megan.

"Yes." Megan's tearstained face contrasted with Greta's dry one.

"I'm very sorry about the loss of your father," Ruth said with kindness.

"We need to see Wayne," Greta demanded. "I need to see my husband."

"Can we see my father?" Megan asked. She tucked her arm through Greta's.

"I'll need to check," Pete said. "Just a moment." He disappeared around the side of the house.

"Why are all these police cars here?" Megan's voice rose in a plaintive note.

"I'm going inside. You can't stop me." Greta pulled Megan toward the house. "It's my home."

"Ma'am." Ruth took two long strides until she stood in front of the women. "I'm afraid you're going to need to wait until I clear that."

Ruth was as tall as Cam, although she carried a good deal more weight on her hefty frame. Cam knew a lot of it was muscle. Not all, but a lot. In her dark uniform and black boots, brown hair pulled back into a bun, Ruth was an imposing presence. She fixed her brown-eyed gaze on Greta. "We're going to wait to hear from Detective Pappas. I need you to stay right here." Ruth glanced at Cam, raising her eyebrows.

Cam nodded, not that she thought she could keep Greta from entering her own house, but at least Greta halted. Pluto trotted around the corner of the house and up to them. Greta leaned down to pet him as Dasha barked from inside the car.

Ruth turned her back, took a few steps away, and spoke quietly into the mike on her shoulder. It crackled back an answer, and Cam thought she heard "living room."

Ruth faced Greta and Megan again. "All right, you can go into the living room. And only the living room."

Another officer appeared at the front door of the house, the door no New Englander ever used, especially not farmers. Everybody used the side door, or the back entrance. He waved the women toward him.

Cam watched them make their way, Megan clinging to her mother, Pluto following, toward the house where, somewhere, Wayne lay lifeless.

Chapter 5

Ruth walked back to where Cam stood near the car.
"Did you notice that Greta seems more mad than sad?" Cam asked. She watched as the front door closed behind Greta and Megan. "I guess people deal with death in different ways. Although when I visited here yesterday she didn't seem that happy with him. So if their marriage was already in trouble . . ."

A door slammed somewhere and Dasha barked. Cam glanced into the car to see him standing alert on the front seat, his face intent on the house.

Pete strode toward them from around the side of the building. "That was a good call, Cam."

Cam blew out a breath. "It really was just dumb luck, if you can call it luck. I was driving past the church after picking up Dasha when they came out. I almost told them myself. I didn't think it was particularly nice to let them come home to a dead man and a bunch of police."

"It's a good thing you didn't. You could have eliminated a piece of evidence." Pete pressed his lips together and waved his hand.

"What do you mean?" Cam asked.

"How the nearest of kin react to the news of a suspicious death is evidence," Ruth said.

"The daughter—Megan—is very upset. She was crying the whole way here," Pete said.

"And Greta appears grim about it, almost angry." Ruth frowned.

When Dasha whined, Pete opened the passenger door. Letting the dog out, he rubbed his head and accepted a few kisses, then stood, his hand on Dasha's head, the leash trailing on the ground.

"How did Wayne die?" Cam asked. The sun was in her eyes and she held up a hand over her eyebrows as a shield. Between the sun and the rising temperature, snow was melting from the corners of the barn's roof and off the branches of a tall sugar maple at the side of the house.

"Not sure yet. ME's on her way." Pete tapped his fingers on his leg.

"But you think it was murder? Not a heart attack or a stroke or something?"

Ruth and Pete exchanged a glance. "It's an unaccompanied, unexplained death. We have to investigate," Pete said. When Dasha trotted away, nose to the ground, Pete called him back and took the leash in his hand.

"Maybe it's connected with the real estate deal," Cam said.

"What's that?" Ruth asked.

"Wayne told me Judith Patterson wants to buy part of the property, where it abuts hers. He and Greta argued about it in front of me yesterday. He didn't want to sell at all, and Greta thought they should let Judith have a piece of the land."

Ruth nodded slowly. "Or it could be connected to the animal rights folks."

"Was he shot or stabbed or something?" Cam asked.

Pete shook his head.

A tall man appeared from around the side of the house, hands on his hips, a neatly knotted tie over a white shirt visible under his jacket. When he saw Pete, he opened his hands to the sides in a "What's keeping you?" gesture.

"Listen, I have to get back inside. Ivan calls. But you need a ride home. And I can't spare anybody." His jaw worked.

"I actually need to get back to my truck, which is at Daisy's. But we'll walk. Right, Dasha? He's got his leash, and it's only a couple of miles down Garden Street."

"Oh, good." Pete's face looked like a weight was lifted off it. "You sure?"

"Of course. On a gorgeous day like this? No problem."

"Thanks. I owe you." He handed her the leash, then turned toward the house. "Dodge, I want to show you something." He beckoned for Ruth to follow.

They disappeared around the side of the house as Cam slung her canvas messenger bag over her head and one shoulder and headed down the long drive with Dasha. Something felt unusual in her pocket. Patting it, she swore and turned back.

"One sec, Dash. I have Megan's keys." She approached the front door of the house and slowed to a halt. Did she want to insert herself in that scene again? Pete would surely prefer that she didn't. She could leave the keys in the car, and text Pete about where they were. As she headed away from the house again, the leash went taut. Dasha had his nose buried in something near a shrub. She tugged on the leash but he didn't budge. He looked up at her with a snout covered in snow and she laughed. He barked and put his nose back on the ground, pawing at something.

"Okay, let's see what you found." Cam knelt next to him. He'd uncovered a slim cylinder about the size of fountain pen, with a band on one end. "Wonder what that is?" She knew better than to touch it. "Good boy, Dasha. I'll tell Dad." She rose, and this time Dasha went with her. She didn't want to disturb the investigators right now, who were not only looking into Wayne's death but also dealing with Greta's and Megan's grief. But if Wayne had been murdered, this could be a piece of evidence. After Cam left the keys on the driver's seat, she slid the leash strap onto her wrist and dug her phone out, texting Pete both about the object and the keys.

"That's done. Let's get some fresh air and exercise, shall we?"

Dasha yipped his approval. The supple leather leash in her hand was smooth from years of Pete's hand holding it, and Cam smiled.

"And we have chicks to take care of, too."

After their vigorous walk to the truck, Cam and Dasha drove back to Attic Hill Farm. The dog had spent enough time with her in the winter that she knew she could leave him off leash on the property. He and Preston had also arrived at a truce. They didn't cuddle up together, but Preston allowed Dasha to exist without either challenging him or feeling the need to flee.

She greeted the mature hens in their yard. "How's it going, girls?" At an indignant crow from Ruffles, she added, "And boy?" She cleaned out their water feeder in the coop, gave them a scoop of food, and collected the eggs in a bucket like the one Wayne had been carrying only the day before.

Wayne. A pang of sadness wound its way around her heart at the thought of that gentle light snuffed out too soon, and violently, if Pete was correct. If Wayne wasn't shot or stabbed, was he choked to death? Or could it have been poison?

One of the Ameraucana hens, whom Cam had named Hillary because she acted as a leader to the other hens, wandered over to Cam and gargled inquisitively.

"Your food's in the coop, Hil. You know that." Cam bent down to pet her but the bird slid under her hand and marched up the ramp to the open door of the coop. Wayne had an entire chicken house full of several hundred birds. Was Greta up to taking care of them?

She headed into the barn and busied herself checking each of the almost week-old chicks, making sure their vents weren't clogged. Luckily none were. The chicks were growing fast, and already looked bigger than the day before. After she topped up their feed and water, she laughed watching them climb over each other.

"Yoo-hoo," a woman's voice called from the main part of the barn.

Cam left the office, closing the door behind her, to see Felicity Slavin walking toward her. Cam greeted the petite woman, one of her first volunteers and a founding member of the Westbury Locavore Club.

Felicity threw a long gray braid over her shoulder. "Thought I'd stop by and help. It's been a long winter, and I miss my farm work." She was dressed to work, in a purple sweatshirt and old jeans tucked into turquoise muck boots.

"I can always use help, thanks. How have you been?" Cam knew Felicity's husband, a tall, aging hippie, had gotten in trouble with the law last fall, but she hadn't heard if he'd gone to trial yet.

"I'm okay. It's hard with Wes, you know." She gave a little smile but her eyes looked pained. She made a waving gesture, as if brushing away the thought of her husband. "Give me a job," she said in a bright tone.

"Starting seedlings is next on my list. Come on out to the hoop house." Cam led the way.

The pipes and plastic of her high tunnel hoop house had survived the heavy snows of winter, and now held long rows of seedling flats sitting on the ground. Beyond the flats were beds of spinach and other cold-hardy mixed salad greens like mizuna, tatsoi, and arugula direct seeded in the ground. She'd been able to cut them over and over again, since they kept growing, to offer to her winter CSA customers. The sun-warmed air inside was humidified by moisture rising up out of the soil, and both women shrugged out of their jackets.

"What are those?" Felicity asked, pointing to the closest flats.

"Leeks and onions. I started them in January." The needle-like leaves of the pungent alliums were greening up nicely and reaching for the light. The lettuces next to them were younger but looked healthy, a mix of bright and dark greens with reds, and curly-leafed varieties next to rounded. Cam checked the composting worm bins on the north wall, scooping up a handful of rich dark castings off the top and scattering it on the greens beds.

"I was going to start tomatoes today." Cam pulled a couple of fat seed packets out of a box on the table. "The flats are here, and the seed-starting mix is all set in this barrel. I already moistened it." She emptied half of one packet into a shallow bowl.

"Do you make your own mix?" Felicity set one flat of seventy-two cells in a supporting tray, then scooped out a measure of mix, spreading it over the inch-wide cells.

"I do. It's a mix of a bunch of stuff—screened compost, peat moss, vermiculite, perlite, greensand, and so on."

"I heard about Wayne Laitinen. Terrible news," Felicity said as she worked.

"It's incredibly sad. He was such a sweet-hearted man. Where did you hear about it?"

"My cousin's sister-in-law is a dispatcher. She knew I'd bought roasters from Wayne and thought I might want to know."

"So you heard they're suspecting he was murdered?"

"I did. I expect your Pete is on the case."

"He is." Cam smiled at the "your Pete." She took the filled tray from Felicity and began placing one tomato seed atop each cell. After they sprouted and were established, she would pot up each seedling into a four-inch container, and eventually transplant half into the hoop house and the rest outside. With any luck, by July her salads and those of all her customers would be graced by sweet, juicy, deep-flavored tomatoes. The New England season was a short one, but with the hoop house, she could get an early start on everybody's favorite summer crop.

"Are these Sun Golds you're planting?" Felicity asked. "I love those cherry tomatoes. They're more like candy than a vegetable."

"That's for sure. But, no, these are Black Prince. I grew them last summer."

"Of course. Incredible flavor, and that deep reddish black color." Felicity smoothed the mix over the cells of another flat. "I was Wayne's high school teacher. Did you know that?"

"I didn't even know you were a teacher," Cam said. She stopped seeding and looked over at Felicity. "You don't still teach, do you? You always seem to have time for Volunteer Wednesdays."

"I took an early retirement package three years ago. But I taught English at Westbury High for more than three decades. Wayne was in one of my first classes. He and Paul Underwood."

"Interesting. I was wondering how old Wayne was."

Felicity stopped, too, and narrowed her eyes at Cam. "Let's see. They were juniors, so about sixteen, seventeen. And I was twenty-four. I'm sixty now, so that makes Wayne fifty-two or so, right? Paul, too." She resumed work, setting a finished flat aside and starting a new one. "Those two, Paul and Wayne." She made a tsking noise.

"Were they friends?"

"They were, and then they weren't. Never really understood what happened between them. Paul was the rowdier . . . no, not rowdy. It was more so like he was unscrupulous. And you know Wayne, he always took the ethical high ground."

"Did Paul cheat on a test or something?" Cam asked.

"Not in my class, he didn't." Felicity whistled. "I may look like a nice older lady, Cam, but I was a tough teacher. Nothing slipped past me." She beamed one of her sweet smiles, which did, in fact, make her look like a nice older lady.

"That seems like Wayne, to take the morally right path. It's even more ironic, then, that someone took the lowest and killed him."

Felicity shuddered. "Who would have killed a nice man like Wayne?"

Cam eased herself into the chair in front of her computer two hours later. Dasha wandered over and sat on the floor next to her, while Preston watched them both from the couch. With Felicity's help she'd seeded over six hundred tomatoes, which would yield big red slicers, small gold orbs, dry-fleshed oblongs for sauce, early medium-sized reds, and the delectable Black Prince. She and Felicity had chatted as they worked, but she hadn't learned anything else about Wayne. Or about Paul. Cam remembered seeing him driving away from Wayne's as she'd arrived the day before, and he hadn't looked happy. Too bad Felicity didn't know what the two boys' falling out had been about.

She ought to be out pruning the blueberry bushes and her antique apple tree, but she was tired. She could do that tomorrow, as long as it was before the weather warmed up for good. Felicity had suggested they call the Laitinen house and offer to help out with end-of-day chores. Cam had agreed, even though she should be doing her own chores. She'd called and talked to Megan, who said she'd be happy for help in the hen house. Surely the police wouldn't mind if they stayed in the chicken house and the barn. She took a bite of the cheese sandwich she'd fixed, then pulled up the Wicked Local news site, which already had a story about Wayne's death. Munching, she scrolled slowly through, then stopped.

"Local resident Paul Underwood discovered Laitinen's body this morning. Underwood is being questioned by authorities."

Cam leaned back in her chair. What was Paul doing over at the poultry farm again this morning? Could it be connected to whatever had happened decades earlier? She glanced at the time in the corner of the monitor. Three-thirty. She had forty minutes before she needed to pick up Felicity, time enough to dive into Google and see what she could find out. She sat up again.

Thirty-four years earlier. A time of big lapels and shoulder pads. Of men still sporting the longer hair of the decade before, but now adding a gold chain around their neck. Of tight economic times, disco dancing, and Pac-Man. Two years before her own birth. Cam shook her head. She needed to go local if she was going to dig up anything about a couple of high school boys, one apparently a straight arrow, one not so much.

Twenty minutes later she sat back again and kicked the leg of the desk. Nothing. She hadn't been able to uncover any news articles about Paul or Wayne being arrested, being charged, getting in a fight, nothing. Their names weren't in the police logs. Not in Westbury, not in Newburyport, not in

Boston. If she wanted more, she'd clearly have to spend time in the microfiche at the library, since the local paper wasn't digitized that far back.

Cam's phone rang in her bag on the kitchen table. In her dash to find it, she cracked her knee on the desk leg as she stood. Swearing, she limped to the table and scrabbled in the bag. Sure enough, it stopped ringing by the time she held it in her palm. The ID showed Alexandra's name. Cam grabbed an ice pack out of the freezer and sat with it pressed against her knee, then poked Alexandra's number.

"Sorry I missed your call. What's up?"

"Cam, they're looking for Katie. And I don't know where she is." Alexandra's voice rose.

"Calm down. Who's looking for her?" Cam asked.

"The police! Detective Pappas."

Oh. "Did he say why?"

"No. I hope she hasn't done something really stupid," Alexandra said.

"Was she part of the vandalism last night?"

"Probably, knowing Katie. She said she was going to spend the night at a friend's, so she wasn't home, anyway. I have to find her."

"Call her friends. Think about where she likes to hang out. Coffee shops, parks, whatever. Okay?"

"You're right." Alexandra exhaled over the phone. "I will. I hope she doesn't think she needs to hide or something."

"Let's assume she's not hiding. That she's at the mall trying on boots with a girlfriend. Or out having coffee. It's Sunday, so she's not at the library, but—"

"Library? My big sister?" Alexandra barked out a laugh. "Katie's not exactly the library type."

"I'm just trying to help."

Alexandra didn't speak for a moment, then said, "She might

be at a farm gazing at animals, though. That's how she got into this whole mess with those fanatics. She loves animals more than she loves people, and hates the thought of them being penned up or hurt."

"Your parents might be able to help you find her," Cam said.

"That's not going to happen. They're on vacation on Saint John."

"Oh. If I think of somewhere she might be, I'll take a look, okay? Or if I see her around town, I'll make sure she calls you."

Alexandra agreed and disconnected.

Pete was good at his job, Cam thought. If he wanted to speak with Katie, he must have good reason to.

On the way to pick up Felicity, Cam realized Pete had never called back. But she knew by now that when he was on a case, she might not see him for days on end. And Dasha was fine with her. She'd taken to keeping kibble, food and water bowls, and a spare dog bed at her house, and Dasha was good company. Not to say that Preston wasn't, but dog and cat energy couldn't be more different. Maybe she'd see Pete at the Laitinens', anyway.

"You were asking me about Paul Underwood earlier," Felicity said as they drove. "I know he was a rowdy teen, but he's sure settled down. Did you know he's a single dad?"

"I don't really know anything about him."

"He's raising three boys all by himself. I heard his wife went off the deep end after his youngest was born."

"Postpartum depression?" Cam asked.

"More like postpartum psychosis. She's still in an institution."

"That's so sad. At town meeting he said the children were all young, under eight, I think." Cam steered the truck onto

Wayne's road, and five minutes later she and Felicity were bumping along the dirt entrance to the poultry farm.

"Do you think the police are going to let us in?" Felicity asked.

Cam pulled the wheel left to avoid a pothole. "If they don't want us there, we can go out for a beer." She glanced at Felicity, who smiled, nodding.

"Uh-oh," Cam said a minute later. Once again a Westbury police car was parked crosswise at the end of the drive, but this time several news vans and other vehicles were parked on the near side of it. Ruth stood, feet apart, arms folded, speaking to a clutch of what looked like reporters, with camera people standing behind them.

Cam pulled to the side of the road and parked. "Wonder if Ruthie will let us through?"

"No way to find out except by trying," Felicity said in her trademark bright tone. She opened her door and jumped out.

Cam climbed out, too, and nearly had to lope to keep up with Felicity's short, fast stride. When they reached the group, they slowed.

"The family is not available for interviews at this time," Ruth was saying. "And, as I said, official news of the investigation will come from State Police Detective Peter Pappas. You'll be notified, and it'll probably happen at the Essex County DA's office, not here. People, just go home, okay? Let Ms. Laitinen and her family grieve in peace." Ruth caught sight of Cam and Felicity and beckoned them over.

Felicity slipped by the right edge of the phalanx of news crews with Cam close behind. A clutch at Cam's elbow made her whirl.

"You're Cam Flaherty, aren't you?" A slim, neatly coiffed, and perfectly made up female reporter gazed at her. "You had a murder at your own farm last year. Would you care to comment?"

Cam shook her head and extracted her arm.

"Leave these folks alone," Ruth said. "They're friends of the family." She held out her arm and ushered them beyond the police car even as another reporter called out a question.

"What are you doing here?" Ruth asked Cam in a low voice.

"We came to help with the chores," Felicity answered. "Megan said it was fine. We don't have to go in the house at all. But it's a lot of work, and Greta won't want to be out there feeding, watering, and collecting eggs."

"Can we?" Cam asked, raising her eyebrows.

Ruth let out a breath. "Let me check." As she'd done earlier in the day, she moved a few steps away and spoke into the mike on her shoulder, then turned back. "It's okay. But only the chicken house and the barn. And don't touch anything you don't have to."

"What'll we do with the eggs?" Cam asked. "We can wash them, assuming there's a sink in the barn, but once they're clean they need to be refrigerated."

"Just leave them in the barn," Ruth said. "I'll ask Greta what to do with them later."

Cam thanked her before she and Felicity began the walk down the hill to the chicken house. Cam glanced toward the farmhouse. What had Dasha uncovered earlier? She turned back toward Ruth.

"Do you know if Pete checked the thing Dasha found under the bushes earlier?"

Ruth shook her head. "No idea what you're talking about. What thing?"

"It was about the size of a pen but not a pen. I left it there and texted Pete about it."

"You'll have to ask him."

"I will." Cam turned away again. The red-splashed side of the long chicken house faced north, so snow still lay in the shadows and the air tasted more of winter than of impending spring. She pulled her work jacket closed at the neck and took long strides to catch up with Felicity.

Felicity slowed before they reached the door. "I don't get these activists, do you?" She gestured to the spray-painted words that read, "Stop Eating Animals," accompanied by several obscenities.

"No, I don't. When I saw Wayne on the television news this morning, he said they'd opened all the doors. Freeing the chickens." Cam snorted, her hand on the door. "As if domesticated hens would even know what to do in the wild." She gazed at the house. "Poor Wayne. I still can't believe he's gone."

Chapter 6

Cam made her way down the long row of nesting boxes. The house held about four hundred hens, dozens already perched on roosting bars, some pecking the red nipples of the watering system, a long pipe that ran the length of the house about a foot off the ground with nipples set into it at regular intervals to provide fresh water on demand. Other hens roamed around the open space or dug in the bedding underfoot. The air was ripe with the smell of livestock, but not overpowering. She had no idea what system Wayne used for changing the bedding or how often he did it. This operation was ten times larger than her own small flock. In her coop, Cam simply shoveled out the floor, adding the soiled bedding to the compost pile, and then spread clean stuff around.

As she reached into the pine shavings to pull out the last two eggs, the chicken house door at the end of the building squeaked open.

"Ladies," Pete said. He stood silhouetted by the late afternoon sun.

Felicity called a greeting from the other end of the building where she was scooping pelleted feed into a cylindrical feeder.

The hens in that area clustered around her, gargling with excitement. Cam gently set her eggs in the now-full bucket and carried it toward Pete.

"How's it going?" She set the heavy bucket down and stretched.

Pete glanced at Felicity before speaking in a voice meant only for Cam's ears. "This is a tough one." He frowned. "I retrieved that object Dasha uncovered, but I haven't had a chance to investigate what in heck it is."

"Won't the autopsy show how Wayne died?"

"Should. But that won't get done until tomorrow, if we're lucky." He tapped the fingers of his right hand on his leg. "Dasha's okay?" A softer look replaced the one of professional worry.

"Of course. I think he likes being on the farm."

"He likes you." Now Pete's soft look included Cam. "As do I." He let out a sigh. "But I'm not going to be free tonight. I can predict that right now. Do you mind keeping him?"

"Not at all. As long as you need me to. How are Greta and Megan doing?"

His frown returned, with his heavy, dark eyebrows meeting in the middle. "Greta doesn't like us treating this as a suspicious death. Not one bit."

Felicity strode toward them. "Detective, have you apprehended the perp?"

Pete's frown turned to a smile. "What kind of television are you watching, anyway?"

Felicity smiled. "I don't get to say 'perp' all that often." Her smile fell away. "But it must be murder if you're involved, right?"

"I'm not at liberty to say. And I need to be getting back to work."

"I'm going to wash these in the barn and then we'll clear out of here." Cam gestured at the eggs.

Pete picked up the bucket. "I'll carry them for you." He led the way out the door toward the barn a few yards away up the hill.

Cam stepped ahead of him and slid the wide door open enough for them to get through, then took the bucket from him. "Thanks. Call when you can."

"You know I will." He cast a longing look at her before sliding the door closed after him.

The creak of the wheels in the rusty track at the top of the door gritted in Cam's ears.

"I think you snagged a good one," Felicity said.

"I did." Cam smiled at her.

"I know you liked Jake, but he was way too volatile."

"Yeah." A year ago Cam had met the bigger-than-life chef when she'd arranged to sell him some of her produce for his high-end restaurant, The Market. Their relationship had grown closer than just farmer-to-restaurateur, but Jake had proved to be the hot-tempered jealous sort—jealous without provocation—and Cam had stopped seeing him. When she and Detective Pete later started spending romantic time together, it was a surprise, but an exceedingly pleasant one, and she'd known she'd made the right choice about Jake.

"Now, where's the washing station?" Cam glanced around. "It's got to be here somewhere." The illumination from two high windows facing west let in enough light to see by as she wandered through the building with Felicity. The air smelled of old wood and a hint of manure, with an overlay of motor oil. The barn had held horses or other large livestock at some point, with a row of now unoccupied stalls lining one wall and tack cupboards set into the wall opposite. Behind the stalls an antique red tractor sat in a corner of the open central space and bags of chicken feed were stacked on a palette, still in clear plastic shrink wrap. Now that Wayne was gone, would Greta continue the poultry operation? Maybe their son would step in and take it over.

"There it is." Felicity pointed at an industrial sink and drain board in an alcove in the far corner. A refrigerator hummed next to it.

"Oh, good, there's a fridge, too." Cam set the bucket next to the sink.

Felicity filled the wide deep sink with water and the two women worked together, carefully scrubbing each egg, then setting the orb into twelve-by-twelve cardboard flats Cam had lifted off a stack on a shelf near the sink.

The wide door creaked open, then closed. Cam couldn't see it from where they worked, so she dried her hands on her jeans and walked around the corner of the alcove. Greta's hand stretched into one of the tack cupboards.

"Greta—"

Greta whirled, eyes wide, holding a small bag in one hand. When she saw Cam, she whipped the bag behind her back. "What are you doing here?" She'd changed out of her church clothes into dark jeans and a sweatshirt.

"We collected the eggs and we're washing them."

"Who's we?" Greta's voice was tight and she almost barked the words.

"My friend Felicity and me. The officer outside said it was okay."

"Well, nobody asked me. This is my farm."

"Of course it is. I called earlier and Megan said it would be fine. We just wanted to help. I thought you would be too upset by Wayne's death to want to come out and do his chores."

She nodded slowly. "I'm sorry. You're right. Thank you,

Cam." She edged toward the door, keeping the bag out of Cam's sight. "I am upset and I appreciate your help. But I can handle the morning chores tomorrow. You don't need to come back."

"What's in that bag?" Cam asked.

"This?" Greta laughed and flashed it at Cam before stuffing it in her pocket. "It's the dog's thyroid medicine. He has to take it twice a day. Wayne and Pluto spent more time out here than in the house, but it's easier for me to keep it in the kitchen." She opened the door and stepped through.

As it slid shut after her, Cam stared. If it was really thyroid medicine, why was Greta trying to hide it?

Cam dropped Felicity at her house and headed back toward her farm on the other side of town to put her own chickens to bed. She dutifully slowed to the posted twenty-five miles per hour going through the small center, where the Food Mart held court across the street from the Westbury House of Pizza, which was across the parking lot from the post office. And that was about it for downtown, except for a barber shop, an insurance company and, a little farther down, SK Foreign Auto, her friend Sim's car repair shop.

Cam approached Church Street, appropriately named as it was flanked on one side by the Catholic Church and on the other by the Congregational. Alexandra's idea that Katie might be out somewhere communing with livestock flashed in Cam's brain. She jerked the wheel and veered sharply to the left off Main Street. The car behind her blasted its horn. Cam ducked her head and waved a sheepish hand as she headed downhill on Church Street toward the bridge over the Merrimack River. On the other side of the river was Randalls', the llama farm, on the outskirts of the city of Haverhill. When Katie had helped out building the coop for Cam's rescue hens last fall, she'd mentioned how much she loved the graceful big-eyed South American beasts. Maybe Katie was finding peace communing with the llamas.

The sun angled low on the wide river as Cam drove over the historic Rocks Village Bridge, which looked like it was built by a giant playing with an Erector Set. Cam smiled to herself. She'd overheard a local at town meeting refer to it as the Mother-in-Law Bridge because someone was reputed to have tossed his mother-in-law off it into the Merrimack. In a few more minutes she arrived at the farm, which advertised its own pork, grass-fed beef, honey, maple syrup, and hay.

She parked in the lot, empty now that the farm store was closed because it was March. The Randall corn maze was a big draw in the fall, and in the winter they sponsored horse-drawn sleigh rides. But this month in New England, otherwise known as mud season, was a slow time at farms that had branched out into the entertainment business to make ends meet. Cam grabbed her phone before she set out in search of the llamas, and Katie, too. She supposed it wasn't a good sign that no cars were parked in the lot, but for all she knew, Katie didn't have a car. She and Alexandra had ridden bicycles that time last fall when the volunteers built the coop.

Making her way around the edge of the fenced-in field, Cam was glad for her muck boots. It was definitely mud season. The fence led up a gentle slope, with woods to Cam's left, the bare bark of the deciduous trees black and ominous. She'd better find the llamas soon. If Katie wasn't here, Cam didn't want to be outside in an unfamiliar setting after sunset, with the temperature dropping quickly to a more seasonable chill.

She crested the hill and spied several tall necks sticking up in a clump of furry bodies a dozen yards away. Inside the fence surrounding the field, a tall-backed woman sat cross-legged as if in meditation. She faced the animals but had her back to

Cam. A rainbow-striped knit cap covered her head, with two dark braids trailing out of it down her back. She looked a lot like Katie.

Cam thought about calling Pete or Alexandra, but it would be dark soon. She thought she could talk Katie into coming with her and then they could make the call. Cam examined the fence, on which leaned a mud-spattered bicycle. The four-foot-high welded wire barrier didn't appear to have an electrified top. She pulled her sleeves over her hands just in case before clambering over the top and nearly caught her toe in the fencing on the way down, ever ungraceful. As she approached the woman and the llamas, a white one turned its head and regarded Cam with dark eyes that drooped at their corners. Katie turned her head, too, and then slumped as if deflated.

"Hey, Katie." Cam squatted next to her.

Katie pulled her knees up and wrapped her arms around them. "What are you doing here?"

Cam gazed at the llamas, who watched her now from their position with all four legs tucked underneath them. "Beautiful animals. They seem to like you." She'd never been so close to one before and hoped they wouldn't get nasty. Her parents had ridden camels, a relative of llamas, in West Africa and had said they could be mean. But she had to find a way to reach Katie. And if it meant sitting here a few feet away from a big cud-chewing animal, so be it.

Katie nodded without speaking.

"Do you come here a lot? Do they have names?" Cam asked.

"Yeah. Paloma's that one. Carlos is there, and Francisco is the dark one. Javiera is the little guy."

"This is a peaceful spot."

The sad-eyed white llama named Paloma chewed in a figure-eight pattern as it watched Cam. Javiera extended its long neck until its face was inches from Cam's, way too close for her comfort, so she scooted back a little.

Katie let out a long breath through her lips, facing Cam at last. "I know I have to go back. I'm only postponing it."

"Why?"

"I did something really stupid last night. I never should have gone to Laitinen's with those idiots. They talked me into helping with their action," she said, surrounding the last word with finger quotes. "But Wayne is a good farmer, and it was just stupid. At least I kept them from shooing all the hens outside." She rolled her eyes. "Those guys don't know anything about animals. They thought four hundred hens would want to go wild and roost in the trees. Ridiculous."

"Alexandra told me Detective Pappas wants to speak with you. Do you know why?"

Katie sighed again. "I have an idea why. I went back to the farm this morning."

Cam stared at her. No wonder Pete wanted to talk with Katie.

"I felt bad about the vandalism, and wanted to apologize to Mr. Laitinen. But that pesticide guy was there—"

"Paul Underwood?"

"Yeah. He saw me and, I don't know, I freaked out and left before I saw Mr. Laitinen. And then when I heard on the news that he was dead, I had to get away. I seem to screw up everything I do lately."

"Listen, why don't you come home with me. We'll have a bite to eat, and I'll call Pete, I mean Detective Pappas. You didn't do anything wrong besides the vandalism." Cam stood and extended a hand to Katie. When she didn't take it, Cam said, "Come on. It's getting dark and cold. We'll throw your bike in the back of my truck. And call Alexandra so she stops worrying about you."

Two of the llamas rose, too, and took a step toward Cam.

Katie crossed her legs again and stood in one fluid motion. She stroked each llama on the nose, murmuring soft words, then straightened and faced Cam. "Let's go. Time I faced the facts."

Cam pulled into the Food Mart parking lot and turned off the truck. "I need to pick up a few things for dinner. Want to come in?" She looked at Katie in the passenger seat.

"I guess." Katie reached for the door handle.

"I'll bet you're a vegetarian."

"But not a vegan."

"Me, I eat everything." Cam held up a hand when Katie started to speak. "But I try to mostly eat meat from Tender-crop Farm, so I know it was raised running around in the fresh air and treated well." She glanced at Katie. "And Laitinen's chicken, of course."

"Look, I said I was sorry." Katie's nostrils flared. "You don't have to keep rubbing it in." She wrenched open the truck door and slid out.

Cam leaned across the seat. "I need to call Detective Pappas. He'll want to know where you are. I'll see you in there." The door slammed on her last word.

By the time Cam got into the small grocery store, she spied Katie's hat heading toward the wine aisle. Good. They both could use a glass, although if Katie had to talk with Pete soon, maybe that wasn't the best of ideas. He'd thanked her for the call and said he'd be over as soon as he finished up something.

Cam grabbed a basket and ambled toward the aisle that held pasta and jars of sauce. She added several of each to her basket, a packet of chocolate cookies from one aisle over, and then headed for the cheese section, picking up a block of Romano for grating, and ricotta and pregrated mozzarella just to have around. That was plenty for a simple, quick supper.

When she reached the checkout line, Katie had already paid for a bottle of red, and the steel-haired cashier was sliding it into a narrow paper bag. Katie looked around the woman behind her in line at Cam. "Okay?"

Cam laughed as she set the contents of her basket onto the rolling checkout belt. "We're both over twenty-one." She could caution her about not overindulging once they got home. Cam was digging in her bag for her wallet when the woman standing in between Katie and Cam spoke to Katie.

"I heard you were with that vandalism group last night up at Laitinens'. You ought to be ashamed of yourself, young lady."

The cashier stood with her hand on Cam's box of spaghetti and pursed her lips, nodding.

"Them are good folks, and now Wayne's dead," the woman continued. "What, did you kill him off? Wasn't enough to try to freeze all them hens?"

Katie stared. She opened her mouth to speak, then closed it. Turning, she rushed out the door.

The customer muttered to the cashier about liberals and no-good young people as she swiped her card with more force than was necessary. Cam kept her own mouth shut, as well. It wouldn't do any good to argue with her. Nobody was going to change that woman's mind. Besides, Cam agreed with her about the vandalism. She waited as her own purchases were rung up. She paid and made her way out.

Outside the temperature had indeed plummeted as the sun made its descent, forecasting a night with the mercury dipping below freezing. Katie stood at the back of Cam's truck talking with Greta. And by the looks of it, Greta wasn't a bit happy, her finger pointed at Katie's chest. *Uh-oh*. And what was Greta doing out shopping the night her husband had been killed?

"That Detective Pappas thinks you killed my husband. Either you or one of your crazy friends." She glanced at Cam. "What are you doing driving a murderer around?"

"A murderer? What's going on in this town?" Katie asked. "I didn't kill Mr. Laitinen." She shook her head, hard. "I wouldn't do that. He was a nice man. I don't even kill animals to eat. Why would I—"

"You'll have to ask Pappas that." Greta whirled and stalked toward the store. She called back to Katie, "I'm warning you. Don't you ever go near my property again or you might end up the dead one."

Chapter 7

Cam latched the door of the coop after making sure Ruffles and all the hens were safely inside. She'd left Katie and her glass of wine waiting for the pasta water to boil as Katie spoke with Alexandra. Maybe they could have a calming dinner before Pete showed up. As Cam walked toward the farmhouse, with Dasha poking around the yard, the full Worm Moon lifted its bright, cold head above the trees. The Worm Moon was the name the Algonquins had taught the colonists for the month when the soil softened and worms began to come alive. With tonight's temperatures chilling the ground, though, Cam expected the worms were going to remain in hiding for a few more days. New Englanders preferred to call the first full moon in March the Sap Moon because it heralded the movement of the maple sap in the trees' veins.

Dasha barked and trotted to the driveway, and the crunch of gravel made Cam turn her head. The motion detector light outside her back door sprang to life, illuminating Pete's old Saab. So they wouldn't be having a quiet dinner first, after all.

When Pete climbed out, Cam called, "Yo, Detective."

He glanced over at her with a smile. "My favorite farmer." Dasha ran up for a pet, and Cam walked up to Pete, too.

She'd opened her mouth to speak when the farmhouse door opened.

"Cam?" Katie called, holding the screen door open with one hand, wineglass in the other. "The water's . . ." She stared at Pete.

He lifted a hand. "Nice to see you, Ms. Magnusson."

The screen door slammed as Katie clattered down the steps. "I heard you want to talk to me, Detective. I was part of the vandalism, but I did not kill Mr. Laitinen." Her voice was calm as she raised her chin.

Pete scratched between his eyebrows. "Can we go inside?"

"Of course," Cam said.

Katie turned and strode back to the house. Pete shut the door to his car and followed Cam toward the steps, Dasha at his side, then reached out and touched her arm after the door closed behind Katie. Cam turned toward him.

"You couldn't have known we were looking for Katie," he said in a quiet voice. "Why did you even go looking for her? I never told you we wanted to question her."

"Alexandra called and told me. It occurred to me that, loving animals as much as she does, Katie might be over at Randall Farm. She'd talked about the llamas last fall when she was here helping build my chicken coop."

"Thanks for calling about Katie."

Cam shivered and gazed at the warm light from the kitchen windows pushing out into the darkening night. "Want some pasta?"

When Pete and Cam walked into the kitchen, Dasha eagerly at Pete's side, Katie was stirring the pasta in the big pot.

Without turning, she said, "I put in the whole box, in case he's hungry." A pot of sauce simmered on a smaller burner, and she'd set the farm table in the eating area with three place mats, plates, and silverware.

Cam raised her eyebrows at Pete.

Sighing again, he said, "I am hungry. Very." He drummed his fingers on the countertop next to him. "Okay, I'll eat. But I do need to bring you in for questioning, Ms. Magnusson, and we're not going to do it over dinner."

"I understand," Katie said. "Got a colander, Cam?"

Cam showed her where it was. "I suppose you're working, so no wine?" Cam asked Pete.

He shook his head. "Would love a cup of coffee, though."

Cam and Katie busied themselves getting dinner on the table for a few minutes as Pete retreated to the living room with Dasha. Cam started a pot of coffee, then rummaged in the refrigerator until she pulled out a small jar.

"I'll stir some of last summer's pesto into the sauce," she said. "The little cheese grater is in that drawer," she told Katie, pointing.

A couple of minutes later, Katie set the wide shallow dish full of steaming spaghetti topped with pestoed tomato sauce in the middle of the table while Cam put a chunk of Romano on the table and poured herself a glass of wine.

"Soup's on, Pete." She grabbed a big spoon and the pasta server from the kitchen and served up the mix onto each plate, then passed around the cheese.

Katie sat and grated in silence, Pete taking the chair opposite her. Cam sank into the chair at the end and sipped her wine. She glanced at Pete, who had delivered a forkful of pasta to his mouth. For several minutes, the only sounds were forks on china, chewing, and swallowing.

"Katie, how long have you been hanging out with the llamas?" Cam asked. There had to be something neutral they all could talk about.

Katie's face brightened. "Every chance I get. They are so not like people. They simply sit and chew, and walk around. I feel like I can communicate with them."

"I have trouble communicating with people, myself," Cam said.

"You don't feel any need to open their gate and let them out into the wild?" Pete asked.

That wasn't fair. He'd said no questioning during dinner.

Katie tilted her head to the side before she answered. "No." She gazed at Pete with her mouth set in a determined expression.

Cam racked her brain for what other safe topic she could bring up, since that one had clearly bombed. "What do you do for work, Katie?" she finally asked.

"I'm an assistant for Judith Patterson. A flunky, more so. She works from home and needs somebody to be her secretary. But I also pick up her cleaning and such." She shrugged. "It's a part-time job. She pays me well for my afternoons, but it's not my life's work or anything."

"What's her profession?" Pete asked.

"She's a consultant, does something with finance. She only goes into Boston once a week."

"Did you ever hear her talking about wanting to buy part of Wayne and Greta's land for her daughter's horse?" Cam glanced at Pete before she looked at Katie.

"For sure. She was wicked focused on that. Said Greta wanted to sell but Wayne didn't." Katie pushed her half-finished plate away. Her wineglass still held half its contents, too. "Thanks for dinner, Cam. I guess I'm ready when you are, Detective."

Pete made fast work of the rest of his pasta. "Thanks from me, too. Didn't expect to get a hot home-cooked meal tonight," he said. "A delicious one, too. Now, happen to have a travel mug I can borrow?" Dasha barked as Pete stood. He leaned down to stroke the dog's head. "You're going to stay here, boy, if it's okay with Cam."

"You know it is." She stood, and a minute later brought him a mug full of black coffee with a lid firmly screwed on. She moved to Katie's side near the door, where Katie was buttoning up her coat.

"Are you okay to do this alone?" Cam spoke in a low voice. "Do you want me to come, or to call Alexandra again?"

Katie looked down. "You're right. I'll call my sister. But I didn't kill him. I'm sure I'll be home soon."

"Does she need a lawyer, Pete?" Cam asked.

"It's up to her."

Katie pulled her knit hat on, tugging it down over her ears, and glanced up. "I'm going to leave my bike here, if that's okay."

"Of course."

Katie set her jaw and faced the door. "Let's get this over with."

Cam puttered around the kitchen, spooning the uneaten pasta into a small container, storing the cheese. She poured herself another glass of wine and sipped it in between washing plates, pots, and silverware. Albert and Marie had never gotten around to installing a dishwasher. Living alone, Cam didn't see the need for one, either.

But her thoughts were elsewhere as her hands worked in the warm soapy water. On Katie being questioned. Pete couldn't think she had motive to actually murder Wayne, could he? Cam also mused at Greta's anger, seemingly at the world. Cam could have mentioned the bag and Greta's assertion that it was thyroid medicine to Pete while he was here, but she hadn't wanted to talk about that in front of Katie. She pulled out her phone and texted him about it.

Cam's mind jumped to Judith pressuring the Laitinens to sell, and the couple not being in agreement about the decision. And then there was Paul Underwood driving away from the farm yesterday in a huff. He was also the one who found Wayne's body this morning. Why had he gone back?

After she wiped down the counters, Cam dried her hands and fed Preston and Dasha, then took Dasha out on a leash until he'd done his business. Back inside, she took her wine to her laptop on the desk tucked in a corner of the living room. She found the digital world a comfort, a familiar, logical place to hang out. And, often, to find answers. She'd already struck out trying to discover anything about Paul's younger life. She did a search on Judith Patterson, but all seemed to be as it was. A divorced single mother with a high-powered job. Nothing there.

Greta Laitinen was next. Greta Carlson Laitinen, apparently. A search for Greta Carlson yielded a notice about graduating Phi Beta Kappa with honors in biology from Wellesley College. Wow. The chicken farmer's wife had brains. Cam stared at a picture of a much younger Greta in gown and mortarboard beaming next to Wayne. Had her dreams been dashed? Maybe they'd started a family a little sooner than they'd intended and Greta hadn't seen her way clear to pursuing her own career. Working as an aide in the library wouldn't be much of a challenge for a star biologist, and resentment often led to anger.

Cam thought of the cylindrical object Dasha had uncovered. How to describe it? She typed, "canister three inches" and hit Enter. Nope. She got "kitchen canisters" and "three-inch gun ordnance." The thing had been more like a cartridge, but those results yielded cartridges for guns and printers. It looked a bit like a shotgun shell, but slimmer. She changed the size to four inches, but nothing looked like the cylinder Dasha had dug up. She sat back and sipped her wine.

Preston wandered over and rubbed against her leg while Cam spent a few minutes checking her e-mail and the farm's Web site. She hadn't posted to the blog in a couple of weeks, but March wasn't much of a news month in the life of a New England farm. She'd take pictures tomorrow of the pruning. She checked the time in the corner of the screen. Nine o'clock and time to curl up with an old movie. She'd figure out that cylinder later. Or let Pete do it. It was his job, after all, not hers.

"Come on, Preston." Cam curled up on the couch with her wine, Preston jumped up to join her, and she switched on the television and selected a movie. The TV was one appliance she had definitely upgraded when she moved in, bringing her flat screen with her from Cambridge. Dasha trotted over and settled on the floor next to the couch. The familiar images of *Casablanca* calmed her. It had been a rough couple of days, and she deserved an hour and a half of escaping into the world of the last century.

She'd been enjoying the movie for a while when a white-tuxedoed Humphrey Bogart lit a cigarette. Cam sat up straight and startled Preston, who leapt to the floor.

A cigarette. Bogart smoked a traditional cigarette. But the cylinder Dasha had found was an e-cigarette cartridge. Like the one Judith Patterson had been smoking in the restaurant last night.

Chapter 8

Cam awoke to sunshine warming the old floorboards in her upstairs bedroom, which meant it was after seven, sleeping in for a farmer. She had texted Pete about the e-cigarette the night before, then had resumed watching the movie. She yawned, feeling distinctly unrested. Her sleep had been punctuated by unsettling dreams and several periods of lying awake, wanting to get back to sleep but being afraid she'd slide back into the last dream sequence.

But now she had work to do, since she'd accomplished essentially nothing on the farm yesterday. Twenty minutes later she was dressed, caffeinated, at least the initial dose, and outside opening the chicken coop, with Dasha sitting in front of the barn. Hillary came strutting out, followed by a wing-flapping Ruffles, who flew to the top of the fence and announced the day. Cam freshened up their food and water, glad she had only forty, not four hundred like Wayne and Greta. No, only Greta, now.

Inside the barn, Cam checked on the chicks in the office. The little puffs seemed to have grown overnight. She gave them fresh food and water, too, and added a few handfuls of new bedding. She smiled and cooed to them in their box, laughing when a couple pecked at her fingers.

She wandered into the hoop house and stretched. She needed to do the pruning, start more seeds, and harvest a load of compost from the worm bins. But it was still chilly out and she'd rather prune during the midday hours when she could catch the warmth of the sun. What she wanted to do was go ask Judith if that was her e-cig cartridge that ended up under the Laitinens' shrubbery. It could be innocent. Judith must have visited the farmhouse trying to convince Wayne to sell. Would she go so far as to kill Wayne to get the land, though? Even though Cam had come in contact with more than one murderer over the last year, she still didn't understand how someone could be driven to commit such a horrible deed.

She turned on the hose and watered the greens growing in the long beds, watching the gentle spray from the watering wand wet the variously shaped and colored leaves of the Asian greens, spinach, and lettuces. She didn't have any reason to pay Judith a visit, since she didn't actually know her. And surely lots of people used e-cigarettes these days. When the plants and seedlings were all watered, Cam spent half an hour starting two flats each of Asian eggplant and assorted hot peppers, including the superhot orange habanero and the fiery Bangkok, a tiny red Thai pepper. She wheeled the garden cart over to the worm bins and shoveled out the finished castings, then sprinkled them over the greens to feed their need for nitrogen.

As she walked back to the house for breakfast and more coffee, Preston streaking ahead of her and Dasha trotting at her side, Cam spied Katie's bike in the back of the truck. Katie, who worked for Judith. Cam snapped her fingers. Now she had a plausible reason for going to see Judith. But first she needed to call Great-Uncle Albert. Despite an assisted living residence being his home and despite his eighty-six years, he still had the pulse of the town, even though he hadn't been at the town meeting.

After the last bite of cheese omelet and toast, Cam dialed Albert's number on the old house phone, which had an actual dial.

"Cammy, what a pleasure," Albert said after greeting her.

Cam smiled to herself at her childhood nickname.

"What's this I hear about our friend Wayne? Gone too soon, and murdered, apparently."

"It's terrible news." She wasn't surprised that Albert already knew.

"Does your Pete have a suspect in custody?"

"Not yet. Listen, how about if I come over for a visit this afternoon? I haven't seen you in a couple of weeks."

"I'd be much pleased, but I've got computer club this afternoon. How about tomorrow at four, instead? Bring me some of that—"

"Ipswich IPA. You bet. Four o'clock?"

"We'll have our own private happy hour."

Cam stood at the front door to Judith's designer home. Most of the houses in this part of town were farmhouses several centuries old, some renovated, some, like the Laitinens', not. But Judith had either torn down the prior residence or had cleared woods to build this Colonial-style mansion. A three-car garage connected at the left side, and every detail looked expensive, from the beveled glass of the entryway to the impeccable landscaping of the front lawn and the curved borders of the still-dormant gardens. No cracks marred the driveway pavement, no dirt lurked in the corners of the windows.

Taking a deep breath, Cam pressed the backlit doorbell. She'd waited until nine-thirty before driving here, and had changed out of her work clothes into clean jeans and a sweater. She stood at the door and listened to chickadees beeping as they flitted around one of the pines at the edge of the lawn. The sunshine was rapidly warming the air.

No one appeared at the door. Cam glanced at a small black device mounted above the door. Was that a camera? She took a step back on the pad of irregularly shaped paving stones. Should she ring again, or leave? She should have called first. She'd turned to go when she heard the faint sound of heels clicking inside. Cam faced the door again as it swung open.

"Yes?" Judith also wore jeans and a sweater, although hers were designer versions. She raised her thin eyebrows. "Can I help you?"

Cam stepped forward, extending her hand. "I'm Cam Flaherty, from up on Attic Hill Road. I'm a friend of your employee Katie Magnusson. We had dinner last night and it was too late for her to ride home. I have her bike in the truck. Is she here working?"

Judith pursed her lips, finally reaching out to shake Cam's hand with a firm touch. "Judith Patterson. But Katie isn't here." She pulled her hand back.

"I guess I'll take the bike back home then. She told me you're a financial planner. Do you suppose I could ask you a few questions?"

"I suppose. Come in." Judith led the way down a long hall toward the back.

Cam pulled the door shut behind her and followed, ending up in a huge pristine kitchen lit by skylights and a wall of windows facing a small garden in front of the woods. What looked like a modest stable on the left appeared to be attached to the back of the garage. Inside, stone countertops gleamed and the black-and-white motif was unwarmed by any splashes of color.

Cam couldn't even see a refrigerator, so a collection of goofy magnets and family photos wasn't part of the scene, either.

Judith pointed to a long cherry table at the side of the room. "Sit. Coffee?"

"I'd love some, thanks." Cam pulled out a chair and lowered herself into it.

Judith inserted a pod into a single-serving brewer, brought over milk, sugar, and a spoon in a modern silver set, then set a steaming mug in front of Cam. With an erect back, Judith sat across the table.

"You're the organic farmer, right?" Judith tapped a long red nail on the table.

Cam added a little milk to the dark rich brew, took a sip, then set down the mug. "I am. That's how I know Katie. Her sister, Alexandra, is one of my volunteers and customers."

"Katie's a good girl. So did you see the local news yesterday?"

"About the vandalism at Wayne's farm, and his death?" Cam asked.

"Poor Wayne." Judith shook her head. "I've heard gossip that he was killed, that it wasn't a heart attack."

"I heard the same thing."

"I don't like the thought of a murderer in our small town. Wayne's farm is right through the woods from here, in fact."

"I know." Cam took a deep breath. She had to give this a try. "Listen, about Katie. I think she's a decent girl, but I wondered if you thought she was—"

Judith interrupted. "Capable of murder?" She barked out a laugh. "Are you kidding? If she finds a fly or a mosquito inside, she traps it and sets it loose outdoors. Kill a person? No way. Impossible."

"Good. I feel the same way."

Judith rose and picked up something from a shelf across the

room. She returned to the table holding a slender e-cigarette. "Do you mind if I vape?"

Vape? So that was the verb, for vapor, she guessed. Cam shook her head. "Anyway, my portfolio is small, but I'd love some advice about where to invest it."

"I'm a consultant in the financial sector. I work in high net worth wealth management, primarily. But I could recommend someone, if you'd like." Judith put the tip of the black cylinder to her mouth. As she took a long drag, a purple light shone at the tip and vapor curled into the air. She pulled out the e-cig and inhaled deeply, then said, "I'm fortunate to work from home, and Katie's a big help."

"She appreciates the job." Cam sipped her coffee. "Wayne was a friend of mine, helping me with my small flock of chickens. I heard Greta and him talking about your offer to buy a parcel of their land."

"It's a generous offer, and it's still on the table." Judith sniffed. "It was ridiculous of him to refuse, although I shouldn't speak ill of the dead. He and Greta needed the money badly. But he had a silly notion of keeping all that unused land in the family."

"Does Greta feel differently about it?"

"Yes, but now it will be tied up in the disposal of his estate. I still want that land for my daughter's horse." She gestured with the e-cig toward the woods beyond the yard. "Their property line is only a few yards into the trees there. My Isabella is growing up fast." She put the e-cig to her lips again. "And all she cares about is horses. Not Harry Potter, not ballet, not science."

"How old is she?"

"Eleven going on twenty." Judith barked out another laugh.

"So you must have been over at Wayne's talking with them about your offer." Cam cringed inwardly. She knew she was at risk of sounding like a busybody, but maybe she could help Pete by learning what Judith and Wayne's dealings had been.

"Yeah. We're neighbors." Judith raised a shoulder and let it drop. "In fact, he had asked me over to breakfast the morning he was killed."

"Oh? Did you go?"

"I don't think that's any of your business." She cocked her head, gazing at Cam. "You're awfully curious about all this. Why do you care if I buy part of the Laitinen property or not?" Her dark eyes pinned Cam.

"I don't care, particularly. But they're friends of mine. Anyway, as you said, the land will probably be tied up in probate for a while." Cam stood. "Thanks for the coffee."

"If you see Katie, tell her I'll need her at the usual time today." Judith stood as well. She led Cam down the hall, heels tapping a sharp rhythm.

As the door to her Ford creaked open, Cam glanced back at the house. Judith remained in the doorway, arms folded, her raptor gaze focused only on Cam.

Chapter 9

Cam lopped a sucker off the apple tree an hour later, then stood back to figure out where to cut next. The book open on the ground next to her said to prune only at the junction of one branch with another, to remove any branch that rubbed on another, and to open up the canopy. She looked from book to tree to book. Where was the apprenticeship system when she needed it? Learning pruning would be so much easier with an experienced orchardist showing her how.

Dasha picked up the long thin sucker in his jaws and looked expectantly at her. Cam laughed, wrested it out of his mouth, and hurled it far across the field toward the woods at the back of her property. The sun warming the air was a welcome blessing on the day and lightened her mood, which had darkened from her visit to Judith. Cam didn't know why she'd wasted her time following up on the e-cig cartridge. Judith had every reason to visit Wayne and she could have dropped the e-cig at the house. True, killing him removed the obstacle of his objection to selling, but now it didn't appear that Greta would be able to sell for a while, at least according to Judith.

Cam shook her head. She'd texted Pete about the e-cig, and about Judith's saying Wayne had invited her for breakfast. Let him deal with it. Cam's work was farming, not detecting. She aimed the long-handled loppers at a thick branch, but they only went halfway through. She twisted the branch, and when it finally came free it took a strip of bark from where it was attached. Her virtual teacher, the book, specifically said to avoid doing that, as it opened the tree to infection.

Cam blew out a breath. This apple tree was the last to survive of the small orchard of antique varieties that Albert and Marie had planted when they'd first married sixty-some years ago. It yielded delicious if somewhat misshapen winey fruit, but it was a lot of work maintaining it organically, and she should have sharpened the old loppers before starting this task. She set down the loppers and picked up her hand pruners. These she'd ordered new in the winter, so they were sharp and nicely oiled, and the smooth red handles felt perfect in her palm. She focused on the smaller branches, clipping the suckers that shot straight up in the middle.

"Yo, Cam!" a female voice called after she'd been working about twenty minutes. Alexandra and Katie appeared from behind the barn and strode toward her. Alexandra was taller than her older sister but they shared the same forthright gait.

Cam waved her pruners. When they reached her, she greeted them.

"You survived last night?" she asked Katie.

Katie shoved her hands in the pockets of her navy pea coat and nodded. "They let me go home, so I guess I survived it."

"What kind of questions did they ask you?" Cam asked.

"They went over and over the vandalism, how I knew those people, and why I went back in the morning." Katie's face was pale under her knit hat and she chewed on her lower lip.

"She kept telling them the same thing," Alexandra added. "That she felt bad, went back to apologize, and then freaked out when she saw Paul Underwood."

"I wonder what he was doing there." Cam frowned. "I know he and Wayne were old friends. Felicity told me they hung out together in high school, anyway."

"No idea," Alexandra said. "I was just glad when she called for a ride. It was late, almost ten o'clock."

"I came to pick up my bike." Katie pulled her phone out of her pocket and checked it. "I need to get to work by noon and it's already eleven-thirty."

"Work at Judith's?" Cam asked.

"She gets wicked upset if I'm late."

"I can imagine. I dropped by to see her this morning."

"Why would you do that?" Katie's face scrunched up in bewilderment.

"Oh, I'll tell you later." Cam cleared her throat. "But she said you do a good job."

"I would hope so." Alexandra sounded protective. "I need to get back to my work, too."

"Thanks for the ride, A." Katie smiled at her sister.

"No probs. See you Wednesday, Cam." Alexandra waved and started for the barn.

"Wednesday?" Cam asked.

"Volunteer day, right? Or don't you need me this week?"

"I almost forgot. Of course. I can always use your help. Thanks," Cam said.

Dasha ran up with the stick in his mouth. Alexandra laughed and threw it toward the driveway.

After Alexandra left, Cam turned to Katie. "Did Pete seem satisfied with your answers to his questioning?"

She didn't meet Cam's gaze. As Cam's cell phone rang in her back pocket, Katie turned away.

"Can you wait a minute?" Cam asked.

Katie shook her head as she almost ran toward the barn. She didn't look back. Cam watched her go as she retrieved the phone and connected to find one of her favorite people on the other end.

"Lucinda, cool to hear from you."

"You know what today is, *fazendeira?*" Her Brazilian friend always called Cam "farmer" in Portuguese.

"Monday?"

"No, silly. Saint Patrick's Day. Let's go to the pub tonight."

"I guess I'd better, with a name like Flaherty."

"Yeah, and you know I'm really O'Silva." Lucinda DaSilva's laugh was as big as her personality. "I'll pick you up at seven."

"I'll be wearing my green overalls. See you tonight." Cam disconnected. Not that she owned green overalls, but she had a green sweater somewhere. A relaxing night at the pub, with Irish stew and green beer, was just the ticket for taking her mind off murder. Katie didn't seem to want to dwell on it, either. But she'd avoided Cam's eyes. Why?

After a couple of hours of pruning, Cam was about to make lunch in the house when Dasha alerted, then ran to the door barking. She pushed up from the chair at her computer to see Pete climbing out of his car. As she opened the door, Dasha ran out. Cam waited, watching dog and human exchange greetings, before calling out her own.

"Done for the day?"

Pete glanced up from Dasha. "I only wish."

"Well, come on in for a minute." Pete, carrying a paper bag, trudged up the stairs like it took his last ounce of energy. His hair was as rumpled as his shirt, and a dark growth was emerging on his usually clean-shaven face. She held the door open, then wrapped her arms around him once they were inside.

They stood together for several moments of respite before Pete disengaged, shucked off his coat, and sank into a chair.

"Have you slept at all?" Cam asked.

He gazed at her with his chin on hand. "I got a few hours last night. I wanted to thank you for that tip about the nicotine cartridge."

"That's what it was? I wondered why Dasha was drawn to it."

"We haven't learned whose it was, but if whoever dropped it was nervous or frightened, Dash would have been attracted to that. Dogs are expert at picking up the chemicals we leave behind."

"I read somewhere that smelling is to dogs as seeing is to us."

"That's right," he said. "Anyway, the information came in time to check for nicotine in the autopsy."

"In the lungs?" Cam sat opposite him.

"No, in the blood. Wayne was poisoned with nicotine." He shook his head and leaned back in his chair.

"So it definitely wasn't a heart attack. Any kind of poison sounds nasty."

"Very. Smoke shops now sell little vials of pure liquid nicotine. It's highly toxic. Two are enough to poison a grown man." He rapped his fingers on the table.

Cam whistled. "Why is it even legal?"

"Shouldn't be. But you know how people are in this country. Can't step on individual rights and all that."

"And vaping keeps smoke out of the air. That's gotta be good, right? Although I wonder if it introduces chemicals into the body."

"Whatever." He waved a tired hand. "Any chance of a cup of coffee? I brought lunch." He held up the bag.

"Sure. I'm hungry." Cam rose and headed to the kitchen. After she ground the beans, she called back to him, "Wouldn't they automatically check for any poison in the blood?"

"No. There are hundreds of toxins that can kill, and lots of the tests are different. They only test for what's suspected. Thanks to you, we had a suspicion of nicotine."

Preston ambled into the kitchen as Cam poured milk into her mug. He gave his tiny mew, then reared up to rub his head against Cam's knee. "One minute, Mr. P." She poured a little milk into his food dish. When Dasha let out a bark and trotted in, Cam dug a dog biscuit out for him. "Treats for all."

She brought Pete a mug of coffee along with one for herself, then carried plates to the table. Pete drew two subs out of the bag and handed her one. "Turkey and cheese for you, an Italian for me."

"Thanks. This is perfect. House of Pizza?"

"You nailed it," Pete said before taking a big bite of his sandwich. "Think they use local turkey?" he asked after he swallowed, with the first smile Cam had seen on him since yesterday morning.

She laughed. "I doubt it, but they make great subs." She dug into her own lunch.

They ate without speaking for a minute to the sound of Dasha crunching his biscuit and Preston lapping up his milk.

Cam washed down a bite with a sip of coffee. "How are you going to find out who poisoned Wayne?"

"The usual way. Hard work. Interviews. Searching for evidence, motive, possibility."

"Speaking of interviews, how did it go with Katie last night?"

"She stuck to her story. Which I don't have any good reason to doubt. Except . . ."

"Except what?" Cam set her chin in her palm, elbow on the table.

"I don't know. There's something she's not telling me. I don't know what and I don't know why." A pulse beat in

Pete's temple and his jaw worked. "In addition, my new boss is breathing down my neck to close this case quickly. Him and his protégé, Ivan. I don't have the best working relationship with either of them. The commander is ambitious, and I think being stuck north of Boston isn't his idea of getting ahead."

"So he's taking it out on you?"

"Something like that. He implied that I'll be demoted if I don't make an arrest by the end of the week." Pete's mouth pulled to the side.

"Maybe this will help you. Remember I told you I saw Judith Patterson at Phat Cats when we were there?"

He frowned. "Yes."

"She's a vaper. She was doing it that night, and also this morning when I visited her."

"What? Why did you go to see her?" Pete set down his mug and stared at Cam.

She cleared her throat. "Well, Wayne and his wife had had that argument about selling to Judith. I wanted to bring Katie's bike over there since she said she works for Judith. And while I was there I asked for some financial advice."

"Cam. That's police business." He leaned toward her across the table. "You're acting like an investigator again. Please leave it to us. Please?" He reached out his hand and covered hers. "It's great when you tell me things—like about the cartridge, like about Ms. Patterson being an e-cig user. I can always use another set of eyes and ears in the community. But you can't go around visiting someone who may very well be a suspect. Or a murderer." He squeezed her hand.

"You're right. I guess."

"I don't want you getting hurt."

"All right. But let me tell you what Judith said. For one thing, she thinks Katie is completely incapable of killing someone, and I agree." When Pete opened his mouth, she held up a hand. "And Judith also said Wayne had asked her over for break-fast the morning he was murdered, like I texted you. She hoped it was to tell her he'd changed his mind about selling."

"Did she go?" Pete's voice quickened and the look in his eyes lightened.

"She wouldn't tell me. If that e-cig cartridge is hers, maybe she did."

"Maybe. I hate to say it, but this is useful information. Thanks, *agapi mou*."

Cam scrunched up her nose. "What did you say?"

Pete laughed. "Means 'my love' in Greek." He rose, bent over to plant a kiss on Cam's head, and turned toward the door, sliding his arms into his coat.

Cam smiled as Dasha trotted in from the kitchen and looked up at Pete expectantly.

"Sorry, my friend. Still working." Pete ruffled Dasha's head. "Still okay to have him?" he asked Cam from the doorway.

"Always. *Agapi mou*," she added softly.

Chapter 10

Cam finished the apple pruning after another hour of work. She gathered up all the clippings into the garden cart and dumped them on the rapidly growing brush pile at the edge of the woods. The branches were too thick and woody to compost, and the pile provided shelter for birds until the wood dried out enough to burn in the fall. She could use the wood ash to amend the asparagus bed, which benefited from a slighter higher alkalinity, and also sprinkle it around several of the other beds, since her soil ran a bit too acidic except for the blueberry bushes and the potato plants. She hated having to set a fire, given her past bad experiences, but it was the only way to sensibly dispose of the brush. She'd burned the brush last November on a windless day with the hose nearby and survived it. Maybe this year she'd corral a volunteer to do it.

She hadn't collected her hens' eggs in a couple of days, so after she hung the pruners and loppers on their hooks on the barn wall, she grabbed a small bucket and headed into the coop through the people door. Then stopped and wrinkled her nose. She hadn't cleaned the bedding in a while either, apparently. The odor of chicken waste was nearly overpowering and she tried to breathe only through her mouth. At least the hens didn't seem to mind. Hillary jumped out of a nesting box when Cam approached, but she had to nudge a few others out of the way to collect the eggs from underneath them. All around her they made their funny noises, scratched in the bedding, bumped into each other, and ran in and out the small door.

She latched the door behind her, gazing at the eggs. Yesterday she had collected eggs for Greta but had been told quite plainly not to come back to help. What if Cam, instead, brought over a friendly condolence casserole? It was only four o'clock. She had time to put a dish together and deliver it before she was to meet Lucinda at the pub. And maybe she could find out what Greta had been trying to hide. That wouldn't violate Pete's ban on investigating.

But what could she cook on short order? A quiche? No, bringing an egg-based dish to a poultry farm was a bit redundant. Cam put the eggs to soak in cold water in the barn and headed to the house. Dasha trotted beside her.

"Almost your dinnertime, too, isn't it, boy?"

Dasha cocked his head and barked his agreement.

Once inside, Cam fed him and then stood in front of the open refrigerator. The rest of last night's pasta dish sat in a small container. Pasta. That was it. She could whip up a fast vegetarian lasagna, since she'd picked up the cheeses last night as well as extra sauce. She checked the cupboard, glad she always kept a box of lasagna noodles on hand. She set a pot of water on the biggest burner, started the oven, and began to prep the other ingredients.

As she chopped parsley and grated Parmesan, she thought about Judith refusing to tell Cam if she'd gone to breakfast with Wayne. Why not simply say if she had or not? Maybe Judith had poisoned Wayne with her nicotine. Greta had said she cooked his breakfast before she went to church. Judith could be trying to frame Greta. But if Judith was trying to hide her breakfast with Wayne, she never would have told Cam about the invitation. Unless she was trying to appear innocent.

Cam dumped the noodles into the boiling water and stirred so they wouldn't stick together. Preston wandered over and rubbed his head against her knee.

"Sorry, P, no pets right now. I'm cooking." She broke two eggs into the ricotta, added the parsley, and mixed it a little harder than necessary. The facts of this case seemed just as mixed up. Katie was hiding something, too, Cam was sure, as was Pete.

The timer went off for the noodles, and in five minutes the lasagna was in the oven. Time for a shower. With any luck she could wash these roiling thoughts down the drain, too.

Cam drove up to the entrance to the Laitinen farm with caution, but the reporters as well as the police were gone. It was nearly six o'clock, and even though the sun didn't officially set for another hour, it was well below the tree line and the shadows were blue and cold.

Leaving her bag in the car, she made her way with her offering toward the farmhouse. At the side door, which opened into a screened porch, she juggled the towel-wrapped Pyrex pan full of warm lasagna onto one arm so she could ring the doorbell with the other hand. Nobody answered. Cam tried to peer through the porch screening into the window of the house, but the curtains were drawn. A sliver of light shone from within, though, so she rang again.

After another minute, she shifted the casserole to both hands. What was she going to do with this hot dinner if they weren't home? She couldn't just leave it on the stoop here or animals would surely find it. She shifted it back to the other hand and tried the doorknob, letting out a sigh of relief when it turned. At least she could leave it inside the porch and then call to let Greta and Megan know it was there.

Cam stepped in. A small table sat at the end of the space. But the sliver of light she'd seen was from the inner door being slightly ajar. Maybe Greta hadn't heard the doorbell. Cam moved toward the door, but stopped when she heard a voice. It was Megan's, not Greta's.

"You have to come home, Henry. Daddy's gone and Mom's acting . . ." Megan's voice was anguished.

Cam heard only sniffling for a moment.

"I know it's a big deal to be at Disney World, but our father was murdered, for God's sake!" A sound of something slamming down came through the door, then silence.

Should Cam interrupt Megan, or slide the lasagna onto the table and leave her to her troubles? She took a step backward and knocked into a chair with her hip. The chair fell over with a clatter.

"Who's there? Mom?" Megan called out. The overhead light flashed on and Megan pulled the door open. "Oh! It's you." She knit her brows together. "What are you doing here?"

Extending the lasagna, Cam said, "I made a casserole for you all. It's still hot."

Megan's face crumpled. "That is so sweet of you." Tears streaked her cheeks and she sniffled. "Come on in." She gestured to the open door.

Cam followed her in and set the lasagna on a straw hot pad on the long weathered table, now cluttered with papers, empty coffee cups, a juice glass half full of wine, a large bottle of Jim Beam, and a flower arrangement. Only two days ago she had sat here with Wayne. It felt like a month had gone by.

"Please sit down. Would you like a cup of coffee? Or a glass of wine? Whiskey?" Megan swept the papers into a pile and set the whiskey bottle on the countertop. "I'm having wine."

"That sounds good."

A moment later Megan handed Cam another juice glass filled with red wine and sat across the table from her. "Sorry about the glasses. Mom isn't much into wine." Megan's reddened nose matched her eyes, and she blew her nose on a tissue. Her fine blond hair lay in disarray on her shoulders. Pluto emerged from the hall and sat alert next to Megan's chair.

"You're having a tough time," Cam said.

"I'll say. My brother won't come home from his vacation. Mom is out somewhere. You're like almost the only person who has done a kind thing for us." Megan took a deep, ragged breath and blew it out. "And my father is dead. He was so sweet. Who could have . . ." She stared at Pluto, stroking his head.

"I'm so sorry." Cam took a sip of wine. "Wayne was a decent, gentle man. How is your mom taking it?"

Megan wiped her eyes. "She's really angry. I don't think she's cried at all for him. I don't get it." Looking like a lost dog, she gazed at Cam. "I mean, I know she and Dad weren't getting along that great, but still. They'd been married for thirty years." She picked up her glass and took a long drink. "Cam, would you help us?"

"You mean with the chickens?"

"No. I mean help find who killed Daddy. I know you've been sort of involved in a few cases this last year. The police won't tell me anything. And since you're not official, maybe you can find out things they can't."

"Well, it's their responsibility, really, not mine."

"And that other guy, Detective Pappas's partner? He never smiles. He's so abrupt, he's almost mean."

Cam pulled her mouth to the side. "I'm sure Detective Hobbs is only trying to do his job."

"Please, Cam? We need your help."

Cam blew out a breath. "I'll try."

Megan scribbled her cell phone number on a piece of paper and slid it across the table to Cam.

"So has your mom been taking care of the hens?" Cam asked after pocketing the slip of paper. "And the cow?"

"I don't think so. I offered to help with the hens but she wouldn't let me. I've been milking Betsy so far. And then today Mom took off in the car. I keep thinking she'll come back and we can talk, but it's been a few hours and she's not answering my texts. I need to go home at some point. I'm taking this week off work, but I have an unhappy cat at my house."

"I could help Greta with the hens, although yesterday she asked me not to. Do you know who Wayne usually sold the eggs to?"

Megan sipped her wine. "No idea. Once I went off to college, I stopped being involved in the poultry business. When I was in high school, he sold them to a cooperative, I think." She looked at Cam. "Should we at least go out and make sure they have food? Mom can't object if you're with me. Although you're dressed kind of nice. I wouldn't want you to get dirty in there."

Cam looked down at her jeans and green sweater under her jacket. "Not a problem. Let's do it now, if that's okay. I need to be somewhere at seven." She took one more swallow of wine and stood.

"Sure." Megan rose, too, and grabbed a coat off the back of a chair. "I appreciate the company. It's kind of freaky being in the hen house alone after dark, ever since it was vandalized."

They walked down to the hen house together, Pluto ambling behind them.

"Felicity and I fed and watered them yesterday, and collected the eggs, too," Cam said.

"Thank you so much, Cam." Megan sniffled again. "I thought my parents had friends, but maybe not. I'm serious, you're the only person who has offered to help. A couple of women from the church brought by those flowers and a deli platter, but that's it." She shook her head. "Whatever happened to community?"

A twinge of guilt stabbed Cam, since part of her motivation for both visits was to try to get information about the murder. "I wonder if people are unsure because your dad didn't die a natural death. Maybe they're a little frightened. But I'm sure the community cares."

"Sure doesn't seem like it so far." Megan pulled open the hen house door to a chorus of chicken song and a rush of warm, fetid air. She stood as if paralyzed.

"Come on," Cam said softly. "Why don't you collect the eggs and I'll do the food? Buckets are on the shelf over there. Pluto, you stay outside," she added, giving the dog a gentle push and closing the door on him.

Megan nodded like a sleepy robot.

Fifteen minutes later Cam closed the hen house door after them. Pluto sat waiting in the near dark, his tongue out. Megan held a bucket full of eggs but still looked lost. Up the hill the lights from the house pushed out a welcoming beacon.

Cam took the bucket from her. "I know where the sink is in the barn," she said. "You go back to the house. Eat a plate of lasagna and then go home."

"Okay. I haven't eaten all day." She spoke slowly, as if she didn't particularly care if she ate or not.

"I'll pop in and say good-bye in a couple of minutes." Cam watched Megan and Pluto head for the house, and then trudged over to the barn. After she flipped the lights on and set the eggs to soak in the industrial sink, she turned for the door. And turned again, back toward the stalls. It wouldn't hurt to quickly check that tack cupboard while Greta was out. Would it? She might have come back and hidden the item after Cam had left. The real question was why she was hiding something in the barn when she had a whole house at her disposal. Cam hesitated for a moment, then made her way to the stalls area.

Which one of the ten doors had Greta opened? Cam tried to picture the scene yesterday afternoon. It was one of the ones in the middle, she was sure. She counted down three and had her hand on the latch of the fourth one when she heard a noise and froze. She tried to listen over the thudding of her heart. The noise didn't sound like a car coming up the drive. A *click-click* sound came closer.

Cam's laugh was shaky as Pluto came trotting around the corner. "You had me there for a minute, doggie. I must have left the door open."

He stood next to her and panted.

"Don't tell, okay?" Cam pulled the compartment door open and leaned down to peer into the space, feeling ridiculously like Nancy Drew. A disappointed Nancy Drew, as it turned out. The cupboard was empty. She opened the next one over. Also empty. Third time a charm? Not so much. Cam closed it. But there were six more. Cam moved down the row. Open, peer, close. Open, peer, close. Pluto watched. At the end of the row, she doubled back to the first cupboard. Empty. After she peered into the second one, she was already straightening when she bent down again. Something was lodged against the back. It was in the shadows but looked like a cube-shaped box.

Cam dug her phone out of her jacket pocket and hit the flashlight app. The bright white light illuminated the whole space. The red, black, and tan cube-shaped box read, FED-

ERAL PREMIUM, .410 HANDGUN, .410 3 IN BUCKSHOT. There were two more lines of details, and at the bottom it read, PERSONAL DEFENSE.

Straightening, Cam switched off the phone light. Handgun ammunition. Cam could see why Greta might not want that in the house. But where was the gun? And why did she feel the need to own one? Certain farmers owned shotguns to ward off prey like coyotes or woodchucks, but a handgun was a different matter. Well, that was Greta's business. And since Wayne hadn't been shot, it should stay Greta's business, although Cam would let Pete know, just in case.

Cam left the barn, Pluto at her side, and made her way back to the house. Megan sat at the table with more wine in her glass and a half-full plate of lasagna. Swing music played from a phone plugged into a small speaker.

"Is that Postmodern Jukebox?" Cam asked. "I love that group."

Megan nodded as she swallowed, then said, "This is perfect, Cam. Thank you so, so much."

"It's my pleasure. Listen, I left the eggs soaking, but I don't have time to scrub and flat them. You can tell your mom you collected them if you want."

The back door flew open. "Tell her mom what?" A frowning Greta stood in the doorway with her bag over her shoulder.

"Hey, Mom. Where you been?" Megan waved her fork. "Cam was nice enough to bring us dinner. Want some?"

Cam greeted Greta with a smile. "How are you?"

Greta did not return the smile. "How do you think?" She set her fists on her waist. Her round face was pale and her eyes as reddened as Megan's had been. "My husband's dead and my son doesn't seem to care. I'm broke and stuck with a business I don't want. I hate hens," she spat.

"Mom." Megan's eyes pleaded with Greta. "Sit down and eat with me."

Greta pulled out a chair and sank into it. She smiled a little. "I wish I could point my wand at the bank and say *Accio* dollars! I wouldn't have to worry about money ever again."

"Mom's a huge Harry Potter geek," Megan said, looking at her mother with soft eyes.

"You both take care." Cam took a step toward the door. "I have to get going."

"Thanks for the food," Greta's voice was gruff. "Appreciate it."

Chapter 11

It looked like every patron in Connolly's Irish Pub was wearing green. Cam and Lucinda's server was a young woman with pale skin, startling blue eyes, and black hair. When she approached their booth, Cam noticed she even sported a pair of green skinny jeans.

Cam looked up from the menu. "I'll have the Irish stew, please."

"You got it," the server said.

"Can I have the fish and chips?" Lucinda examined the back of the menu. "And we'll take a pitcher of green-colored Sam Adams, right, Cam?"

"Of course. Will it be green?"

"Is it Saint Patrick's Day?" The server laughed. "Green all the way." She gathered their menus and turned away.

A trio played Celtic music in the far corner. A seated man held a flat frame drum vertically with his left hand inside, his right playing the skin with a stick. A man in a tweed cap coaxed an elaborate tune from a flute, and a petite, energetic woman in a short dress and boots played the fiddle and danced her feet at the same time.

"Sorry I was late," Cam said.

"Not a problem." Lucinda folded her arms on the table, leaning toward Cam. "What do you know about the chicken farmer's murder, the Laitinen man?"

Cam pursed her lips. "Wayne, poor guy. Why do bad things happen to the people with the biggest hearts?"

"I know. He was a really nice guy. I used to buy roasters from him. Can't get much more local than that."

"I was late because I took a lasagna over to the Laitinens. Their daughter is pretty upset." She decided to keep news of the ammunition to herself, along with any mention of Greta's behavior.

"How'd he die?"

"The family thought it might have been a heart attack." Cam gazed at her. Lucinda could keep a secret. She kept her voice low. "It took the police a while, but Pete told me this afternoon it was nicotine poisoning."

"Nicotine, like in cigarettes?"

"Like in cigarettes. But you know, with those e-cigs, people buy little vials of pure liquid nicotine."

"Those things they call vaping? People who do that look ridiculous, if you ask me."

"That's it. And apparently liquid nicotine is so toxic it only takes a couple of those vials to kill someone."

"It should be illegal." Lucinda's dark eyes flashed.

"Agree. Pete thinks so, too." Cam sat back, nodding. "So how's your locavore year going?" Cam asked Lucinda, who had vowed last June to eat only locally produced food for a year.

"Eh." She lifted a shoulder, then dropped it. "I have to make lots of exceptions. Like tonight, although with any luck the fish is at least from the Atlantic. I wouldn't be able to eat

97

out hardly anywhere if I stuck to it. But it's okay. It's been a real learning experience."

"A couple of restaurants around here like to feature local ingredients."

"But those are fancy, expensive places, Cam. I'm a librarian at a private school, remember? With a librarian's salary."

Their server arrived with a pitcher and two pint glasses and set them on the table. "Enjoy."

After Lucinda poured, Cam raised her glass. "Here's to the Irish."

"To the Irish." Lucinda clinked her glass with Cam's and took a long drink. She tapped the table to the music.

The woman now held her fiddle at her side and sang in a language that must be Gaelic. Cam glanced around the room. Every seat at the bar was occupied and all the tables and booths seemed to be, too. As a man approached their table, Cam looked up.

"Mind if I join you, ladies?" Paul Underwood smiled at them. He wore a long-sleeved green shirt with pressed jeans, and his neatly trimmed brown hair looked, as with every time Cam had seen him, as if he'd come straight from the barber. He beat the rhythm of the music on his thigh with his hand. "All the seats are taken, and I'm a huge fan of that group."

Really? He wanted to sit with a couple of organic farming types? "Um, sure," Cam said. She glanced at Lucinda and raised her eyebrows. "Have a seat."

Lucinda shot her a look. She had organized the forum in the winter at the school where she worked, the forum where Cam and Paul had faced off over the question of using chemicals like G-Phos on a farm. Cam and Lucinda shared the view that glyphosates should be banned, but Paul had firmly defended his position, and that of his employer.

"Thanks. This is my favorite holiday. I know Underwood

doesn't sound Irish, but my mother was from County Cork."
Paul sat between Lucinda and Cam. "How are you, Lucinda?"
He smiled at her.

"Good." She pushed her dark curly hair away from her forehead with a quick gesture.

"What's the name of the group?" Cam asked.

"Keeltori." Paul gazed at them, now beating the table in
time with the drum. "I used to play with them."

"What do you play?" Lucinda looked at him with eyebrows
raised, as if he'd suddenly acquired a new dimension.

"Guitar, banjo, mandolin. I especially like the mandolin,
even though it's not really traditionally Irish."

"Are you in a group now?" Cam asked.

"No. I have three little boys, and it's hard to do anything
without them beyond going to work." He smiled. "They're
super guys, but they take a lot of time. Well, all my free time,
unless I get my dad to come over and babysit, like tonight."

"It must be good to get a break once in a while," Lucinda
said.

He nodded. "Katrina there is an old friend of mine and we
try to jam from time to time, usually at my house so I don't
have to get a sitter." His voice turned wistful. As if she'd heard
him, the female lead caught sight of Paul and waved at him.

Old friends. "I heard you were old friends with Wayne Laitinen, too." Cam watched as Paul turned to look at her.

"I was. Who'd you hear that from?"

"Your high school English teacher."

"Mrs. Slavin?" He frowned.

"Yes," Cam said. "She's one of my farm customers. Said you
and Wayne were pretty close buddies in school."

"We were. For a while. May he rest in peace."

The server returned with Cam's and Lucinda's dinners.
"Can I get you something, sir?" she asked Paul.

"A double Irish whiskey neat, with water back." At the waitress's look of confusion, he groaned. "Just bring me a small glass of water when you bring the whiskey."

When she'd gone, Cam remarked, "I don't know what a water back is, either." She took a bite of the stew and let a chunk of meat dissolve on her tongue as she savored the stew's rich flavors.

"Adding a little water to whiskey opens up the flavor," Paul said. "I should stop saying it anyplace but at the bar itself. The server ought to know the term, but . . ."

Cam swallowed. "So you weren't friends with Wayne anymore? But I saw you driving away from his place Saturday afternoon."

"Yes, I went to see him." Paul looked at the band. "We were trying to sort of work through a couple of things."

"You mean the reason you stopped being friends?" Cam asked.

"Yes," Paul said without meeting her eyes.

"You didn't look too happy when you left."

"Happy, not happy. What does it matter?" He chewed on the inside of his lip.

"I read online that you found him dead Sunday morning," Lucinda said as she swirled a French fry in ketchup. "Why'd you go back?" A little smile played around her mouth.

Paul looked from Lucinda to Cam. "What's with you girls? You sound like the damn detectives." He stood. "Excuse me. I came here to listen to music, not to get grilled." He intercepted the server and exchanged money for his drink. He splashed water from the glass into the whiskey and gave the water back to the server, then took up position standing near the band, his back to their table.

"A little touchy about that, wasn't he?" Lucinda asked.

"I guess. But who wouldn't be? We barely know him and

here we were both pestering him with questions." Cam watched Paul as he sipped his whiskey, his foot tapping to the music. She pulled her attention back to the most delicious beef stew she'd ever tasted.

"Is that good?" Lucinda asked, popping another French fry into her mouth.

"Very." Cam poked her spoon around in the bowl. "Beef, carrots, onions, potatoes, of course. But the flavor is what does it. I wonder what their secret is."

"I read a recipe that calls for a bottle of stout in it. Can you taste beer?"

Cam rolled a spoonful around on her tongue. "That might be it. I'm going to try this at home. Make it for Pete whenever he solves this case."

"You could do it all local, too." Lucinda waggled her eyebrows.

"Absolutely, and then give the recipe to the shareholders next summer or fall, when I harvest carrots and potatoes. Good idea." Cam glanced up when the music stopped.

The woman took the microphone. "Sure and I hope you're all havin' a grand time tonight," she said in accented English, her short dark hair spiked up off her head. "We're after askin' an old friend to play with us. Will yeh join us now, Paul Underwood?" She strode to Paul's side and grabbed his hand.

He shook his head hard and tried to pull back, but the fiddler won out, and a minute later a mandolin was in his hands. And a minute after that he was picking out an intricate tune with the rest of the group. Cam watched him, his head down as the fingers of both his hands flew over the frets and the strings. He had real talent.

"He's pretty good," Lucinda said. "Wonder why he's selling chemicals instead of touring with that group."

"I imagine it's because it's hard to support a family being a wandering musician." Under the table her own feet were dancing to the song. "I've heard him talk about his sons. Felicity said he's essentially a single dad, so it'd be that much harder."

"Sure would," Lucinda said before draining her glass. "Fill 'er up?" She lifted the pitcher.

Cam nodded, but her thoughts were on Paul. How could she find out what his issue with Wayne had been? Pete had said Paul found Wayne's body Sunday morning. The police obviously didn't think Paul had killed Wayne, but why not? She shook her head. Tonight was supposed to be an escape from those thoughts, an evening of green beer, a good friend, and excellent music, not thinking about murder.

The next morning dawned windy and raw, with a gunmetal sky pressing down on the farm. Cam had stayed at the pub a little later than she should have, and now at eight she yawned as she trudged to the barn, her knit work cap pulled down over her ears, a travel mug full of French roast in one work-gloved hand. Dasha trotted at her side while Preston stayed behind on the back steps watching them.

After yesterday's warm weather and with the longer days, the outside worms were moving again and the compost should be warming enough to turn. Two of the three slatted bins sat full of last fall's spent plants, plus horse manure, leaves, and all the other vegetable matter a farm produced. She'd also bought a load of crushed lobster body shells to mix in. The compost wouldn't have broken down much over the winter, but it should be thawed by now. All it needed was air to get cooking again so the temperature would rise enough to kill weed seeds and break down the woody matter of stems.

Cam made sure all the chicks were alive and fed, and did the same for the adult chickens before grabbing a pitchfork and heading for the bins around the back of the barn. She dug into the middle three-sided bin, which she'd constructed of free shipping pallets almost four-foot square, and forked a heap of the rough mix over into the empty bin on her right. And another and another. The repetitive work freed up her brain to work overtime.

Paul had gotten defensive about Lucinda and Cam asking him questions last night. Maybe Albert would know something about Paul's past. She'd have to remember to ask Pete if his team had followed up on Paul's connection. Interesting that Paul was such a good musician. He'd played with the group the rest of the evening and had looked like he enjoyed himself. Cam thought she picked up on flirting between him and the woman he'd called Katrina, but maybe it was only the energy of old friends sharing something they both loved.

She wrestled a big chunk of matted-together leaves over the bin wall, shaking it as she dropped it so they would separate. Pete. It was Tuesday and he'd said his boss had threatened him with demotion if he didn't have someone in custody by the end of the week. And the days were ticking by. He didn't want Cam to go out into dangerous situations. Heck, she didn't, either. But if she could gather information that might help him, he couldn't argue with that. Could he?

Cam came to a layer of nearly finished compost, dark and crumbly, which was easy to toss over the side. The pile in the empty bin was growing into a cone, with the new material sliding down the sides. Then there was land-hungry Judith. Judith who vaped. Judith who seemed to expect she would get her own way. Judith who could apparently afford anything she wanted. Cam sure wouldn't want to be her daughter. Maybe

Ellie knew Isabella and could . . . But, no, Ellie was on vacation in Florida.

After the rightmost bin was full, with a mound now heaped above the rim of the bin, Cam moved to the one on the left. She forked the loose leaves from the top into the now empty middle bin, then paused to stretch her back. Stretching made her think of Katie, who must be a dancer or do yoga or something, the way she'd stood up from the ground in one movement at the llama farm on Sunday. Katie hadn't wanted to tell Cam if Pete seemed satisfied with her answers. Cam removed her cap and rubbed her head. It seemed like everybody was hiding something. And speaking of hiding, Greta had been trying to hide something, Cam was sure of it. She had no idea how she was going to help Megan. She was pretty sure Pete wouldn't encourage such help, either.

As she resumed digging, the tines hit an obstacle. Maybe the middle of this pile was still frozen. But the other one hadn't been. She poked some more but couldn't get purchase on the blockage to move it or lift it out. Sometimes a clump of grass clippings or a collection of kitchen garbage glued itself together. But this seemed more solid.

A gust of wind rustled the dry leaves on the grapevine behind her and the cold air chilled her cheeks even as she was sweating in her coat from the work. Cam took her hands off the pitchfork handle. A murderer was out there, a killer who wanted to keep his or her identity hidden. What if someone had hidden something—a piece of evidence, an incriminating object—in her compost? She shook off the thought. Her imagination was getting out of control. She'd been through this before, this living with a killer on the loose, and if she let herself become paralyzed with fear, she'd never get any work done.

She jabbed the pitchfork in at a different angle and lifted a clump of what had been lobster shells. That was all the obstacle was, and it wasn't actually solid. As she tossed the forkful over the side, something glinted, something nonorganic.

"What in heck?" Cam threw down the fork to sift through the top of the material in the middle bin, finally drawing out a simple gold bracelet, dirty and dented. Cam rubbed at the bracelet, a quarter-inch wide ring of gold, with her glove, thinking she saw letters engraved on the inside, but she couldn't make them out. She slid it into her pocket before she resumed work. Compost was an aggregator. That bracelet could have come in with the lobster bodies or the horse manure, both of which were off-farm inputs. Or she supposed it could have been lying in the soil of her own farm for years. She imagined Great-Aunt Marie losing the bracelet while hoeing up potatoes a decade or two earlier. Albert would know, and she was going to visit him this afternoon. She'd clean up the bracelet and take it along to show him. Cam smiled at the memory of Marie, who had loved her, taught her, and laughed with her. The sturdy little woman had been more of a mother to Cam than her own, a tall, spare academic who lived in her head and never seemed comfortable with affection. That Marie had been taken by pancreatic cancer in her early seventies still didn't seem fair to Cam. But death was never fair.

She picked up the fork and kept on transferring the forkfuls to the other bin. She was almost to the bottom when one forkful made something long and ivory-colored fly through the air onto the new pile. What was that? She set the tines of the fork into the ground and took a step closer, narrowing her eyes at it. The something was a bone.

She took one more step. She stuck her hands in her jacket pocket as she leaned over to examine it. The bone was about nine inches long. She tried to think of animals with legs that long. A coyote, maybe, or a baby deer, both of whom roamed the woods. Not the fox. But she should get it out of there—it clearly wasn't going to break down, and maybe she could find someone who would know what kind of bone it was. She reached her gloved hand toward it.

And froze. The bone looked exactly as long as her forearm. It could be a human bone. The one that had worn the bracelet.

Chapter 12

What an awful thought, that she might be looking at part of a human. Cam shuddered as she slowly pulled out her cell phone. She snapped several pictures of the bone, then called the nonemergency number for the Westbury Police Department. She wasn't handling this alone.

After an officer picked up, Cam identified herself and gave her address. "I found a bone in my compost pile. It's about nine inches long and I—"

"Do you know how it got there?" the officer asked.

"No. This pile includes manure from a local horse stable, and a load of lobster shells, too, so it might have come in with one of those." Cam cleared her throat. "But I just, you know, wondered if it might be human remains."

"What makes you think that?" The officer's voice was sharp. "Don't you have animals on your farm?"

"None that size. I only have chickens, and two very much alive pets. I called because right before I saw the bone, I found a gold bracelet. And then I thought maybe the bone and the bracelet went together."

"Don't touch the bone. We'll send someone out as soon as we can." He disconnected.

Cam headed for the house to wait for the police. Inside, she drew the bracelet out of her pocket and laid it on a paper towel on the kitchen counter while she still had her gloves on, then stowed her outerwear. Despite having found a bone that might be human, her stomach was reminding her she'd only had toast for breakfast. She threw together a quick cheese-and-pickle sandwich while she waited for the police, and ate standing, gazing at the bracelet. Who had lost it, and where? She didn't think girls these days would wear something so old-fashioned as a gold bracelet, so it probably hadn't come in with the horse manure. Or it could be Sue Genest's, the stable owner who was in her sixties. If the jewelry had come in with the lobsters, could it have been in the salty ocean and not be corroded?

She set down her plate and picked up the bracelet with a tissue. Would the police want to take this, too? Of course. She shouldn't get fingerprints on it. She tried to wipe it off with another tissue, but dirt remained, so she gently cleaned the inside with the dish brush, then picked up the bracelet with the tissue. She carried it to her desk and switched on the light. What she wanted to see were the letters on the inside. She peered at them. The engraving looked like an embellished *FL*. So it wasn't Marie's. She snapped a picture with her cell phone, then another, trying to catch the letters.

Sue might know something about it. Cam pressed the number for the stable owner, but the call went to voice mail. Sue was no doubt out in the riding ring or tending to the horses.

With a sigh, Cam laid down the phone and opened her laptop. A search for the properties of gold revealed that it didn't corrode in salt water. Interesting. Or in horse urine, presumably. She ran another search and learned that salt water preserved bone, but that sea creatures could degrade it, whatever that meant, after twelve years. She glanced at the time display, which read ten-thirty. When were the police going to show up?

She gazed at the bracelet again. Someone had lost it. Was anyone missing it?

At the sound of a door slamming, she grabbed her coat and headed outside. Chief Frost climbed out of a Westbury police car, and Ruth walked around the front of it toward Cam. At least they hadn't come roaring up with lights and sirens on, but why was the chief here? Cam walked up and greeted both of them.

"Ms. Flaherty, I understand you believe you uncovered human remains," George Frost said. "Can you show us, please?" Trim iron-colored hair showed under his hat, and his lean face looked tired.

"Well, I found a bone. I don't know if it's human or not. It's just that I had uncovered a gold bracelet right before that. And when I saw the bone, it looked the same length as my forearm, so . . ." Cam gestured toward the back. "The bone is out in the compost pile. Follow me." She led the way. "How are the girls, Ruth?" she asked as they walked. She wasn't going to pretend she and Ruth weren't friends just because this was a business call. The chief knew they were.

Ruth glanced at the chief before answering. "They're great and growing fast. First grade has really opened them up."

"I haven't seen them in a couple of months. You should bring them by for lunch on the weekend. They'd love to see my little chicks."

"They sure would." Ruth smiled. Chief Frost, on the other hand, was all business, and by the set of his mouth Cam expected he disapproved of the friendly chat.

When they arrived at the compost piles, Cam pointed at the bone. "There it is. I expect it's an animal bone, but you guys must have a way of determining that, right?"

Ruth squatted and peered at the bone. She straightened and turned to the chief. "Looks close enough to human to call in the teams."

"Got it." He stepped away, pulling a phone out of a case on his duty belt.

"Which teams?" Cam asked Ruth.

"Crime scene and evidence collection units. I'll take pictures to document the area, and we're going to have to investigate the rest of the property. The chief might choose to bring in a cadaver dog, too."

"Really? All that?" At a cold gust of wind, Cam pulled her coat tighter around her. "Don't you need to make sure it's a human bone first?"

"It looks a lot like an ulna. You know, one of the bones in the forearm. I did a rotation in the forensic anthropology unit at the state police training facility last year. In animals of that size, the radius and the ulna are usually fused. They're always separate in humans."

Chief Frost returned to where they stood. "Teams are on their way. Canine unit, too. Now, what was this you said about also finding a bracelet?"

"I did. It's in the house." Dasha trotted up. "If you have a dog coming, should I put Dasha in the house?"

"Yes," the chief said. "Officer Dodge, please secure the bracelet and take a statement from Ms. Flaherty. I'll wait out here for the units."

Cam offered tea to Ruth in the house, but her friend declined.

"Sorry, we have another call we need to get to after this."

Ruth pulled out a digital tablet and a paper evidence bag, which she proceeded to label. After she used the tablet to shoot a couple of pictures of the bracelet, she lifted it with a pencil and slid it into the bag. "Okay, tell me exactly how you found this item."

"At least sit down, won't you?" Cam said, sliding into a seat at the table.

Ruth sat, fingers hovering over the tablet's virtual keyboard.

"I was turning the compost an hour ago."

"For the record, what does that mean?" Ruth glanced up and smiled. "Not many officers are big into gardening."

"Compost is a mix of organic materials—leaves, grass, plants. I get manure from a local horse farm, and I also got a load of lobster shells last fall. Anyway, it's a mix, and with air, moisture, worms, and soil organisms, it breaks down into a rich soil amendment. Organic farms depend on compost for nutrients, and it improves the structure of the soil, too."

"And you turn it why?"

"To keep that activity going, you need to expose more of it to air, mix it up. So anyway, I was turning one pile into the next bin when I saw that bracelet."

"You'd never seen it before."

"No. I saw it had initials on the inside, though, and when I brought it in here, I kind of scrubbed it a little." Cam winced, expecting what came next.

"Cam. Do we have to send you to the Citizens' Police Academy? You of all people should know that you never touch a piece of evidence."

"Evidence of what?" Cam's voice rose. "I didn't think of it being related to a crime until I unearthed the bone. I simply thought it was an interesting piece of history. And I didn't really think it was human bone."

"Okay."

"I didn't touch the bracelet without gloves on."

"There's that. So where do you think the bracelet came from?" Ruth looked up.

"It had to be in the manure or the lobster shells. Or maybe it's been in the soil here for a long time and it only now surfaced. That's possible, too. Winter frost heaves push up all kinds of things from deeper down."

"Like maybe it was your great-aunt's?"

"Maybe. I'll ask Albert when I get a chance."

"Be sure to let me know what he says."

"Ruth." Cam gazed at her. "I don't mind finding a gold bracelet. But what if the bone is the arm it was on? How long has the person been dead? And where's the rest of the skeleton? Could someone have been buried right here on the farm?"

"That's why we call in the teams, Cam. To find out exactly that as best we can. But that's something else you can ask Albert. Maybe the previous owners had a home burying ground on the property. People used to do that kind of thing, way back when."

Cam gazed out the window. "I can see farmers a century earlier interring a deceased grandmother, or maybe a child who had died of fever. A grandmother buried wearing her favorite gold bracelet. But wouldn't they have had markers, or a fence around the graveyard?"

"Who knows? Markers fall down. Fences rot."

"I hate the thought of tilling up ground that people's earthly shells were buried under," Cam said. "On the other hand, what better way to honor the dead than by growing food for the living above them?"

* * *

Cam pulled into the long drive of Sue Genest's stable on Middle Road near the Newburyport border and hit the brakes. The police had finally let her leave at a little before two. Her driveway had been full of cruisers and other vehicles, and officers had swarmed the property. She'd told them it was unlikely that other bones were around, if the one in the compost had come in from off the farm, but they didn't listen. They'd even sifted all the rest of the compost, both the stuff she'd already turned and the fresh pile. Which was actually a help to her, since the small particles of sifted compost integrated much more easily into the soil. She just never had enough time to do it herself.

The stable and riding ring sat on a hill, with pasture sloping down all around it like a full skirt in midtwirl. A skirt with a pattern of fence lines and the coloring of camouflage cloth, blotches of brown mud mixing with early grass greening up. It being mud season, Cam was grateful for the graded and well-graveled drive as she accelerated toward the top of the hill. She'd only been here twice: late last spring and again in the fall, when Sue Genest had used her small front loader to scoop manure into Cam's truck.

A minute later she climbed out of the Ford and opened the door to the big structure that let riders and steeds practice their techniques and gaits all winter long. The air inside was somewhat warmer than the chilly outside, and the smell of sweat and manure was present but not overpowering. Sue stood in the middle of the ring, wearing a heavy green-cabled sweater over cream-colored riding pants and low black boots. She pivoted gradually, keeping her narrow face toward the horse and rider who rode following the perimeter of the barn. Cam closed the door behind her, staying near it and watching for several minutes. The rider, an adult wearing a black helmet and short jacket, seemed to stand up in the stirrups and then sit over and over. Cam had never ridden a horse. She didn't know if this was cantering or trotting or posting, words she'd read in books as a child but had never learned from doing it herself. All she knew was that it didn't look like the galloping horses she'd seen in movies.

Sue occasionally called a comment to the rider, who then altered her position slightly, or sped up a little. Sue caught sight of Cam and waved at her, indicating that she should stay where she was. Finally the lesson ended with Sue clapping twice, then walking toward the horse. The rider coaxed the horse to a stop and dismounted, holding the reins with one hand as she pulled off her helmet with the other. Cam was surprised to see Judith under there. Didn't she have a full-time job? Or maybe she could set her own hours, since she worked from home as a consultant.

Sue and Judith conferred in the center of the ring, then started toward the side of the building that housed the stalls, with Judith leading the horse. Cam walked toward them.

"What, you need a load of early manure?" Sue said when she was within earshot. She shot Cam a warm, toothy smile. Sue's graying blond shoulder-length hair was pushed off her forehead with a comb, as she always wore it. Despite the heavy sweater, her thin frame was apparent.

"Hey, Sue. No, not quite yet. The stuff from last fall is starting to cook again." Cam glanced at Judith. "Hi, Judith."

"I wondered what you were doing here," Judith said. "But of course a farmer needs manure." The corners of her mouth curled up but she didn't particularly look like she was smiling.

"That's a beautiful horse," Cam said. The horse's coat was a glossy black, and it had a finely shaped head over a smooth, muscular body. She reached out a hand to stroke its velvety nose, but the horse tossed its head with a snort.

"Thanks. He doesn't like strangers." Judith led him around Sue in the direction of the stalls. "See you Thursday," she called over her shoulder.

"Gotcha," Sue replied. "What's up, Cam?"

"I wanted to ask you something."

"Can you ask it over coffee in my office? I need to sit down."

"Of course."

Sue headed for the steps that led to an upstairs hallway. When she opened the door to the office, warm air and the aroma of overcooked coffee spilled out. The office featured a window overlooking the riding ring. Sue bent over to remove her riding boots while still in the passageway, then straightened. "This is my little refuge from manure." She gestured to Cam to come in. "You don't have to take your shoes off, though."

"Thanks." Cam had seen the window on the riding ring but had never been up in the office before. It was a cozy room, with a desk and chair, a small couch covered in red next to an end table with a lamp, and a shelf holding the coffee machine and supplies atop a dorm fridge. Pillows in bright primary colors lay on the couch and a painting on the wall pictured two women at a produce market that looked distinctly Caribbean. An electric blue pillow on the couch matched the upholstery of the desk chair.

"Have a seat." Sue pointed to the couch before carrying the coffee carafe through a doorway into a small bathroom. After clattering about and running water, Sue reappeared with the carafe full of water and proceeded to start a new pot.

"So what's up?" Sue asked, sinking into the desk chair when she was done.

"I found a gold bracelet in my compost pile. I wondered if you or someone here might have lost it in the manure and it got onto my farm by accident." Cam drew out her phone and brought up the pictures. "I took two shots of it before the police took it away."

"The police?" Sue's blue eyes flew wide open.

"Well, I found a bone, too. There's an off chance it could be human, so I thought I'd better turn it over to the authorities."

"Good idea. I hope it's not, though." Sue reached for the phone. "I've never owned a gold bracelet, but maybe one of my riders lost it." She squinted at the first picture, swiped to the second and back to the first, then glanced up at Cam. "What does that say? I don't know where my glasses have got to."

"It has the letters *FL* engraved on the inside. Do you have any horse owners with those initials? Or any of the girls who work for you?"

Sue turned to a phone list pinned to the wall above her desk and scanned it. "Not presently." As the coffee sputtered, signaling the end of the brewing, she stood and poured it into two mugs, extending one to Cam. "Milk? Sugar?"

"A little milk if you have it, thanks." Cam accepted the quart of whole milk Sue extracted from the fridge and added a glug to her coffee.

"Long time ago, though, when I was starting out, there was an Irish girl who loved horses, and she worked mucking out stalls for me to earn riding time," Sue said. "Fionnoula Leary. And I'm thinking she used to wear a bracelet like that."

Cam sat up straight on the couch. "Really? Does she still live in this area?"

"I don't think so. I remember the bracelet because I told her she shouldn't wear it in the stalls, that it would get trashed with the manure and all." Sue smiled at a memory. "She said in that accent of hers that she never took it off because it was her grandmother's, who'd had the same name. And that gold would last forever."

Chapter 13

Cam peered at the microfilm screen on the second floor of the Newburyport Library half an hour later. She'd had an hour to fill before going to see Uncle Albert, and she wanted to dig into the long-ago conflict between Paul and Wayne just in case it helped Pete with the case, and thereby helped Megan, too. After she texted Ruth with the name of the Irish girl, Cam had located the year Felicity said Paul and Wayne had had their falling out. But a year's worth of a daily paper could take a while to scan. She didn't need to peruse the features or sports pages, but it was too bad she couldn't run a search. Cam shifted in her seat. Might as well start with January.

She clicked the Next arrow through page after page, scanning for a mention of either Paul's or Wayne's names. She checked the news headlines and the police logs for each town in the paper's coverage area, looking for a mention of high school boys getting in trouble. She was well into April with nothing to show for it when her phone buzzed where she'd laid it on the table next to the keyboard. She'd set the timer for three-thirty, which was now. Time to head back to Westbury for her date with Albert.

Clicking onto one more day, Cam froze. The top news headline read, POLICE SEEK INFORMATION IN LOCAL GIRL'S DISAPPEARANCE. And the first paragraph contained the name Fionnoula Leary.

Cam stared. Fionnoula Leary. The Irish girl who had worn a gold bracelet to muck out horse stalls. Cam read every word of the article and then read it again. Fionnoula had been on an informal exchange year, the article said, staying with relatives in Westbury and attending the high school as a junior. The relatives, the Brennan family, had reported her missing after a day, saying only that she'd said she was going out with friends but that she'd never come home. No friend had as yet come forward to say what had happened. The story ended with the usual plea for anyone with knowledge of Fionnoula's whereabouts to call the local authorities.

The poor thing. A sixteen-year-old exchange student. How could a girl like that just disappear? Had she been abducted? Or run away because she wasn't happy with the family? Maybe she'd been in an accident and had suffered from amnesia.

When Cam's phone timer buzzed insistently again, she shook her head. She was dying to find out if Fionnoula had ever surfaced, but she had to get going. Google might get Cam somewhere once she got home, since she now had specifics of name and date. She hadn't learned anything about Paul and Wayne, though, which was what she had come for. She shook her head again.

She quickly sent the page to her personal e-mail account and logged out, then gathered up her bag and coat and headed downstairs, through the lobby, and out the front doors. As she walked briskly along the sidewalk toward her truck, she glanced over at the wide, lit windows of the library's children's room and stopped. Greta, with a thin black cloak thrown over her sweater and slacks, stood in front of a circle of elementary-aged girls and boys, each of whom wore round black Harry Potter glasses and held a wand. Greta held one, too, and waved it as she spoke. The children followed suit. It had to be an after-school Spells class or something similar. But what was Greta doing back at work so soon after her husband's death?

Albert cracked open first one beer and then the other. "Fetch those drinking glasses from the cupboard, will you, dear? And the bag of chips." He stayed in his big padded re-cliner, his customary red plaid blanket draped over his lap, his one remaining foot peeking out from under the blanket.

Cam handed him a glass, poured the potato chips into a bowl and brought it over, then sat in the accompanying chair in his cozy assisted living room at Moran Manor. It included a sitting nook with his desk in one corner, a tiny kitchen area with sink and minifridge next to the bathroom, and the bed-room area beyond. It smelled cozy, too, a whiff of Albert's Old Spice aftershave mixing with the leather of his chair. A photo-graph of a dark-haired Albert and Marie at the farm hung on the wall. They stood in the classic *American Gothic* pose in front of the old barn, Albert in overalls, Marie's hair pulled back in a bun. Except that she wore overalls, too, they both held pitchforks, and rather than looking stern, they were smil-ing into the camera as a breeze ruffled their hair.

"When was that taken?" Cam asked. "I don't think I ever asked you." She popped a salty chip into her mouth and crunched.

Albert smiled. "Why, I'd say I was about forty, so forty-six years ago, give or take a couple."

"You look happy."

"We surely were."

She poured the beer into her glass and held it up. "Here's to happiness."

Albert poured his own and clinked his glass with hers. He peered at her. "Are you happy, Cammy?" He took a swallow and set the glass down.

Cam blinked. "I guess so." She gazed out the window, then back at Albert. "Sure, I'm happy. Pete says he loves me. I have work, I have friends. I have you." She had found Albert unconscious on his floor a couple of months ago while the most recent murderer had been at large, and Cam had been afraid she would lose him.

"I hear a 'but.'" He reached over and patted her knee.

"Good ears." Cam sipped her own beer before she went on. "Wayne's murder is disturbing. I'm sad he's gone, but it's also frightening to have another killer wandering around out there. Plus, Pete's boss is putting a lot of pressure on him to solve the case quickly. So I'm basically happy, but it's an unsettling week."

"I understand. Want to talk about something else?" At Cam's nod, Albert asked, "How's spring pruning and planting going?"

They chatted for a few minutes about the farm, about a Moran Manor trip to the Boston Museum of Fine Arts Albert had been on, about the chicks, about Albert's computer club activities—about anything but murder.

"And how's Marilyn?" Cam asked. She liked Albert's new lady friend, a smart and gentle woman who didn't let her fondness for Albert get in the way of regularly beating him at games of Scrabble.

"Excellent. She's up to Ipswich visiting her daughter and grandsons just now for a few days." He took a handful of chips and began to eat them one at a time.

Cam cocked her head. "Do you remember news about a young Irish exchange student going missing about thirty-five years ago?"

He narrowed his eyes. "Can't say that I do. Why are you interested?"

"I was turning the compost this morning, and a bracelet emerged." She leaned down to her bag where she'd set it on the floor and fished in it until she found her phone. She brought up the pictures and handed it to him.

Albert took the phone in his gnarled, age-spotted hands and peered at the picture. "That's a nice piece of work. Someone must be missing it. Any idea how it got into the compost?" He handed it back to her.

"That's what I'm trying to figure out. Three ways it could have gotten there. One, it was already on the farm, buried in the soil, and got in with the roots of a spent plant—"

"I never saw it, but that doesn't mean it wasn't there."

"Right. That particular batch of compost also has two sets of off-farm inputs. Horse manure from Sue Genest's stable, and a load of lobster bodies I ordered from Seacoast Organics." She showed him the initials on the bracelet. "I went over to see Sue earlier this afternoon, and she told me an Irish girl named Fionnoula Leary used to work and ride there when Sue was getting started."

"*FL*. But surely if she lost the bracelet all those decades ago it wouldn't have come over in a load of manure this year?"

"No. But then I was at the Newburyport Library looking at their microfilm for the *Daily News* for that same time period—"

"Why were you doing that?"

"Tell you in a minute. I was about to leave to come here when I saw an article about a Fionnoula Leary disappearing. She was staying with relatives and going to high school here in town, and she didn't come home one night."

Albert frowned. "An Irish family in Westbury? Now that does ring a bell. They were only here for a few years. The father was an executive for a European company and was working in Boston for a while. He wanted the children to live and go to school somewhere safer than the city, so they took up residence here in Westbury. Can't say that I heard about the visiting girl, though. Did she ever show up?"

"I don't know. I was running late to come over here and didn't get a chance to keep reading. I'll go back tomorrow." Cam took another sip of beer and savored the bitter hop flavor as it went down. "So the Irish family had children. I don't suppose you remember their names?"

He tapped a finger against his glass. "The older one came to the farm one time, said she was interested in growing vegetables. Marie showed her around. Now what was the girl's name?" He tapped some more. "Katrina, maybe. Although that sounds Russian, doesn't it?"

"There was a Katrina playing at the pub last night. And she knew Paul Underwood—remember, the chemical salesman I debated in the winter?"

"Yes."

"The other thing I wanted to ask you was the reason I went to the library in the first place. And it might have to do with the murder."

Albert raised his bushy white eyebrows.

"So it turns out Paul Underwood and Wayne were friends in high school, according to Felicity Slavin, but had a falling out at the time. Paul was visiting Wayne on Saturday right before he was killed, and I want to know what happened between them all those years ago. Which, as it turns out, was the same year Fionnoula Leary went missing."

"And the plot thickens. This Katrina playing Irish music— that certainly might be Fionnoula's cousin. I can't say that I remember either of those boys, though, so I'm not much help to you, dear."

"I knew it was a long shot. But if any old memory pops up, you'll let me know?"

Albert nodded. "And you'll let me know what you find out about that missing girl."

"There was something else in the compost. A bone as long as my forearm."

Albert's eyes widened. "You don't say."

"I do, and I wondered if it might have come with the bracelet. I called the police and, boy, did they ever investigate. Ruth came and said she thought it was likely a human bone. The teams are probably still there. They even brought in a cadaver-sniffing dog. I had to shut Dasha and Preston in the house."

"My goodness, honey. Did they find anything?" Albert asked.

"I don't know. They said they'd call." She frowned at her glass. Her phone dinged and she picked it up off the side table. "Speak of the devil. It's the police." She connected and said hello.

Ruth was on the line. "Wanted to tell you we didn't find any additional remains on your property."

"Okay, thanks. I found out something about the bracelet today. It belonged to an Irish girl named Fionnoula Leary about thirty years ago. She was apparently staying with cousins here in Westbury."

"How did you find out?"

"It's a long story. Can I come and talk about it tomorrow?"

"How about tonight?" Ruth asked.

"If I have to. I'm at Albert's. I'll stop by the station after I leave here."

After Cam disconnected, she glanced at Albert. "They didn't find any other remains, as they put it."

"Well, that's good. Wonder if they'll figure out whose bone it was. Maybe it was this Fionnoula's."

She cocked her head at her uncle. "You never heard of anyone being buried on the farm, did you? Like before your time?"

Albert laughed. "I most certainly did not."

"Ruth wanted me to ask you that. But if the bracelet was Fionnoula's, that's kind of a moot point."

"I have a thought." Albert reached into the drawer of the end table and pulled out a slim pamphlet. "There's a lady here who used to teach at the school. History and social studies, if memory serves. Let me see if I can find her number in the directory." He scanned the pages, running a knobby bent index finger down the lines of names. "Here she is. Nina Bertoli. I'll give you her phone number along with her room number. She's in the other wing." He scrawled the number on a notepad, tore off the page, and handed it to Cam

"Thanks. I'll give her a call, or maybe stop in and see her."

"Tell her I sent you." He glanced at the clock next to his bed and drained his beer. "It's almost time to go down for dinner, and as you know it takes a one-legged man a good deal of time to get anywhere. Will you join me for the meal?"

"Thanks, Uncle Albert, but I should get home to the chickens and the pets."

"Pets plural?"

"I have Pete's dog, Dasha, while he's working this case." Cam helped Albert up and into his wheelchair, although she knew he was perfectly capable of managing it himself. Having his foot amputated had meant he could no longer farm, and was the reason he'd offered the property and business to Cam, but it hadn't slowed him down much once he'd moved here.

"Get along then. I'll join the line of old folks waiting for the elevator." He winked at her, and then his smile went serious. "You watch your back, now, honey. Lock up tight. You're the most precious thing in this life of mine."

Cam, her throat suddenly thick, leaned down for a hug. "Right back atcha. I'll be careful, don't worry." She walked out into the hall with him, then waved as she headed for the wide central staircase. "Love you," she called.

Cam knocked on Nina Bertoli's door. At the bottom of the stairs she'd glanced at the slip of paper and decided to try and find Nina now rather than call her later. Cam made her way to the room on the first floor of the wing opposite Albert's.

"Come in," a quavery voice called out.

Cam pushed open the door to a faint scent of vanilla and a room as feminine as Albert's was masculine despite an identical layout. Pink flowered curtains lined the windows, and the two stuffed armchairs were upholstered in a dainty blue and pink floral print. A tiny woman sat in the one near the window, her pink-slippered feet resting on a round pink ottoman. One hand held an embroidery hoop with a piece of needlework stretched on it, the other hand grasped a needle threaded with yellow silk. A brightly lit gooseneck floor lamp illuminated the work. The woman glanced up at Cam above the red-rimmed reading glasses perched on her nose.

"Hello, dear. Do I know you?" She smiled. Her snowy hair was pulled up into a bun on the very top of her head, giving her an old-fashioned look, although the decidedly modern powder blue fleece sweat suit she wore countered that effect.

"Ms. Bertoli, I'm Albert St. Pierre's great niece, Cam Flaherty."

"Oh, the farmer. I've heard about you, dear." Her eyes twinkled with delight. "You're the one who solves crimes about town, isn't that right? Do sit down."

Cam sat on the edge of the other chair. "Thank you. I don't want to interrupt what you're doing."

"Oh, it's no problem at all. I don't get many visitors, you see. Now, what can I help you with? Are you working on a new case?"

"I don't really work on cases—"

Nina batted away the suggestion. "You can trust me. I won't tell a soul. I've been reading mysteries all my life, don't you know? I started with Agatha Christie as a girl and just kept on going. It's important to be able to keep a secret. Now, what can I help you with?"

"Albert said you taught history and social studies at the high school. I'm trying to find out what happened to an Irish girl who was visiting several decades ago."

"Fionnoula Leary?" Nina's pale face was remarkably unwrinkled for someone who had to be at least in her seventies if not much older, with only fine lines drawn around her eyes and mouth.

"You remember her?"

Nina nodded.

Cam went on to tell her about finding the bracelet and the bone, and about the news article she'd unearthed. "I assume you knew about her disappearance?"

"Oh, yes, indeed. I followed it closely. The family Fionnoula stayed with was the Brennans. They were tore up something fierce when she never came home." She pointed a knobby index finger at the dark wooden piece of furniture the television sat on. Two doors in the front were closed. "Do me a favor, dear. In that cabinet is a scrapbook. Would you pull it out for me?"

Cam knelt and opened the doors to a mess of papers, needlework catalogs, and envelopes. She glanced up at Nina.

"In here?"

"It's in there somewhere." Nina laughed. "I'm not very organized anymore, I'm afraid."

Cam's hand finally landed on a book. She held the avalanche of papers back with her other hand as she pulled it out, and then shut the doors quickly before the contents of the cabinet spilled out. The book was an old-style photo album, with black pages and a weathered green cover. The book's binding was secured by metal fasteners so it could be loosened to add more pages. Standing, she handed the book to Nina and then sat on the chair again.

Nina slowly flipped through the pages. They were full of newspaper clippings that had been pasted in.

"Here's one of the ones I was looking for." Nina extended the book to Cam.

Cam gazed at an article from the *Daily News*, describing the Irish exchange student. It included a picture of a slender blond girl and a darker-haired one of about the same age, laughing into the camera with arms around each other's waists. The caption read, "Fionnoula Leary enjoys American high school life with cousin Catriona Brennan." Cam looked closer at the picture. On the hand that peeked out from Catriona's side was a band of metal that had caught a flash of light. The gold bracelet. Then she studied Catriona's face.

Cam sat back, still gazing at the picture. That was Katrina, the fiddler. It had to be. Catriona must be pronounced Katrina if you were Irish. And she'd bet this year's tomato crop that Paul and Catriona had been friends in high school. And Fionnoula. And Wayne. They had to be the friends Fionnoula went out with the night she disappeared.

"What is it?" Nina asked.

"I think I saw Catriona last night."

"Yes, she plays around here."

"And Catriona didn't know what happened to Fionnoula?" Cam asked.

"She claimed not to."

"Claimed?"

"They were not only cousins but friends. Fionnoula was living with the Brennans. How could she not know? I'll tell you something, young lady." Nina jabbed her finger in the air. "I never did believe Catriona. She'd been one of my best students. I thought she was going to have a career in law, or maybe politics. After the disappearance, though, she changed. It was like she didn't care anymore."

Chapter 14

Six o'clock on a cold, overcast day felt a lot later. Cam had stopped by the station on her way, as she'd promised, and told Ruth everything she'd discovered about Fionnoula. Now she let Dasha out of the house and watched as he moseyed around the yard, sniffing at this and pawing at that before finding a suitable place to do his business. She made her way to the barn and checked on the chicks, where all was well. At the outside coop, most of the hens were already inside. Ruffles and Hillary usually vied for last place to go in at night, but she didn't see the rooster in the yard. Cam held her breath as she poked her head into the coop, since she still hadn't cleaned it, but didn't see him.

"Ruffles," she called, standing up in the fresh air again. "Where are you?"

Dasha trotted up and barked.

"Not you, doggie. I'm looking for—" Cam stopped when she heard a squealing sound behind the barn. "What's that?"

Ruffles crowed from somewhere. Dasha alerted and barked again, then headed for the back of the barn, with Cam close behind. She pulled up short when she rounded the corner.

Ruffles had his talons sunk into the back of a furry animal about the size of a small cat. The little guy wriggled and squealed, but Ruffles hung on tight. He flapped his wings and crowed again. Cam had had those talons on her own leg once and knew how sharp they were. The poor little pup. She peered at the animal. Its face still had baby proportions: a round face, big eyes, soft-looking gray fur. But its ears were clearly that of a fox, and its eyes had a feral look in them.

"Ruffles, let go of that baby." She clapped her hands twice, as loud as she could. Ruffles ignored her. Where had he found the kit? If the mother fox showed up, Ruffles would be the one under attack. But the rooster was too aggressive for Cam to be able to lift him off the fox kit, at least not without thick leather gloves.

Ruffles flapped again. Dasha took up what looked like a defensive stance and growled. A shadowy shape a couple of feet tall emerged from the line of maples a few yards away. It moved toward them with slow, deliberate steps. The vixen was here. Cam took a couple of steps back. She'd rather Dasha came with her, but he wasn't wearing a leash and she didn't particularly want to grab his collar while he sounded like that.

In a blur of reddish rust, the vixen raced to the kit. Dasha sprang forward but halted, still growling, a yard away from the scene. The vixen leapt into the air, grabbing Ruffles' neck in her sharp-toothed mouth. He let go of the kit with a screech as the fox landed on the ground, swinging her head back and forth with Ruffles' neck in her jaws until he went limp.

The fox stared at Cam with pale orange eyes for a moment. The white around her snout and neck cut a clean line under the red-tinged rusty color of her head, making it look like a mask.

"Dasha, come," Cam said in a low voice.

The dog gave one more look at the fox, then walked back to where Cam stood.

The vixen dropped Ruffles on the ground and turned to her kit, giving it a couple of licks, then picked up Ruffles again in her jaws. She used her snout to nudge the kit ahead of her to-ward the woods. The kit scampered ahead of its mother with its still-stocky little legs, glancing back at Mom once in a while as if for reassurance.

"Good boy," Cam said to Dasha, laying a hand on his head. "You let that mother take care of her baby, didn't you?" She watched as the foxes disappeared into the woods, then shud-dered. "I guess that's it for Ruffles." The natural world could be a fierce and dangerous place. As was, at times, the human world.

Cam frowned as she stood in front of her refrigerator door. Why hadn't she assembled two lasagnas yesterday? The possi-bilities for dinner were scant, and she was exhausted from the day of working and talking. And then seeing Ruffles' life snuffed out in a flash, not that he didn't have it coming. But she'd grown almost fond of his brash, strutting personality and she'd miss him. Her customers had liked buying fertilized eggs, too.

The cold air in front of Cam reminded her that she still stood with the fridge open. She drew out eggs, smoked turkey breast, mayo and mustard, and cheddar. She busied herself buttering whole wheat bread and slicing cheese. Preston si-dled over and reared up, rubbing his head on her knee a cou-ple of times, then gave his tiny plaintive request for a morsel of turkey, please. Cam smiled and tossed him a few small tid-bits. She heated a frying pan and slid one of the slices of bread into it butter side down, then added a swipe of Ipswich Ale mustard, layers of turkey and cheese, then the top bread, to which she'd added mayonnaise on the unbuttered side. After the bottom side was golden and crisp, she flipped the sandwich, pressing it down, and cracked an egg into the pan next to it. Dasha lay on his bed in the corner of the kitchen looking interested but not making any demands. He'd had his dinner.

A few minutes later she sat at the table with a glass of Pinot Noir and a plate holding her quick-and-dirty version of a Croque Madame, with the fried egg topping the grilled sandwich. She'd already brought over a jar of salsa and a knife and fork. She spread a forkful of salsa over the top of the sandwich, cut into it, and brought the bite to her mouth, a drop of gooey cheese and a splash of egg yolk hitting the plate as she did. Perfection in one small corner of the world.

She spread out today's *Daily News* to read as she ate. Which might have been a bad idea, because the top headline on the front page read, NO LEADS IN LOCAL MURDER CASE. It quoted Detective Peter Pappas as saying they were following up several avenues of investigation and persons of interest, but were not ready to make an arrest at this time. Cam hadn't talked with Pete since yesterday afternoon. Maybe his team had discovered evidence leading to persons of interest. She ought to call him, anyway, and tell him about the box of ammunition. Would he be interested in the bracelet, too? Cam had a feeling it was related somehow to the murder. But she didn't know how.

She ignored the rest of the news article and turned to the feature section. The gardening column always was about what chemical products to apply. A story about a local woman devising a way to spray bicycle frames with highway-quality reflective paint was fascinating, as was an article about the two-hundred-and-fiftieth birthday of Newburyport and the great fire of 1811. Cam shuddered inwardly at the thought of flames consuming half the downtown. She'd had two bad experiences with fire in her life, one as a child of six and one only last June. She never wanted to have to face her worst fear again.

Cam took her wine to the computer and dove deep into Google, looking for more details on Fionnoula. She found another news story from a week after the first one. It said Fionnoula was still missing, and that the family, devastated, was sending out a plea for information from anyone who might have seen her. And then the trail went cold. She couldn't find anything else that mentioned Fionnoula Leary. How strange. Nina had said Fionnoula had never surfaced. Had she run away? Or been abducted? Surely her return would have been reported. If Paul or Wayne, or both, had killed Fionnoula for some reason and buried her, they could still be in conflict about it, about letting the news out.

Cam tapped the monitor and narrowed her eyes. Nina had been convinced that Catriona knew what happened to Fionnoula but had refused to say. Cam ran a search on Catriona Brennan but couldn't find her. She'd likely married and changed her name. But she was part of a band, a lively popular group that played locally. How hard could it be to find her? Cam couldn't remember the name of the group even though Paul had mentioned it. But the pub would know. She found the number and dialed it. Whoever answered the phone said the group was called Keeltori.

A few more taps of the fingers, and bingo. Catriona Brennan's last name was now Watson. Cam found both the band and Catriona on Facebook. She stared at Catriona's face on her personal page, a close-up of her playing the fiddle on an outdoor stage that looked like it might be Boarding House Park in Lowell. Large dark eyes in a petite face made the musician look younger than she must be if she was Paul's age. Cam clicked the About tab, but Catriona had privacy locked down, so the information only showed to friends. Cam didn't click Add Friend—Catriona didn't know her from anybody. Switching back to the band's page, she checked the Events tab. They weren't playing tonight, but would be at the Grog on Wednesday night.

Wednesday. Was something happening Wednesday? She glanced at the calendar on her phone. Oh, yeah, it was the continuation of town meeting, but maybe she could stop by the iconic Newburyport bar and restaurant afterward. Cam sipped her wine. She should be doing farm business instead of delving into past history that might mean nothing. Paying bills didn't stop just because not much was growing, neither did updating the Web site and Attic Hill Farm's own Facebook page with fresh postings. The last was easy enough, even though she'd forgotten to take pictures while she was pruning yesterday. She clicked over and wrote a quick update about the spring greens, adding a picture she'd taken inside the hoop house last week. Maybe she'd stop blogging on the Web site. Facebook seemed to have taken over for blogs.

As she hit Enter, she heard a noise and glanced up. Dasha was sleeping on a corner of the rug and Preston lay curled up snoozing at her feet, so it wasn't either of them. She removed her fingers from the keyboard and listened. There it was again, sounding like a scratching on the window. Except there hadn't been a breath of wind all day. The drum of her heart beat faster and faster even though she knew she had a good lock on the door.

She'd drawn the curtains and didn't particularly want to look out from a lit interior into the darkness. She switched off the lamp and closed the computer, then moved to the back door where she flipped the override switch for the normally motion-controlled outdoor floodlight. Peering out the window, she examined the stairs and driveway as they flared into existence. No figure skulked away into the night. No animal scurried away. And no human stood there hoping to gain entrance, either. She'd installed the motion-controlled light last June when there had been a person out there one time. The next time the light had come on it had illuminated only a skunk.

Cam shook her head and turned the light back to motion-controlled. When her phone rang on the desk, she took three long strides to pick it up. Pete was on the other end.

After she greeted him, she said, "What's new?"

"I wondered if you'd like company tonight. I'm beat and don't feel like going home to a cold, empty apartment."

"I haven't heard a nicer offer in a long time. Come on over." She opened her mouth to tell him about the noise, then shut it. He didn't need to hear about a false alarm.

An hour later Pete sat with the remnants of his own Croque Madame on a plate in front of him at the table. He still wore his blazer but he'd untucked his shirt and his feet were shod in the fleece slippers Cam kept for his use in the house. Dasha, who'd been overjoyed to see his main human, sat happily at Pete's feet.

"Cam, you're an angel." He wiped his mouth with a napkin, then took a sip of beer, gazing at her.

Cam snorted. "Hardly. I can put together a pretty mean hot sandwich, though." She had refilled her wineglass and sat with him while he ate. "So what's happening with the case? Or can't you talk about it?" She wet a finger on her tongue and ran the finger around the rim of the wineglass until it sang.

"We're stuck. The commander is pissed. I went to talk to Judith Patterson and she wanted a lawyer there. And Ivan's driving me nuts. Plus I was in court all afternoon on a different case entirely." He shook his head. "What have you been up to?"

"Besides farming, I've been wondering what beef Paul

Underwood had with Wayne. I told you I saw him drive away looking angry the day before the murder, right?"

"No, I don't believe you did. What time of day?"

"It was as I was heading there to talk with Wayne about my two chicks that died. Maybe four or five o'clock. You must have questioned Paul about finding the body."

"We did. Wayne was already dead when Underwood says he got there, although we're still following up on confirming when he actually showed up and where he was before that. What's this about a beef?"

"Felicity Slavin was their high school teacher." Cam went on to tell Pete what her friend had said about the falling out. "I was at Connolly's Pub last night for Saint Patrick's Day and Paul asked to sit with Lucinda and me. Our table had the last empty seats, I guess. I asked him what their falling out was over but he didn't really want to say, only that he went to see Wayne on Saturday to sort a few things out. It didn't really look like they had sorted out anything or he wouldn't have looked like an angry bull driving away. And then Lucinda asked him why he went back over there Sunday morning and he got up in a huff."

"Interesting. Felicity doesn't know what went on between them?"

"No. But then today I found a gold bracelet in my compost pile. An old, dented, dirty gold bracelet, with the initials *FL* inside."

"And this has what to do with Paul Underwood? Or with Wayne?" Pete yawned. "Sorry. I haven't slept much since Sunday."

Cam held up her hand. "Hang on another minute. I also found a bone about as long as my forearm, also in the compost."

Pete sat up straight, looking more alert. "What did you do with it?"

"Exactly what I was supposed to. I didn't touch it, and I called the Westbury police. They came and picked it up, and took the bracelet, too. They called teams in to check out the entire farm."

"Good. I wonder why I didn't hear about that. Guess because I was in court. Did the bone look human?"

"Ruth Dodge thought it did. I've never seen a human ulna without skin on it. But I called because after seeing the bracelet, I thought maybe they were connected."

Pete nodded. "Good move."

"Then I went to see the stable owner where I got the manure that went into that batch of compost." She relayed what she'd learned from Sue Genest about Fionnoula Leary, her stay with the Brennan family, and when Fionnoula disappeared. "I spent time with the microfilm in the Newburyport Library, too. I read an article that said only that Fionnoula was going out with friends that night. She would have been the same age as Paul, Wayne, and Catriona. It's so strange. I couldn't find anything that said she ever turned up."

"Who is Catriona?"

"She's Fionnoula's cousin, and Fionnoula was staying with them for a year in Westbury. Now Catriona's a fiddler in an Irish group. They were at the pub last night, and it turns out she and Paul are old friends. She made him go up and play with the band."

"So Wayne was probably friends with all of them, too." Pete tapped his fingers on the table.

"That's what I was thinking. Albert steered me to a friend of his at Moran Manor today who was also a teacher at the high school when Fionnoula disappeared." She told him what Nina had said about the change in Catriona.

"Interesting."

"I should call Felicity and ask her about Catriona and Fionnoula, too." Cam checked the old wall clock. "Too late tonight. She's told me she goes to bed at about nine, and that was half an hour ago."

"Interesting stuff. Not sure how it bears on Wayne's murder, but sometimes stuff from the past goes live again and affects how people act."

"One more thing I should tell you. I took a lasagna over to Greta yesterday. She wasn't there, and I helped Megan with the hens and the eggs. While I was in the barn I happened to see a box of ammunition for a point four ten revolver. Or at least that's what it said. Not that there's anything wrong with a farmer owning a gun."

"You just happened to see it? This box was lying out in the open on a shelf somewhere?"

"Well, not exactly." She swallowed.

Pete laughed. "I can't keep you from detecting, can I?"

Cam pulled a small smile. "On Sunday, Greta was trying to hide something in a tack cupboard near the stalls. She said it was the dog's thyroid medicine but I'm not so sure it was. Since I was there, anyway, and Greta was out, I thought I'd take a look." No need to go into more details about how many cupboards she'd checked before finding the box.

"I'll check out her gun ownership. Wayne wasn't shot, so owning a gun doesn't make her a suspect, although of course we're looking at everyone, including the wife. Gun could have been Wayne's, of course."

"Of course. Here's something else. When Greta did come home, she blurted out that she was broke and stuck with a business she doesn't want. And that she hates hens."

"Noted."

"I also thought it was odd that she was already back at work

138

today," Cam said. "I saw her leading a children's session at the Newburyport Library."

"Certain people deal with their grief best when they're working." Pete yawned again. "And I'd like to deal with my exhaustion by sleeping. Not going to be good for much else, I'm afraid."

Cam covered his hand with hers. "You know I like you in my bed even when all we're doing is sleeping."

Chapter 15

Pete left at seven right as the sun peeked through the trees. Ruffles' cries did not herald this morning, though, and the farm seemed too quiet without him. Cam stepped outside. The weather report forecast a mild, sunny day and the air smelled of growth and promise. She sat with her coffee on the back stoop, listening to cardinals chirp and flit about and busy chickadees buzz in the big maple. Returning inside, she spread a couple of pieces of toast with peanut butter, honey, and banana and ate before heading out to work, reflecting on how she had the best commute in the world.

She let the hens out, then changed the chicks' bedding after scooping them all up and setting them in a big cardboard box for a few minutes.

"Cam, you in there?" Felicity's voice rang out. "I'm here for Volunteer Wednesday."

"Come on in. I'm in the office."

Felicity popped her head in, and then said, "Ooh, look at those cuties!"

"You didn't see them the other day?"

"No. They're so sweet and soft. Can I hold one?"

After Cam said she could, Felicity scooped up a chick and stroked its downy back. "Are these the next batch of layers?"

"Right. They're only a week old. I lost two on Saturday, and took them over to Wayne to ask for help. But now he's not here anymore." Cam tsked as she poured new pine shavings into the chicks' usual box under the light, adding clean water and food receptacles. "Help me put them back."

She and Felicity lifted the chicks two at a time and set them back into their home.

"Any news on the murder, Cam?"

"Not really."

"Well, give me a job. I'm here to work all morning."

"Thanks. Let's go out to the hoop house." Cam led the way out of the barn, Dasha trotting alongside.

"Does he live here now?" Felicity asked, gesturing at the dog.

"No. But when Pete's working a homicide, he barely gets home, and I like having Dasha around." She glimpsed the compost area behind the barn and stopped. "Got something I want to ask you. I was turning compost yesterday and I found a gold bracelet with the initials *FL* inside."

Felicity waited, hands in purple pants pockets.

"When you were teaching Wayne and Paul, did you also have a Catriona Brennan in your class?"

"Yep. Nice girl, smart. Schools are more rigorous in Ireland, so she was ahead of the rest of her class. A musician, too. Why do you ask?"

"Did you also maybe have her cousin, Fionnoula Leary, for a while?"

"The other Irish girl." She stared at Cam. "I did, now that you mention it. The one who disappeared." Felicity's eyes went wide open. "*FL*. That's it. She wore a thick gold bracelet all the time. Seemed old-fashioned to me. How in the world did you connect that bracelet with Fionnoula?"

"A process of elimination." She told Felicity her theory of the three ways the bracelet could have gotten into her compost, and about her talk with Sue, the stable owner. "And when I learned Fionnoula hadn't been seen for more than thirty years, I ruled out the manure idea."

"But if the bracelet came in with the lobster stuff, that means it was in the ocean."

Cam cocked her head. "When they were in high school, were Wayne and Paul also friends with the cousins? I know Paul is friendly with Catriona now."

"They were a gang of four. A sweet, rowdy gang who hung out together. There might have been some flirting going on, but mainly they all seemed like friends."

"Until Fionnoula went missing?" Cam asked.

"That's right."

They reached the hoop house and Cam held the door open for Felicity. With today's sunshine, it was already warm and smelled of rich, moist soil. "Did the authorities locate her? Did she ever show up?"

"Not that I'm aware of." Felicity set her fists on her hips. "But remember when you asked me what had happened to make Wayne and Paul no longer friends and I didn't know? Now that you bring up the girls, I think it was after that. Losing Fionnoula split them apart like an ax."

Felicity and Cam had been starting more seeds in the hoop house for an hour when Alexandra pulled the door open.

"Am I too late? I have muffins." With a sheepish smile she held up a paper bag in one hand. In her other hand was a cardboard tray holding three paper cups with lids.

"I'm ready for a break. You?" Cam asked Felicity. "It's never too late for muffins, especially if you made them, Alexandra."

"Whole wheat carrot cinnamon," the tall young woman said. "The storage carrots are getting pretty old. Thought I'd grate them up and bring breakfast. Including coffee."

"Then it's definitely time for a break." Cam upended a yellow plastic crate, then pulled two more into a circle before heading to the hose to rinse her hands. Felicity followed suit.

After they were seated, Alexandra distributed coffees and muffins. "All have milk and sugar. Seemed easier that way." She shrugged. "Farming burns up the calories, right, Cam?"

Cam nodded with her mouth full.

"Superb, Alexandra," Felicity said a minute later, after swallowing a bite of muffin.

"Hey, I stopped to say hi to the chickens on my way out here. I didn't see Ruffles around. Where is he?" Alexandra asked.

"He's gone."

"Gone?" Felicity asked. "Like he ran away?" She brushed a speck of carrot off her cheek.

"No. Yesterday afternoon, almost evening, he was outside the fence and he'd caught a fox kit. Had his talons right into the little thing. But then the kit's mother streaked out from the woods and broke old Ruffles' neck in her jaws. I saw the whole thing."

"Whoa," Alexandra said. "I guess he had it coming to him. Was the kit okay?"

"Yeah. The mom made sure it was, and then took Ruffles back to their den with them. Rooster Tartare for dinner."

"Were you scared of the vixen?" Felicity asked. "They can be ruthless."

"A little. Dasha was with me, and luckily he only watched, too. I wouldn't have wanted to see him and the fox fight."

"Remember this winter when Ruffles came racing in the barn's cat door after Preston?" Felicity started to giggle.

"What I remember is him chasing me down the driveway

and getting his talons into my leg for a minute," Cam said. Her laugh turned into a snort.

"And seeing him, um, fertilize the girls was really something." Alexandra added her own giggle. "He was such a stud."

"A real man's man. Ah." Felicity smiled. "This is fun. I didn't know we were going to have a wake for Ruffles."

Cam held up her coffee. "Here's to Ruffles. May he rest in peace."

"To Ruffles!" Felicity and Alexandra held up their cups, too.

Cam popped the last bite of muffin into her mouth and savored the moist spiced crumb. She brushed her hand off on her work jeans. "How's Katie doing?" she asked Alexandra.

The smile slid off Alexandra's face. "She went back to class, but she's way upset about everything that went down. Getting sucked in by that group, and then suspected by the cops. I know she didn't do anything wrong, other than throw red paint on the Laitinens' barn. She's not that resilient of a person, though. She still seems really shook up."

"Did she tell you what exactly she saw that morning when she went back?" Cam asked.

Alexandra gazed down the rows of six-inch-high greens for a moment, then back at Cam. "She said she drove over there to apologize to Mr. Laitinen. She saw that chemical guy—"

"Paul Underwood?" Cam asked.

"Yeah. She saw him getting out of his car at the house. She said when he saw her he looked angry, so she turned around and went home."

"She didn't talk to him?"

"I don't know. I don't think so."

"That seems pretty straightforward, then." Felicity looked from Alexandra to Cam. "Right? What can the police—or it's the staties, so Detective Pappas, right?"

"Right," Cam said.

"What can he think Katie did?" Felicity continued. "Went over there and killed Wayne?"

"I don't know. He isn't supposed to talk with me about it, anyway. Do you think she's hiding something, Alexandra? Something she's not telling?"

"She could be. I'll see if I can get more out of her tonight."

Cam finished her last sip of coffee and stood. "Thanks for the muffins, Alexandra. Time to burn off those calories, girls." She had darkened their light mood by asking about Katie, and wished she hadn't. But she had a working farm to run, murder or no murder. And it was time for farming, not detecting.

The door to the hoop house swung open, and a tall man filled the doorway. "Am I in the right place?" he asked.

"This is Attic Hill Farm. Come on in and close the door," Cam said.

"I heard you take volunteers on Wednesday." He shut the door behind him and sauntered toward Cam in jeans and a hooded sweatshirt with a U Mass logo, a black scarf wrapped around his neck. He looked about Alexandra's or Katie's age: midtwenties, clean shaven, with short dark hair and a wide smile that flashed perfect white teeth.

"Hey, Tam." Alexandra stood. "Cam, this is Tam Haskell. He's a friend of Katie's. Tam, Cam Flaherty, farmer in chief, and this is our friend Felicity Slavin."

"Very nice to meet you both," he said, extending his hand first to Felicity and then to Cam.

Cam shook his hand. "Always happy to have more help. So Katie told you about our Wednesdays?"

He bounced on his heels. "I'm really interested in learning more about organic farming. And helping with your hens, too. I'm thinking of getting a few chickens for my backyard, and

I'd love to learn how you manage them." He gave Cam the attentive gaze of a serious student.

"Sounds good to me."

"Tam's an interesting name," Felicity said.

"Short for Tamlin. Old family name my parents stuck me with." He lifted one eyebrow.

"Got it. Come on." Cam beckoned. "I'll show you how to change the chickens' bedding. It's overdue. Felicity, can you show Alexandra what we were working on?"

At Felicity's nod, Cam led Tam out and toward the coop. "I have about forty hens now, but another couple dozen chicks are in the barn."

"Can I see them, too?"

"Sure. So what do you do for work, Tam?" she asked as they walked.

"I'm a student like Katie, studying political science. But I don't have classes on Wednesdays."

"Are you in grad school?"

"No, still getting my undergrad degree. I took a few years off to travel." As they neared the barn, he said, "Just look at that beautiful door."

Cam slid open the barn door and made her way to the office. The chicks seemed to have grown even more. "Here are the babies." She turned when Tam didn't reply, but he wasn't behind her. She poked her head out the office door to see him lingering at the wide door, one hand on the latch. "Tam?"

He turned, then strode toward her. "I'd love to photograph your barn someday."

By the time Alexandra, Felicity, and Tam left, a few minutes after noon, they'd had a productive morning. The seeding was all done, and Tam had completely mucked out the coop and spread fresh bedding on the floor without a word of complaint at the smell. Cam might have to hire a part-time worker when the season ratcheted up to full gear come summer, but for now, a few congenial and competent workers who were happy to help out was all she needed. And it had taken her mind off murder, even if all that socializing over work had the capacity to drain her. Silence was a huge blessing.

The end of the week was looming for Pete, though. How else could she help him? Helping him would be helping Megan, too, and Cam had promised her she would. She'd told Pete everything she'd learned. Well, except for Felicity saying it was Fionnoula's disappearance that had split up the group of friends. And she wasn't sure that was even related to the murder. But it might be. She pulled out her phone and texted Pete about it, then sank onto the bench outside the barn and closed her eyes. She soaked up the welcome warmth of the sunshine. Spring was almost officially here, and summer heat was guaranteed to follow. For now? She could sit here all day.

Dasha had other ideas. He pushed his muzzle into Cam's knee. She opened an eye to see him sitting up watching her. When she opened both eyes, he barked.

"Want to go for a real walk, big guy?" Cam smiled at him as she stood. It was too nice a day to waste it sitting on a bench. And the company of a quiet, agreeable dog was as restorative to an introvert like her as being alone.

She grabbed an apple and a hunk of cheddar cheese from the house, along with Dasha's leash. Fifteen minutes later she and the dog strolled out across the meadow at Maudslay State Park, a large former private estate right over the border into Newburyport. Riding trails and walking paths wound through wooded hills and open meadows, with miles of rhododendron planted on either side. One trail ran through a huge stand of mountain laurel, and another presented breathtaking views as it curved high above the Merrimack River. None of the flowers were blooming yet, of course, but it was a perfect day for a long thinking walk. Cam had cross-country skied here in the winter, an easier experience than in her own woods because someone had always been along the Maudslay routes breaking trail before she arrived. And a change of scenery was always a good thing.

As Dasha trotted along at her side, Cam mused on how she'd be glad for more than one reason once this murder was solved. She wanted to get back to that easy pattern she and Pete had fallen into. His work as a detective consisted of investigating any unattended or suspicious death. Often the unattended deaths were simply elderly people who died alone and Pete's became a regular day job like anyone else's, with time in the evenings and on weekends for Cam. But during a murder investigation, routine went out the window.

She led Dasha through the woods and headed up the Castle Hill loop for an aerobic workout, something she rarely got unless she was skiing. Daily farm work was exercise, but it was more in the drudge category than the uplifting get-your-heart-rate-up sort. A horse whinnied somewhere in the distance and a black-and-white woodpecker rapped at the trunk of a tall fir just ahead. Dasha looked like he was enjoying the walk as much as she was, his tongue out and his focus on the narrow trail. She was tempted to disconnect his leash, but he didn't seem to mind it, and the posted rules said all dogs were to be leashed, curbed, and cleaned up after.

They topped the hill and headed down the perimeter of the other side where the winding trail perched at the edge of a steep slope. Cam had nearly slammed into a tree here in the winter when the snow had been slick and momentum had taken her faster than she wanted to go. From around the bend a horse and rider clopped uphill toward Cam and Dasha. Cam took a second look and realized it was Judith astride the same black horse she'd been riding at Sue's stable the day before. Odd that she'd run into Judith two days in a row. When the horse drew near, Cam waved.

"Hi, Judith."

Judith pulled the horse to a stop ten feet away. It snorted and stamped its front feet as if it didn't agree with the decision. Cam didn't move close enough to stroke the horse this time, sticking her hands in her pockets instead.

"Beautiful day, isn't it?" Cam said, when Judith didn't speak.

"Yes. You ought to mind your own business, you know." She gazed down at Cam with narrowed eyes. She wore the same short black jacket as she had at the stable, with black knee-high boots over riding pants, and an orange silk scarf tied around her neck.

"What do you mean?"

"The police came to talk to me. They think I had something to do with Wayne's death. I've never heard anything more ridiculous." Judith sniffed and her lip curled.

Oh. She'd told Pete about Judith's vaping. "That doesn't involve me, though," Cam said. "You said you were in conflict with Wayne about the property. The police are only doing their job, their due diligence."

"I think you told that detective something that made him interested in me. I don't like it, Cam. You ought to stick to farming. It's unbecoming to turn snitch." She clucked to the horse, which started moving again, fast. And it was moving straight at Cam.

"Hey! What are you doing?" Cam yelled. Dasha barked. Cam leapt to the side and grabbed at a branch to keep from sliding down the hill. Dasha planted his feet downhill from her and kept barking. Cam barely hung on as Judith steered the horse past her so close Cam could feel the heat of its body on her face.

Once they were past, Cam blew out a breath and climbed back onto the trail, staring as Judith and the horse disappeared over the crest of the hill. Cam's heart was thudding in her ears like a loud, fast bass rhythm.

"Geez, Dasha." She picked up the dropped leash. "What was that all about? She's crazy." Or guilty.

Dasha barked at the trail ahead.

"Good idea. Let's go home."

Chapter 16

Cam was about to leave the farm after dinner for town meeting when she realized she hadn't tucked the hens and chicks in for the night. She rushed out to the barn to secure them before climbing into the truck. She rattled down the hill and then right on Main Street a quarter mile, hurrying into the vestibule of Old Town Hall twenty minutes after seven. She checked in with the registrar at the door, but when she entered the hall, the meeting wasn't yet in session. Committee members milled about on the stage, and clumps of townspeople stood talking in the back. A scattering of folks occupied seats, some reading, a few knitting, others chatting. Detective Hobbs stood in a back corner, hands clasped behind his back, eyes scanning the room, his trimmed dark-blond hair combed with exaction. Why was he here?

Cam spied Felicity sitting near the side aisle and made her way toward her. Taking a seat, she greeted Felicity. "Why haven't they started?"

"No quorum. We need at least thirty percent of the voting population in order to decide financial matters over five thousand dollars."

"Guess I didn't need to worry about being late, then."

Felicity laughed. "Nope. Hey, stroke of luck getting that new fellow in as a volunteer, wasn't it?"

"Seemed like it. I can use all the help I can get."

Felicity frowned at a crossword puzzle on a clipboard in her lap. "What's an eleven-letter word for 'before you eat'?"

"Preprandial?"

Felicity entered the letters on the puzzle and glanced over at Cam. "That's it. How do you know that word?"

"Great-Aunt Marie liked to use it." Cam laughed. "When she and Albert would have their cocktail at the end of the day, she'd always offer me a preprandial libation, too. In those exact words."

"It's a good one. Preprandial. I like the way it rolls off the tongue." Felicity turned her gaze back to the puzzle.

"There's also postprandial and intraprandial. One of their friends who came over for dinner sometimes used to excuse himself in between courses. He'd say he was going outside for an intraprandial cigarette. Cam turned sideways in her seat and scanned the hall. She whistled.

"What?" Felicity looked in the same direction.

"Over there. Greta Laitinen and Judith Patterson talking together." Cam shook her head. "I was walking in Maudslay today, and Judith almost ran me down with her horse."

Felicity wrinkled her nose. "Why would she do that?"

"She thinks I got her in trouble with the police." Cam frowned "I wonder if she's hiding something. Innocent people don't care if the police question them, do they?"

"Not usually." She glanced at Cam. "Seems kind of early for Greta to be out and about. It's only four days since Wayne was killed."

Cam nodded her head slowly, still gazing at the two women.

"That's right. She was already back at work at the library on Tuesday, too. I think I might go over and say hello to them. See what Judith has to say about running me down, too."

"Don't get caught in the crossfire." Felicity pointed. "They don't look that happy with each other."

"They sure don't." Cam had never seen either of them look particularly happy with anyone, come to think of it. She rose and made her way up the aisle and across the back of the hall. She passed Ivan Hobbs and slowed. She was about to say hello to him, but since they hadn't been introduced, she decided to skip it. Pete could do the formalities if they were ever all in one place.

Greta stood halfway down the aisle along the side of the room with arms folded across her chest, chin in the air, jaw clenched. Judith, standing a couple of inches taller than Greta and impeccably attired in a black pantsuit, waved a hand in the air with her back to Cam. Cam slowed as she approached. She was about to clear her throat to announce herself when Judith spoke.

"Leasing the land to me benefits both of us, Greta. You know that. I thought we were in agreement about letting me have the land before . . ."

"Before my husband was murdered? That changed everything. Now I'm not so sure I want to let you take part of my children's inheritance."

Judith blew out an aggrieved sigh. "I wouldn't be taking it. I'd be paying you for it, and paying you well."

"I'll ask my lawyer about it." Greta turned and stalked down to the third row of seats.

Judith turned on her heel. Her nostrils flared when she saw Cam a few feet away. "What are you doing eavesdropping on us? That was a private conversation."

"Hold on. This is a public hall. I just came over to say hello. And to ask what you were doing running me down on the trail today. I almost fell down the hill."

Judith gave Cam a pitying look. "You have quite the imagination. There was plenty of room on that trail for both of us. Now, if you'll excuse me?" She stepped forward.

"It wasn't my imagination." Cam folded her arms and occupied the center of the aisle, with seats on her right and the wall holding ten-foot-tall windows on her left. "Why are you so worried about talking to the police if you've done nothing wrong?" She kept her voice low.

"None of your business." Judith turned again. Cam watched as she made her way down to the front and back up the center aisle, her heels clicking on the wooden floor. When she drew even with Cam, Judith glanced at her and mouthed, "Don't mess with me."

Cam glanced toward the back to see Detective Hobbs, his gaze firmly fixed on Judith.

Cam sipped her beer downstairs at the Grog, tapping her toe to the lively tunes of Keeltori. Town meeting had never reached quorum. She and Felicity had worked on the crossword together while they waited, with Cam occasionally supplying a word. At around eight o'clock the moderator had used the microphone to plead with everyone present to each please call another resident and ask them to show up. But by eight-thirty there still weren't enough voters in the hall, and the meeting had been continued to the following Saturday.

So Cam had driven over to the Grog, hoping she could talk to Catriona about Fionnoula and what had happened to her cousin. Not that she wanted to, but she felt she had to. Cam yawned. Surely the group would take a break soon. Couples and small groups occupied the rough wood tables, chatting quietly or simply listening. Glasses clinked and someone laughed back near the door. The room was half full, not bad for a Wednesday night at nine o'clock.

Cam watched the fiddler. She moved her whole body with her playing, sometimes bending low over the fiddle, some- times facing the guitarist as if their instruments were talking to each other, a few times sashaying toward the tables and en- gaging a listener here and there. Catriona wore a pink and black flowered dress this evening, with pink tights and low black boots, a pink flower pinned in her dark hair.

Cam had finished her beer and her bowl of complimentary popcorn, and was considering giving up and heading home when the group finished a song with a flourish.

Catriona leaned into the mike and announced into the ap- plause, "We're after taking a short break now. Catch you in fif- teen, then." She carefully set her fiddle on the stand, drank down a bottle of water, and dabbed a handkerchief on her forehead and neck.

Cam took a deep breath. This wasn't going to be easy. She stood and took a step toward the front of the room when Catri- ona glanced around as if searching for something. Cam fol- lowed her gaze and saw her head for the restrooms. Well, Cam had to use the facilities, too, so she followed Catriona.

A couple of minutes later she was washing her hands at the sink next to Catriona. Cam caught her eye in the mirror and smiled. "Great music you all play. I'm a big fan."

"Thanks, dearie. We're loving doing it, for sure."

"I saw Paul Underwood playing with you on Monday. You're old friends with him?" Cam asked.

Catriona pulled out a paper towel and faced Cam, drying her hands. "We are, that."

"This might sound odd, but I'm a farmer, and I found a gold bracelet on my land. It had the initials *FL* inside it."

Catriona stopped drying her hands. She stood without moving.

"And then I learned that the girl who wore it was named Fionnoula Leary. She used to ride at my friend's stable, but my friend said she disappeared. And a news article said she lived with you and your family. Is that right?"

"Who are yeh, then? Are yeh a private investigator?" Catriona's mouth hung open and her face had gone pale.

"No, not at all. But my friend was murdered this week—"

"Wayne." Her eyes filled as she stared at Cam. "He was my friend, too."

"His daughter asked for my help. I wondered what happened between Paul and Wayne all those years ago. You might be the only person who knows, besides Paul."

"Yeh think Paul killed him?"

"I don't know. But something caused them to split apart, and I know they were still dealing with it when Wayne died. And it seems linked to your cousin's disappearance."

Catriona set her hands on the sink and hung her head down for a moment.

"Please talk to me," Cam urged.

Catriona straightened and turned toward Cam. "I will. I shouldn't, you know, but I will. I can't do it now, though. We're after having another set to play, and it's a long one."

"Can I meet you for lunch tomorrow?"

"All right."

"Here at noon?" Cam asked. If she didn't set the time and place now, it might never happen.

Catriona nodded. She tossed the towel in the receptacle near the door. With her hand on the door, she said, "None of us killed Fionnoula, and we all did."

Chapter 17

Cam lay in bed with her eyes wide open. "None of us killed Fionnoula, and we all did." Catriona's words echoed in her brain. What in the world did that mean? The "us" had to be Catriona, Paul, and Wayne.

She'd thought she was tired, but sleep was a distant train whistle compared to these nearby sirens of thoughts in her head. She turned and glanced at the red numbers of her alarm clock. Was ten-thirty too late to call Pete? She knew he'd want her to. She grabbed her phone and sat up, pressing his number.

He answered with a slow, deep, "Pappas."

"Did I wake you?" she asked.

"Yeah, but it's okay. Are you all right?"

"Yes. I can't sleep and wanted to tell you what happened tonight. All day, actually."

"Go." His voice already sounded more alert.

"So I had a run-in with Judith Patterson today. I took Dasha for a walk in Maudslay this afternoon, because it was such a nice day."

"I'll bet he loved that."

"He did. But then Judith came at me on a horse. First she

said she was unhappy that I had snitched on her to you. Her word, not mine. And then she rode her horse so close to me I almost fell down the hill. And it was a steep one."

"But you were okay?"

"Yes. Did you make any connection with Judith and the murder weapon?"

He groaned. "Not yet. She claims . . . Well, I can't really talk about it. Now, what was the other thing you wanted to tell me?"

"Well, after town meeting— Oh, I should also tell you that Greta and Judith were arguing there. Greta seems to have changed her mind about letting Judith acquire a portion of the land."

"Hmm. Interesting." Pete didn't quite muffle his yawn.

"And then Judith denied that she ran me down. But the other thing is, after the meeting was postponed because they didn't get a quorum, I went to the Grog. I wanted to talk to Catriona Watson, and her group played there tonight."

"The fiddler. The one who knew Fionnoula."

"Exactly. I wanted to ask her about Fionnoula and the bracelet."

"What did she say?" Pete asked.

"She asked me if I was a private investigator. She seemed really upset by my asking, like she'd seen a ghost. She didn't have time to talk, though, so we set a lunch date for tomorrow. She said she'd tell me then."

"That's good, at least."

"But what I wanted to tell you was the last thing she said. She said, 'None of us killed Fionnoula, and we all did.'"

Pete fell silent. When he spoke he was terse and sounded official. "That's a very incriminating thing for her to say. What's her last name again?"

"Watson. Her maiden name was Brennan. And her first name isn't spelled like it sounds." Cam spelled out Catriona for him.

Sounds of tapping came from the phone, as if Pete was typing into a laptop or tapping out a text message.

"What did the "we" refer to?" he asked.

"We'd just been talking about Paul Underwood and Wayne Laitinen. I assumed she meant the three of them."

"Got it. Do you know where she lives?"

"No, but she plays around here, so it must be somewhere local."

"I'll call it in. We'll find her."

"What? Call what in?"

"Anybody who says she killed someone is our business. I don't care how long ago it was. There's no statute of limitations on murder. They likely never closed the Fionnoula Leary disappearance case."

"But she also said she *didn't* kill Fionnoula."

Pete was silent for a moment.

"Dare I ask if you've made any progress in finding Wayne's murderer?" Cam asked.

"You can dare, but the truth is that we haven't. No real progress, anyway." He let out a low, groaning breath.

"That's too bad."

"It is what it is. I've gotta get off the phone, Cam. Thanks for the tip about Catriona. Glad you're safe. Talk to you tomorrow." With that, he disconnected.

The tip? Cam sat staring at the phone in her hand. Was he going to go find Catriona right now at eleven o'clock at night? And Paul? What can of worms had she opened? He'd said there was no statute of limitations on murder. Murder. A shudder rippled through her at the image of three teenagers murdering their friend.

Chapter 18

Cam headed out to do the morning chores as soon as she was awake, dressed, and caffeinated. Yesterday's mild weather had disappeared overnight, and the iron-clad sky had returned. Such was March in New England. It would be as typical for this gloom to disappear and the temperature to double by the afternoon as it would be to get more snow in a couple of hours.

Halfway to the barn she halted. Something didn't look right. The outside wall of the barn had color on it instead of being plain wood. And was the door open? She knew she'd closed the sliding door before she'd left for Town Meeting yesterday. She slid a hand inside the open door and flicked on the light switch. And gasped.

The office door stood open. Red spray-painted letters above the office door read, "ARF. FREEDOM FOR ANIMALS. STOP CRUELTY NOW." And little yellow and black puff balls dotted the large interior of the barn. Her chick babies.

"Oh, no. You poor things." She reached down and picked up the closest chick, which shivered in her hand. "Who would do such a thing?" *ARF* were the same letters as at Wayne's, the Animal Rights Front.

She hurried to the door and was about to pull it closed when she glimpsed movement in the far corner where the light barely reached. Were the ARF vandals still here? She stuck her other hand into her pocket, grabbing her phone. If there was ever a time to dial 911, it was now.

She froze as a high-pitched sound came from the same corner, then the sound abruptly cut off. A fox emerged into the light. It trotted straight at her, a bit of yellow fluff in the corner of its mouth.

A chill ran through Cam. She took two slow steps back and watched as the fox stopped to snatch up another chick in its powerful jaws. The chick wriggled for only a brief moment before going limp. The fox gazed at Cam.

Why hadn't she paid attention to that article about what to do if you met a wild predator in the woods? Was she supposed to puff up and look larger? Freeze? She did not want to experience those jaws, those sharp teeth. Keeping her gaze on the fox, she ran her free hand over the wall behind her, but it wasn't the one where she hung her tools. What could she defend herself with? Throwing her phone at the animal wouldn't do much good.

The fox started moving again, but not at her, instead trotting straight out the door. Cam swore and pulled the door closed, making sure it latched securely. So not only had those idiotic radicals put her chicks at peril, they'd also enabled a fox to come in for dinner. That was stopping cruelty?

The chick in her hand kept shivering. The temperature couldn't be above fifty degrees in here, and outside the air had dropped to below freezing. Solar panels powered the radiant heat in the cement floor, but she had it set only low enough to keep the chill off. She carried the chick to the office, picking up a couple more on her way. Their box was upended and the light turned off. Cam righted it, set the chicks inside, switched the heat light back on, and set out to collect the rest, cursing the ARF people as she went.

A few minutes later she shut the office door and counted the chicks. Only twenty-two remained. The rest had either been eaten by the fox or had hidden from it in some of the many hidey-holes that a working barn offered: piles of bushel baskets, the curved tines of a rototiller, sacks of soil amendments, even the extra bags Cam kept around for customers who forgot their own. She'd never find them, and if she did, they were unlikely to survive.

The remaining chicks in the box huddled together in a clump under the light. She petted several of them until they seemed calmer, then set up their food and water in the middle of the box again, swearing aloud at the group who'd invaded her private property and maliciously caused harm.

Oh, no. They must have left the doors open for the adult hens, too. She blew the remaining chicks a kiss and closed the office door carefully.

Once outside, she rushed around the corner to the coop. Sure enough, red paint splashed the coop roof, and the fence door stood open along with the coop door. But when she peeked inside, all looked well. The girls sat on their roosting bars and slept. She did a quick count. They were all present and accounted for. The PETA splinter activists in ARF apparently didn't know that mature hens much preferred roosting in their customary spots at night over escaping into the dark wilderness. And maybe Cam had surprised the fox early in its foraging for fresh meat.

She latched the fence and pulled out her phone to call the Westbury police again. It was about time she put a lock on the barn, too.

* * *

The police said they'd be there shortly, so she waited in the driveway, hands in her work coat pockets. Dasha poked around the yard, relieved himself in the far corner, then joined her in the driveway.

After two officers climbed out of a cruiser a couple of minutes later, Cam showed them the red letters and paint outside the barn and then led them inside.

"You discovered this just now, you say?" the burly male officer asked, gesturing around the main area of barn where they stood. He pulled on a pair of blue latex gloves.

"About half an hour ago," Cam said. "It must have happened during the night."

The other officer, a young woman, said, "Were you home all evening?"

"No, I left at about seven last night and didn't get home until ten. I suppose it could have happened while I was out and I didn't notice the paint on the outside in the dark."

"Tell us what you saw this morning."

Cam described seeing the chicks all over the barn floor, and the fox with one in its jaws. She watched as the male officer moved methodically around the space, shining a big flashlight into the dark corners and under things like Red, Albert's rusty old rototiller.

"So you have material property loss." The female officer typed into a tablet with a flying index finger. "We'll need you to estimate the cost, both of the livestock and the cleanup. You didn't see any of the vandals, is that correct?"

"I didn't."

The male officer walked up with a stiff chick in his gloved hand. "Sorry. Here's one of them. It was under the tiller." He extended a kind smile along with the tiny body.

"Aw." Cam received it into her own glove. "Poor thing."

"Aren't you the one who called in finding a bone recently?" The female officer looked up from her iPad as the man went off examining the barn again.

"I am. Do you know if they figured out if it was human or not?"

The officer shook her head. "We'll need to call in the crime scene and evidence teams again. You must be real popular with the staties by now."

If only she knew. Cam smiled to herself.

"Who's been in this barn lately?" The female officer looked up from her tablet.

"Who hasn't? I mean, I have volunteers every Wednesday. My customers come in to pick up their shares. And then, of course, your people only two days ago."

"I'll need the names of the volunteers and the regular customers, then. Numbers and addresses if you have them."

"I have a list on the computer in the house. Okay if I print it out for you? Or e-mail it?"

"Perfect." She handed Cam a business card, pointing at the e-mail address.

"I'll be back in a minute, then." At the officer's nod, Cam pulled open the sliding door and slid it shut after her. She turned toward the house and halted at the sight of a news van in her driveway. Wonderful.

The same female reporter who had accosted her on Sunday at Wayne's farm now walked toward her, a camera person behind her already filming. The reporter, in a trim red jacket and black pencil skirt, smiled and extended the microphone to Cam.

"We hear there's been an animal rights action here at Attic Hill Farm, Cameron Flaherty. When did you discover it, and how much damage did you suffer?" Her perfect red lipstick glistened as she waited with an expectant open mouth.

Cam glanced behind her at the safety of the barn and then back at the reporter. "I discovered it this morning. A number of my baby chicks died from the cold, and from a fox that got into the barn. Plus, as you can see, there's red paint everywhere." She ran a hand through her hair. Had she even remembered to brush it this morning? "I don't consider it ethical treatment of animals to set loose a few dozen chicks into a cold barn, chicks that have enough trouble regulating their body temperature even with a heat light."

"Did you see any of the vandals? Did they accost you?" The woman's low voice was tinged with drama bordering on excitement, and her gaze bored into Cam's eyes.

"No. I wasn't home when it happened." Cam cleared her throat. "Listen, I need to do something in the house. The police are in the barn and—"

"As you can see, local farmer Cameron Flaherty is upset by her . . ." The reporter turned to the camera with the barn as backdrop and addressed her prospective audience, not Cam.

Cam left her to it and made her way to the house, fuming inwardly. Who wouldn't be upset?

The same evidence team van as on Tuesday was in the driveway when Cam came back out twenty minutes later. It had taken her a while to pull together the customer list and then mark the volunteers on it before e-mailing it to the officer. She'd also taken a moment to call down the list of locksmiths in the phone book until she found Bill at Bill's Locks, who said someone would come out that afternoon. Cam knew she should be able to install locks, but it would go faster and be more secure if she hired a professional, even though her bank account wouldn't like it. She wanted to call Katie and ask if she knew anything about this. The police were waiting for the list, though.

Blessedly the news truck was gone, but a blue Prius had replaced it and a man with a notebook in one hand had his other hand on the barn door.

"Can I help you?" Cam called as she strode toward him.

He turned. "Cameron Flaherty?"

"That's me."

The man, who stood a few inches shorter than Cam, extended his free hand, which Cam shook.

"Ken Wallace. Reporter for the *Boston Globe*." Curly red hair peeked out from a black watch cap, and a green tie was knotted at his throat. "I'd like to interview you, if I might." He pulled a business card out of his pocket and handed it to her.

She examined it to make sure he was who he said he was, then slid the card into her pocket.

"I'm Cam. Do you have press credentials?"

"Of course. Here." He extended a card in a clear plastic sleeve.

Cam read it and handed it back. "Okay. Ask away. It's kind of refreshing to have an actual print reporter here instead of the sound-bite folks."

"TV?"

"Exactly."

"So this vandalism apparently is by the same people as at the Laitinen Poultry Farm on Sunday."

"The Animal Rights Front. ARF. A ridiculous acronym, if you ask me. Wait, don't quote me on that, okay?"

He laughed. "I promise. And I agree."

"The police are still in the barn, trying to find evidence of the people who did it." She pointed with her thumb over her shoulder.

"What damage did you suffer, besides this red paint?" He gestured to the barn wall beside them.

Cam repeated the story of the chicks that were set free and how many she'd lost.

"A fox was inside the barn?" He drew a pen out of his pocket and scribbled something in his notebook.

"Yes."

"They're dangerous, aren't they? I've seen videos of them attacking."

"You bet they are. Mr. Wallace—"

"Please, call me Ken."

"Ken, I don't know the exact agenda of this group, but you can quote me as saying that it is not ethical treatment of tiny defenseless birds to let them loose in the cold and leave the door open to a fierce predator."

He smiled and nodded. "Preaching to the choir, Cam. But that's a good quote, thanks. Do you also have adult hens?"

"I do. Want to see them? Get ready to laugh—they're funny." She led him around the barn to the coop. Hillary came running to the fence, and half the rest of the hens followed.

Ken laughed. "It sounds like they're gargling."

"I know, right?" Cam smiled at the girls.

"No rooster?"

"I had one named Ruffles. But a fox killed him only a couple days ago."

He glanced over at her. "Did you know Wayne Laitinen?"

Cam gazed at the reporter, the smile sliding off her face, but he appeared merely curious and doing his job, not after sensationalism. "I did. He was a decent man who was kind to every living being he encountered, from humans to hens. When he had to slaughter his chickens, he took them to the one slaughterhouse that plays calming music during the killing, and he sold the meat at an affordable price. He died way too young."

Ken scribbled more. "How long have you been farming?"

Cam gestured to the bench on the barn wall and sat, facing the chickens. He joined her, and she told the story of how she got where she was. And that she'd never expected murder to be part of the bargain.

Chapter 19

"Those Animal Rights Front radicals hit my farm during the night." Cam had called Pete after she was done talking with Ken.

"No." He swore. "The PETA splinter group like at the Laitinens'?"

"Yeah. The worst part was the baby chicks. They were all over the barn floor. Pete, they're way too little for that. They were shivering, some were dead, some are missing. And then a fox came out of the corner of the barn with one in its mouth."

He swore again. "Because the vandals left the door open, right?"

"Exactly. Luckily the fox kept right on going out the door. I didn't know what I was going to do if it tried to attack me."

"Oh, Cam." Pete's voice turned husky. "I'm glad you didn't get hurt."

"Me, too. The adult hens were fine, at least, although their door was open. What idiots do stuff like that?"

"Misguided ones."

"No kidding." Cam shook her head, even though Pete couldn't see her.

"Were you home?" he asked.

"I was home all night, of course, but I was out during the evening."

"How long were you gone?"

"From about seven to when I got home at ten. I was at town meeting, but it was canceled because they didn't get a quorum. Then I stopped by the Grog, as I told you last night."

"So the ARF folks could have been watching you and came in right after you left."

"Watching me? That's creepy."

"What they do is creepy, and dangerous. Or they could have hit your place after you came home."

"I'm getting locks installed on my barn door this afternoon."

Cam checked the time on her phone one more time. Twelve-thirty. She'd been in this booth at the Grog for half an hour, and Catriona still hadn't shown up. Had she gotten cold feet, or was she in an interview room at the police station being grilled about Fionnoula Leary? Cam regretted telling Pete what Catriona had said last night, but then again, it was his business. She was obliged to tell him, and she got in the way of that often enough, as it was.

She took a sip of her beer and glanced up as the waiter appeared with her order of fish and chips. Catriona or no Catriona, she still needed lunch. She thanked him as her phone rang. That had to be her. Cam picked it up from the table and checked the display, but there was no name associated with the number. She connected and said hello.

"Cam? It's Megan Laitinen."

Cam let out a breath and greeted Megan. "What's up?"

"I haven't seen you since you brought that lasagna. Have you made any progress? Do you know who killed my father?" Her words tumbled out in a breathless rush.

Why had Cam ever agreed to try to help Megan? "No, I don't. A lot has been happening, and—"

"But you said you'd help us." Megan's voice wobbled.

"Megan, I'm so sorry. It's really the state police's job. You know that, right?"

"I know."

"As far as I'm aware, they haven't made an arrest. But I'm sure it'll happen soon." She wasn't sure at all, but if it didn't, Pete could be demoted. Cam gazed at the galloping horse above the bar, with its gold and blue blanket under a short leather saddle, which must have come from a defunct carousel somewhere. Too bad the investigation wasn't galloping along, too. "And if I hear anything, I'll give you a call. Okay?"

Silence met her ears for a moment.

Finally Megan spoke. "Okay. So are you coming to the wake this afternoon?"

"The wake?" *Huh?*

"Yes. It's at the McClaren Funeral Home from five to seven. I hope you'll be there."

"Of course I will. I just hadn't heard about it."

Megan thanked her and disconnected. Cam popped a perfect crispy fry in her mouth and chewed. A wake. That must mean they had released the body. She wiped her fingers on the napkin and pressed Pete's number, but he didn't pick up. She left him a short message about the wake, and then pressed Lucinda's number. She might be on her lunch break right about now.

"*Fazendeira!* What's cooking?" Lucinda, as always, sounded bright and cheery.

"Wayne's wake is at the end of the day today. Want to go together?"

"Sure. I'd like to honor that farmer. What time, and where?"

"It's from five to seven at the McClaren—"

"Yeah, that one next to the church."

"Right. Let's go at the start, and we can grab dinner after."

"Deal."

"Deal. I'll pick you up at four forty-five." Cam hung up, glad Lucinda had been able to move from Salisbury to an apartment in Westbury. She dug into the batter-fried fish, which was perfectly flaky and moist on the inside and deliciously crunchy on the outside. When a shadow fell over the table, she glanced up, still hoping Catriona would show, but it was only the waiter asking if she was all set.

By the time Cam returned home from the Grog, the police were gone. The female officer had texted her that they were through, and reminded her to be sure to lock up at all times, even when Cam was on the property.

Cam checked on the remaining chicks, who all seemed to have recovered from their very horrible, bad evening. They were cheeping and pecking and running around the box. Which she'd have to replace with a bigger one soon. She wasn't sure what the next stage was, but the *Raising Chickens for Dummies* book was right there on her desk, a welcome Christmas gift from Albert.

Albert. Would he want a ride to Wayne's wake? Cam knew he liked to pay his respects in the community. She pressed his number.

"Cammy, how are things? I saw you on the news."

"Already? Geez."

"And you lost some of your chicks. A pity, that. And a fox in your barn?"

"Right. At least it didn't come after me. But the rest of the chicks are all right, and so are the mature hens. I'm alive. We're okay, don't worry." No, she should tell him about Ruffles. "Actually, a fox took Ruffles. I guess it was right after I came home from seeing you on Tuesday."

"Why, that's a shame."

"Yeah, but he had his talons in a fox kit, so the mom was rightfully upset."

Albert laughed. "That's life in the wild, for you."

"I guess. I called because I heard that Wayne's wake is this afternoon. Do you need a ride?"

"No on both counts, dear, but thanks for asking. Marilyn's back and she'll drive me. I expect I'll see you there. We're going early so we can get back for dinner. It's competitive Scrabble night."

"I'll be there at the start, too. See you soon, then."

"Love you." Albert disconnected.

Cam looked around the office, then closed the door on the chicks and surveyed the rest of the barn. It looked as though the entire space was covered in powder. Dark surfaces like the tools and an old table were dusted with a light-colored powder, and light objects, like the light switch and a couple of white plastic chairs, were smeared with black. How could the police possibly eliminate the dozens of people who'd been through her barn in the last nine months since it'd been constructed?

A heavy rapping at the outer door made her whip her head. Now what? Her heart raced.

"Cam Flaherty?" The rapping resumed. "It's the locksmith."

Oh! Cam slid the door open. Her mouth slid open, too. Bobby Burr stood in front of her with a big grin on his face.

173

"Hey, Cam." He held a hand up, palm out, still smiling.

"Bobby! What a nice surprise. I haven't seen you since, when, last November? Come on the heck in." It finally registered that he held a plastic bag in one hand and had a heavy canvas bag slung over the other shoulder. "Wait. What are you—"

"You didn't know I work for Bill's Locks in the wintertime? Outdoor building slows way down when there's snow on the ground."

"I didn't know." Cam smiled. "Glad you have employment, though. Is there anything you can't do?" Bobby had expertly rebuilt this very barn after the terrible fire last June.

"I can't bake a pie to save my life." He laughed, his dark eyes flashing. He'd been quite the flirt last summer and fall and his attractive looks hadn't diminished.

Cam cleared her throat but kept smiling. "Neither can I."

"Now that that's settled, let's get locks installed."

Cam turned to the door she'd slid open. "The slider is the main one. I got vandalized last night and it's time to be able to lock up this barn good and tight. I told Bill on the phone."

"I heard." Bobby turned serious. "Hope you weren't hurt."

"No, but a bunch of my chicks were. And now I'm going to have to paint over those letters." She pointed to the spray-painted message.

"Yeah. It's got to be soaked into the wood by now. Want me to do it for you? I have primer in the truck."

"Well, that would be fantastic. Do you have time?"

"You're my last job of the day. Let me get these locks done first—you want the back door, too?"

"You bet."

"And then I'll throw some paint up there. You don't want to have to look at that every day."

"I sure don't. Thanks so much."

"For the slider I brought a vintage-looking barn lock that's keyed on the outside and has a thumb turn on the inside. And a regular dead bolt for the small door."

"What's a thumb turn?"

Bobby laughed. "One of those little levers you turn to lock the door. With your thumb."

Chapter 20

Lucinda and Cam walked up the steps of the funeral home a few minutes past five toward a black-coated man holding the door open for them, Cam with a shiny new barn key on her key ring. Once inside, they joined the mourners already lined up in the hallway where somber music played softly from a hidden sound system. Cam bent over to sign the guest book, spying Albert's and Marilyn's names near the top of the page, but she couldn't see them ahead of her in the line. People spoke in low voices as the line moved slowly forward.

Cam glanced down at her black skirt and brushed a few of Preston's hairs off it. "Can't take me anywhere," she said to Lucinda in a whisper.

Lucinda smiled. "How are the rest of those chicks of yours doing? They going to be my dinner next year?"

Cam had told her about the vandalism on the way over. "I expect they will. At least I finally got a good lock on the barn door. You wouldn't believe who works as a locksmith in the wintertime."

"Who?"

"Bobby Burr, that's who. He did a great job, too."

"No kidding. He's cute, that one." She elbowed Cam as she grinned.

"I know. I think he knows it, too."

A voice from behind them said, "Hey, guys. What is this, the farm contingent?"

Cam turned to see a grinning Alexandra next to a pale Katie. She greeted them. "Katie, are you all right?"

Katie nodded slowly, but the skin below her eyes was dark and she chewed on the inside of her lip.

"Ready?" Lucinda asked, pointing. The last people in front of them had gone in.

Cam took a deep breath. "Let's do it." She wasn't that comfortable around groups of people generally, and having to speak about sympathies was not her favorite activity. But it was what one did, and she knew grieving families took comfort in the words. She and Lucinda moved into the room where a man stood next to Megan and Greta. Cam glanced around. She was glad there wasn't an open casket. There wasn't any casket, in fact. The police must not have released the body yet. The air was heavy with the scent of lilies.

Cam introduced herself to the man. "I'm so sorry for your loss."

He extended a remarkably cold hand. "Thank you. I'm Henry, by the way, Wayne's son." He resembled Greta more than Wayne, with a robust build and dark eyes now shadowed by grief.

As Cam shook his hand, Megan glanced over. "Oh, Cam, thanks for coming. You met Henry? He's just in from Florida."

Cam took another step and took Megan's hand, but Megan pulled her in for a hug.

"Still no news?" Megan murmured in Cam's ear.

Pulling back, Cam shook her head. "Sorry." She patted

Megan's arm, then glanced at Greta, her next stop. Greta wore a black knit dress covered in small white flowers, with low black pumps. Cam waited until the man talking to Greta moved on before approaching her, but Greta gazed away from the incoming line of people toward a large framed casual portrait of a smiling Wayne. Cam glimpsed a look of such sadness on Greta's face it tore at her heart.

Cam took one more step and cleared her throat. "How are you doing?" she asked Greta, holding out her hand.

Greta looked at Cam but kept her arms at her sides. "As well as can be expected with my life in shambles." It looked like her hand had slipped when she applied a deep red lipstick, and a line of white edged her scalp at her hairline. "At least Henry came home. I told him he had to."

"Good. Please let me know how I can help you."

"You can tell your detective over there to find the person who killed my husband." Greta spit out the words in a harsh whisper, the look of sorrow instantly replaced by flared nostrils and angry eyebrows.

Over there? Sure enough, Pete stood in the far corner in front of a long table laden with appetizers and glasses of wine at the ready. He was leaning over talking with Great-Uncle Albert. Marilyn was at Albert's side, perched on the seat of her red walker next to Albert's wheelchair. Rows of chairs were lined up, with only a few occupied by chatting mourners.

Cam moved on to the table filled with framed pictures of Wayne and the family, which stood in front of several tall flower arrangements. She gazed at Wayne as a skinny white-blond boy in overalls. Wayne with an unfortunate swooping haircut, long sideburns, and a frilly dress shirt at what had to be a high school prom. Wayne and Greta in wedding attire, him looking adoringly at her as she faced the camera unsmiling. Wayne pushing a little boy and a little girl on a swing set. Wayne holding a hen in one arm and a blue ribbon in the other hand in front of the Poultry Building at the Middleford County Fair.

Lucinda came up next to her. "Such a loss."

"I'll say."

Lucinda glanced up. "Oh, look at that. It's a teacher from my school. I'm helping her learn Portuguese." Lucinda waved at a woman across the room. "We're not in any hurry to leave, right?"

"Not at all." Cam watched Lucinda make her way to her friend, then turned herself toward Pete, Albert, and Marilyn.

"There's my favorite girl," Albert said when she walked up. He pulled her down for a kiss.

"What am I, chopped liver?" Marilyn asked with a smile.

"You're my other favorite girl." Albert patted Marilyn's hand. "And you know it." Albert had knotted a narrow knit tie at his neck and wore the same dark suit Cam had seen him don for previous somber events like this one.

"Nice to see you, Cam, despite the circumstances," Marilyn said. Her pink sweater, worn with a string of pearls under a black cardigan, matched the color in her cheeks.

"Same here," Cam said to Marilyn, then squeezed Pete's hand unobtrusively. "Hey."

"Hey, yourself." Pete gave her a hint of a smile.

"A sad week for this family," Albert said.

"Indeed," Cam said as she glanced at the receiving line. A steady stream of locals moved slowly past the family.

"Will you excuse us for a moment?" Pete asked. At Albert's nod, Pete gestured to Cam to follow him to two unoccupied seats.

"Any news?" Cam spoke softly.

"A little. I had quite an interesting conversation with your Catriona—" Pete clapped his hand to his waist. "Sorry, have to get this." Standing, he pulled his phone out and walked out of the room.

Cam waited a few moments, the hubbub of the room flowing past her, but Pete never returned. She rose and filled a couple of small plates with miniquiches and minicarrots with dip, then brought them to where Albert and Marilyn sat.

"Snacks, anyone?"

Marilyn reached for the plates. "Thank you, dear. Now sit down and tell us what you've been up to, won't you?"

"Yes, do. But first, I'd take a nip of wine, if you would." Albert winked at Cam, who brought three cups of red wine to where they sat.

Albert thanked her. "Cam's been trying to figure out what happened to poor Laitinen. Those same radicals who hit his farm came and vandalized hers, too," he told Marilyn, then gazed at Cam. "I hope you didn't run into them."

Cam sipped her wine. "No, thank goodness. But I lost a dozen of my brand new chicks."

Marilyn shook her head. "The people who do that kind of thing are misguided, but they must have had an unhappy childhood."

"Marilyn always takes the side of the underdog." Albert gave her a fond smile, his pale blue eyes twinkling.

Cam glanced up at the sight of Judith sweeping into the room, heels clicking, trailed by a petulant long-legged preteen girl with a phone in her hand. Cam watched as Judith greeted first Henry and then Megan. When Judith approached Greta, she held out a hand and Cam was surprised to see Greta take it. They spoke for a moment, although Cam was too far away to hear what was said. After Judith pulled her daughter forward and the daughter spoke to Greta, the daughter wandered off, thumbs flying on her phone. Judith leaned in and said something into Greta's ear, then sauntered over to the table of pictures.

With narrowed eyes and tightened lines around her mouth, Greta stared after her.

Chapter 21

After a few minutes of visiting, Albert and Marilyn said their good-byes. Before they made their way toward the door, Albert said, "We want to get home before dark."

"I still own a car and drive all over town," Marilyn added, "but only during the daylight hours. I am eighty-something, after all."

Cam smiled, grateful that Albert had a ride, and a prudent one, too.

Judith and her daughter hadn't lingered at all after paying their respects. The chairs in the room were nearly full now, with folks having turned them around here and there to make small circles better suited for conversation. And the line of mourners kept on coming. Cam sat alone, still pondering what Judith had said to Greta. It had to be about the land decision. Didn't it?

Lucinda strolled over to Cam. "I know we were going to get something to eat. But my friend needs to practice her Portuguese before her test tomorrow," Lucinda said. "Okay with you if I cut out on dinner?"

"Of course. Great you're helping her." Cam stood. "I ought

to get home, myself." After Lucinda left, Cam spied Alexandra and Katie near the end of the drinks table. Alexandra seemed to be trying to convince Katie of something, who shook her head. Cam caught Alexandra's eye and waved to them, then tossed her wine cup in a trash receptacle. She was in the hallway when Ivan Hobbs strode in from the outside. He saw her and extended his hand.

"Ms. Flaherty, I think? Detective Ivan Hobbs." His short-cut hair was perfectly combed and the nostrils of his narrow nose flared slightly as he gazed at her out of oddly dark eyes. He didn't smile.

Cam shook his hand. "Nice to meet you, Detective. I've heard a lot about you." *Wait.* Did he know about her and Pete? How much should she say?

He cocked his head. "Is that so?"

Surely Pete was allowed to have a personal life? But he likely wasn't supposed to be discussing the case with her. Or departmental politics.

"Oh, you know." She waved a hand in a vague gesture. "Tongues start wagging whenever someone new shows up in a town like this."

"Actually, I don't know. But I've noticed you watching the principals in this murder case, and I believe I don't have to tell you to leave the police work to the police. Which means Detective Pappas and myself. As you well know." His voice, reedy and nasal, grated.

"Of course." Everything by the book, Pete had said. Ivan did everything by the book. And that sounded a lot like a warning, straight from the book. "Good luck with it, then." She slid past him and headed for the door.

It was still cold and cloudy out, and the impending twilight made her long for hot cocoa and a good book as she slid into her truck and turned the key. The engine made a weak grinding sound but didn't catch. She pressed the accelerator to the floor twice, as Albert had taught her when he handed off the ownership of the Ford. She took the key out and put it in again, and turned. This time nothing happened except a click. She swore and whacked the steering wheel with the flat of her hand. The battery had been getting a little balky lately and must have finally given up the ghost.

Now what? She drew out her phone and pressed the number for SK Foreign Auto. If Sim was still at work, maybe she could come and give Cam a jump-start, but the mechanic didn't pick up. And Cam didn't have AAA, either—not a smart move for somebody driving a thirty-year-old truck. She climbed out. Maybe Alexandra and Katie could give her a lift home, if they'd come in their parents' car, that is. She'd reached the top step of the funeral home when a black sedan pulled in and parked in the area labeled FIRE ZONE, NO PARKING. As she glanced over, Cam recognized Paul Underwood's car. She waited, half turned on the step, one hand on the railing.

Paul emerged wearing a black wool coat. He walked swiftly toward the building, but put the brakes on when he saw Cam. "You again." He crossed his arms, gazing up at her. "The over-curious one."

"Can we talk a minute?"

"Aren't we?"

She walked down the steps so she could face him. She swallowed. "Megan, Wayne's daughter, asked me to help her. If I knew what happened between you and Wayne when you were in high school . . ." *I could what?* That was the wrong approach. She was already making a mess of this chance to get him to talk.

"You could help Megan find Wayne's killer?" Paul asked. "Well, it wasn't me. I told the police that and it's the truth."

184

"Okay. But your friend Catriona said something to me yesterday about Fionnoula."

"Oh, God." He groaned and dropped his arms. "She didn't."

"She did." Cam glanced around to be sure no one was about to walk by, but the parking lot and entry to the building were both devoid of people. The doorman appeared to have left his post, too.

"She said, and I quote, 'We all killed her and none of us killed her.' Or something like that." She watched him turn his head to look into the distance.

He faced her again. "There was an accident. A bad accident. And we all covered up for each other. But it was an accident. We didn't kill her."

"Will you tell me what happened?"

"No. But Wayne was ready to go public about it. That would have ruined me, ruined all of us."

"Going public about an accident that happened thirty-some years ago?" It was Cam's turn to cross her arms. "Really?"

"Really. On Saturday I was trying to talk him out of it. And that's why I went back on Sunday. But he was already dead."

The door to the funeral home burst open. Alexandra clattered down the steps with Katie trailing behind. They stopped when they saw Cam and Paul.

"Excuse me." Paul pushed by them and headed through the door they'd come out of. He glanced back once at Cam, shaking his head, before the door closed.

"What up with him?" Alexandra asked.

"Nothing." Cam pressed her lips together. *Damn.* She'd been so close.

"Hey, we're going to get a bite at the House of Pizza," Alexandra said. "Want to come?"

"Do you have a car?"

"Yeah, we have our dad's."

"My truck battery died. I'd love to come if you can give me a ride home after. Or maybe we could jump it."

"Of course we'll give you a ride, or we can jump-start the truck if you have cables. Do you?"

"Only if Albert left a set in here." Cam turned back to the truck and rummaged under the seat. She straightened, turning back to Alexandra. "Nope. Do you?"

"No way. My dad's is almost a new car. And he is the least handy person in the universe. He wouldn't even know what to do with jumper cables. Let's go eat and we'll drop you home afterward."

Cam lifted a piece of pizza laden with pepperoni and artichoke hearts and took a bite, then snagged a string of cheese that escaped and popped it in after. The pictures on the walls showed sunny Greek whitewashed villages with bushels of olives sitting in front of blue-splashed doors. The warm scene contrasted with the cold air she, Alexandra, and Katie had come in from. The only available booth was near the door, and whenever someone entered the three women got another dose of chill. In between, the air was redolent with the aroma of fresh-baked crusts, the spice of tomato sauce, and the delectable smell of chicken sautéing, all overlaid with the deep richness of olive oil.

"Love this place," Alexandra said from her seat next to Cam. "How can you go wrong with goat cheese, roasted peppers, and mushrooms?" She wiped the corners of her mouth and took a sip of beer. Two large pizzas filled the table, with barely enough room for plates, napkins, and glasses.

"You can't," Katie mumbled around a mouthful of same from across the table.

Cam sipped her glass of Merlot and watched Katie, whose eyes still held a haunted look, despite her apparent appetite. Her dark hair lay limp on her shoulders, and her navy blue turtleneck sweater sported a smear of tomato sauce near her collarbone.

"Katie, what's wrong?" Cam asked.

"Nothing," she said, but didn't meet Cam's gaze.

Cam glanced at Alexandra, who mouthed, "No idea." Alexandra's flaxen hair was tied back in a messy knot over an embroidered Alpine boiled wool jacket that made her look like a grown-up Heidi.

"Did you hear that my chicks were attacked last night by your friends?" Cam watched Katie.

"They're not my friends." Katie finally looked up. She shook her head. "Cam, they're not my friends. It's terrible you lost your chicks. I'm so sorry those guys went to your place. I . . ." She covered her mouth with her hand.

"I lost a dozen babies, and a fox was right inside my barn eating a couple of them. I was lucky it didn't attack me."

Katie's eyes filled but she didn't speak.

"You need to tell the police who they are," Cam urged. "Give them names. Vandalism like that is criminal."

Alexandra rolled her eyes. "Dude, I've been telling her this all along."

"But it's a different group every time," Katie nearly whispered. "It's like a cell. The one I went with, they said they don't even know the other people."

"Okay, but did you tell the police who attacked Wayne's farm, at least?" Cam asked.

"Of course," Katie said.

Another whoosh of cold air came from the door of the restaurant. A young man ambled in and looked around, then cast a wide, white-toothed smile at their table. Cam realized it was Tam, the guy who had shown up at her farm to volunteer the day before. He approached their table.

"Hey, guys," Tam said. "Mind if I join you?" He slid in next to Katie and sat with a straight back, his hands neatly folded on the table.

Katie shot him a sharp glance, but moved over to give him room.

"Cam, this is my friend Tam," Katie said.

Alexandra laughed. "Sounds like a Dr. Seuss line. Do Cam and Tam like green eggs and ham?"

Katie gave her sister a wan smile.

"How're you doing, Tam?" Cam asked. "It was great to have your help yesterday."

"I'm good, I'm good," Tam said.

At Katie's quizzical look, Cam explained, "He came by and mucked out the coop for Volunteer Wednesday." She reminded herself to add him to the list of people who had been on the farm and to let the police know.

Katie's eyes went wide but she didn't say anything.

"Hungry?" Alexandra asked him.

"Actually, I am." Tam eyed the pizza, slipping out of his jacket. "Got an extra slice or two?" He again wore a U Mass sweatshirt.

"Sure," Alexandra said. "This one is veggie, that one has pepperoni." She gestured.

His lip curled for an instant, and then relaxed. "I'll take a slice of the veggie, thanks." He reached for a slice.

"We were just talking about the vandalism at Cam's farm last night," Alexandra said. "That same radical group hit her place, left her baby chicks out to die."

Tam shook his head as he chewed, his brow knitted. After he swallowed, he said, "Terrible. Do they know who did it?"

"Not that I know of," Cam said. She glanced out the window

at the now-dark night. *Shoot.* She hadn't closed in the hens before she left, since she hadn't thought she'd be out late. At least
the chicks were locked up and safe, and if yesterday was indication, the hens would all be a-roost when she arrived home.
She helped herself to another piece of the pepperoni.

"So, Cam, are your chickens certified organic along with the
rest of your farm?" Tam asked.

"They are, but it's so expensive to buy organic feed, I might
change that." At Alexandra's open mouth looking like it was
about to mount a protest, Cam held up a hand. "Hens that are
free range, local, and chemical free satisfy the vast majority of my
customers, Alexandra. You know that. I wouldn't change being
certified organic for my produce, but if I charged enough for eggs
and meat birds to cover my costs, nobody would buy any."

"You could disinvest from raising livestock. Have you considered that?" Tam asked, then popped the rest of an end
crust into his mouth.

"I like the girls." At Tam's confused look, Cam added, "My
hens. They're funny."

"How can you get attached to them if you're going to kill
them later?" Katie asked.

Tam raised his eyebrows and blinked attentively at Cam.

"I don't know if they'll all go to the slaughterhouse." Cam
sipped her wine. "This is my first year, remember? First half
year with chickens, really. I'm still figuring things out."

"No worries, Cam," Alexandra said. "Hey, did anybody
catch the podcast of *The Moth* finals?"

The discussion from Cam's younger tablemates washed
over her. She didn't have time to listen to podcasts except
while she was working, and then she much preferred to listen
to the birds, insects, and other sounds of a working farm. She
gazed into the sun-splashed Greek tableau on the wall instead, fantasizing about a future vacation with Pete.

* * *

Alexandra dropped Cam at the farm at a little before seven. Katie had left the House of Pizza with Tam after they'd split the bill four ways, which had been Tam's idea.

"How well do you know Tam?" Cam asked Alexandra after they pulled into the drive. Cam rested her hand on the passenger door latch.

"I don't really know him. He and Katie have a few classes together this winter. He seems smart. Harmless. Kind of cute, if you like that type." Alexandra glanced at the time display on the dashboard. "Sorry, gotta run. I'm meeting a friend for a movie."

"Have fun. Thanks for the ride," Cam said, and watched her drive off. The motion-controlled light at the house flashed on as Cam trudged past it toward the barn. Tam's "type" was definitely not Alexandra's, if the sweet, scruffy, thoughtful, ever knowledgeable DJ were any guide. But, hey, didn't they say there was somebody for everybody? And who would ever have guessed that Cam herself would be attracted to a police detective a decade older and few inches shorter than herself?

She unlocked the barn, the new key in her hand making her feel like she had her own personal security guard. She flipped on the inside and outside lights, then went around the corner to lock up the hens. She should install a motion-controlled light out here, too. She didn't want anybody prowling around here unseen ever again. At the chicken yard, only Hillary remained still out, so Cam shooed her inside the coop and latched the door. She returned to the barn to check on the remaining chicks.

"Hey, chickies," she cooed at the fluff balls as she made sure they had food and fresh water. She reached into the box and stroked each one that would let her. She had no idea if they missed their moms grooming them, but she figured giving the livestock on her farm a sense of well-being had to be good for them. "Do you miss your sisters?" None answered, so she went on, "You're safe now, girls. Just eat and grow, okay?" She gave the closest one a last stroke. As she straightened, the image of the fox popped up in her brain, the fox with yellow down on its jaws, and she shuddered.

After locking the barn again, she let Dasha out of the house while she scooped out Preston's dinner and freshened his water. She added Dasha's kibble to his dish and ran clean water for him, too. Preston reared up and rubbed his head against her knee, then looked up at her before trotting to his bowl. Cam laughed and leaned down. It was his time to get stroked, his favorite activity while he crunched his kitty kibble.

At the sound of barking outside, Cam moved to the door but didn't see the dog anywhere. "Dasha," she called, stepping out onto the porch. "Come on in, buddy." His barking pierced the night, sounding like it was coming from the far side of the barn. She called again, but he didn't appear. What was he barking at? And why didn't he come?

Cam swore, suddenly chilled to her core. Were the vandals back? Or maybe the fox? There were other predators out there, too—coyotes and the weasel-relative fisher cats, at the very least. She should have taken Dasha out on a leash. And here she was without her truck. She hurried to the kitchen and scrabbled in a drawer until she found the flashlight, then grabbed her phone, too. She was definitely putting up a motion-activated light on the barn tomorrow. With one hand on the door, she turned back, lifted her keys off their hook, and locked the door behind her.

Hurrying toward the barn, she called Dasha again. His barking ceased, but she couldn't hear any snarling or sounds of an animal fight. *Let him be all right*, she prayed to no one in particular. As she reached the building, she heard a car door slam.

Cam whirled toward the sound. An engine started up out on the road in front of the field that was the beginning of her neighbor's property, and not a very well-tuned-up engine. It gave off a knocking sound as its headlights raced away down the hill.

That was no animal predator. And every residence around here had long driveways with plenty of room to park. Nobody parked on the rural road with its unfinished berms and scraggly underbrush that reached out to scratch car finishes. It had to be her intruder. But who was it?

She heard panting and turned to see Dasha trotting around the barn toward her.

Relief washed over her as tears filled her eyes. "There you are. Are you okay, buddy?" She dropped the flashlight, squatted, and rubbed his head with two hands as he watched her. "Who was out there?" She sniffed and wiped her eye.

He gave a little bark and looked at the house.

"You're not going to tell me, are you?"

Dasha looked back at her.

"Yes, it's dinnertime. And you're an awesome guard dog." She stood and gave him one more pet. "Come on." Cam walked briskly to the house and unlocked the door, letting Dasha in ahead of her. She gazed out at the inky night for a moment. The skies had cleared, and cold stars shone down from their far-off constellations.

A horrible cry ripped out from the woods at the back of her farm. It was a cry like a baby being tortured, the cry of the fisher cat. Cam shuddered as she turned toward the solace of her warm, lit, lockable home.

Chapter 22

Cam poured a glass of wine and settled on the couch with her phone, the animals joining her at opposite ends. She dialed Pete, grateful when he answered. She filled him in on what had just happened.

"Dasha is the best guard dog," she added.

"I'm so glad you both are all right. It might be better to keep him on a leash when you let him out at night, though."

Cam winced a little. "I was thinking the same thing." She wasn't about to tell him about hearing the fisher cat with its huge clawed paws and powerful jaws. She wasn't sure Dasha could hold his own with the fierce carnivorous predator even if it was smaller than he was. "Sorry."

"Don't worry about it. It's my fault he's there at all."

"I'll for sure keep him leashed at night from now on. It was kind of unsettling, too, because I don't even have my truck here. The battery died when I went to go home, so I left the Ford in the parking lot of the funeral home and got a ride with Alexandra."

"Not good to be without wheels."

"You're telling me."

"So you couldn't see the make of the car that drove away from your place? A license plate or anything?"

"No, it was dark out. The moon hasn't risen yet." She thought for a moment. "But the person must have been trying to get into the barn. Which is now locked up tight, thanks to my calling a locksmith this afternoon."

"Good move."

"And when they couldn't get in and Dasha started barking, I guess they sprinted for the car. I'm surprised they made it over Tully's field without tripping on something."

"I thought you said Tully didn't own it anymore," Pete said.

"Yeah, yeah. I can never remember the new owner's name." Tully, an old man, had finally died this winter. "To me, it's Tully's field. But anyway, I don't know who would want to get into the barn if not those vandals. And I thought they usually didn't strike the same place twice."

"They haven't in the past."

"I only hope whoever it was doesn't come back," Cam said. "So you had to leave the wake today."

"I did. But I was starting to tell you that I had a very interesting conversation with Catriona Watson this morning," Pete said.

"I wondered about that. She was supposed to meet me for lunch but she never showed."

"She wasn't particularly happy to be called in for questioning."

"Did she tell you what happened? What she meant by that comment of hers?" Cam tapped her fingers on her wineglass.

"She said there was an accident. Fionnoula died."

"That's what Paul said, too."

"Paul Underwood? I was looking for him this morning, too, but he wasn't answering his phone."

"Exactly. I talked with him tonight when I was leaving the wake and he had just arrived. When I told him what Catriona said, he said it was true. And that Wayne was about to go public with the news. He said it would have ruined his life."

"Possibly true," Pete said. "That group reported neither the death nor the accident. We can't press charges unless it's murder, and we need more information to decide that. If it wasn't murder, it'd be manslaughter at most, and that has a statute of limitations of six years. But if news got out about how a friend of theirs died, even accidentally, I can imagine it would not do good things for Paul's reputation, or Catriona's."

"Did you find out what the accident was?"

"Catriona clammed up at that. I'm still hoping, though."

"How are things with your commander?" Cam asked. "Tomorrow's the end of the week."

Pete groaned. "As much pressure as always. Ivan isn't helping."

"I ran into him at the wake, too. He basically warned me off the case."

"Great."

"Does he know we're, you know, seeing each other?"

"I think so. And there's nothing wrong with that," Pete reassured her. "Me talking with you about the case? Not so much."

Cam caressed the phone with her finger. "I wish this was all over. I wish we could just hang out again. I miss you."

His voice turned gruff. "I miss you, too."

At seven the next morning Cam pressed the number for SK Foreign Auto. She had to get her battery replaced, pronto, and she knew Sim opened early. The mechanic agreed to go to the funeral home and jump-start the truck if Cam would meet her there.

Cam pulled on coat, gloves, and a knit cap. She locked up the house and dragged her bicycle out of the barn. At least the sun was out today, although the outside thermometer read only forty degrees. Fifteen minutes later, having coasted downhill nearly all the way into town, she sat behind the wheel of the Ford with the door open, the bike in the back, and the engine blessedly running thanks to one red cable and one black that ran between the engine compartment and Sim's mobile battery unit.

"Rev it a few times," Sim instructed. Her short dark hair was spiked, as usual, and she wore her usual black, although today's leather jacket looked like it was the auto mechanic version, not the punk band look Sim often sported.

Cam pressed the pedal. A running engine was the best sound, ever.

Sim set to work disconnecting the jumper cables. "Follow me to the shop," she called to Cam when she was done, then let the Ford's hood drop. "It'll only take me a few to swap in a new battery, and I have one of the right size all charged up."

Cam waved her agreement and soon stood in the auto shop down the road. Sim leaned under the open hood of the truck and worked on the battery connections. The place had a gritty smell of metal and oil and rubber. Two racks of tires hung high on one wall, and mote-filled light filtered in through windows in the garage doors.

"Coffee and donuts in the office if you want." Sim pointed with a wrench.

"That sounds perfect." Cam went through the small door, reemerging with a paper cup of coffee in one hand and a chocolate cake donut in the other. She leaned against a metal workbench holding a big red toolbox with its lid open. Shelves above the bench held rows of small boxes and cans of oil. A snapshot of Sim, head down, playing a drum set with both hands and feet, was pinned to the lowest shelf.

"Exactly what the doctor ordered," Cam said. "How have you been?"

"Great. Band has a gig coming up at the Kit Kat Lounge in Haverhill tomorrow night, if you're not busy." Four small silver rings marched up the edge of her right ear and another one adorned her left eyebrow.

"I might be able to do that."

"Bring that detective of yours," Sim added, glancing up with a grin.

"That could be a problem. He's on this murder case. If it isn't solved soon, he definitely won't be free. And might get demoted, too."

Sim heaved the battery out and carried it to a cart, then wiped her hands on a red rag she pulled from her back pocket. She cocked her head at Cam.

"I heard about the murder. You involved in this one, too?" she asked.

"Sort of. Wayne Laitinen was a friend of mine. His daughter asked me to help, but I haven't been much use so far." She shook her head, then nibbled on the donut.

"Who's involved?" Sim asked.

"Well, according to Pete, Wayne's wife could be a suspect. She wasn't that happy with him, but isn't that why they made divorce?"

Sim snorted as she lugged the new battery to the truck. "Yeah. If every unhappy wife knocked off the husband, there wouldn't be many men left in the world."

"And then this rich woman who lives next door apparently wanted to buy part of the farm for her daughter's horse. But—"

"You talking Judith Patterson?"

"Yes. How did you know?"

"She brings her Mercedes here for service. She's okay. A little snooty, but she doesn't give me trouble. Not like Irene did." She raised the pierced eyebrow. Sim had been a suspect

197

in a murder case in the fall after a public argument between her and the victim.

"I'm glad to hear that." Cam sipped the coffee.

"They think Judith might have killed this Wayne guy to get his land?"

"I don't know. There's a connection between her vaping habit and the murder, apparently." Cam couldn't remember if the murder weapon had been made public.

"Funny, those e-cigs. I think people look ridiculous doing that."

"Agree. Well, if you happen to hear Judith talking about the farm or anything, will you let me know?"

"Of course." Sim straightened from the engine compartment and wiped her hands again. "Climb in and start 'er up. Should be all set."

Cam drove directly from Sim's to Seabrook. An hour after she got home, she climbed down from the ladder at the corner of the barn, her two new electronic acquisitions installed. The motion detector light was easy, since she'd done one in the past. She'd decided for now to plug it into a receptacle inside the barn, threading an extension cord through a hole she drilled in the wall, until she could get an electrician to come out. While she was at the electronics store, she'd bought a remote camera, too. With all that had been going on, it seemed only prudent. The camera proved even easier to install, since it operated by a wireless signal, and could use the same power source as the light. She set down the drill, held out her phone, and activated the camera according to the instructions in the slim manual, then brought up the viewing app.

Sure enough, there she was, seen from above, gazing at her phone in her hand. If anybody tried to come near her barn again, they'd be both spotlighted and filmed. And if for some reason the light didn't come on, the camera also included night-vision capability up to twenty-five feet.

She had no idea who last night's intruder had been. But if they came back, she'd at least nab them on camera.

She shook her head. It was time to get to work around here. The midmorning sun shone with all the fervor of nearing the equinox, and she'd never gotten to the blueberry pruning. If she didn't do it while the bushes were still dormant, she'd risk clipping out too much or damaging the buds. And with this sunshine, they weren't going to be dormant much longer.

After she put away the drill and screws, she grabbed the red-handled hand pruners off their hook on her tool wall, locked the barn, and headed out to the row of blueberries along the left side of the property. Albert had planted twenty bushes a couple of decades earlier, a mix of mid- and high-bush varieties, and they were in full maturity now. When the berries ripened in July, the sweet dark orbs were easy to pick, didn't have pests or diseases to speak of, and customers loved them for their flavor and their health properties alike. The bushes, most not much taller than Cam, were healthy and only needed dead branches pruned out. Albert had told her to watch for when the pine trees shed their needles, gather them up, and use them to mulch the acidic-loving blueberries. That was about all the care they needed. Well, plus throwing nets over them in the summer so she didn't lose the crop to birds.

She studied the first bush and began to clip. The theory was to remove any dead wood or any branch that rubbed on another, which could open a wound and let disease get in, and then to keep the center of the plant open, allowing in light and air. Just like with the apple tree, except she didn't need to stand on a ladder to manage these. She inhaled. The air finally smelled like things growing instead of things freezing. As Cam wrestled with a particularly thick branch in the middle of one bush, the pruners slipped and turned sideways, then fell to the ground, nearly slicing her thumb on the way down. She swore. This was a branch for loppers, not hand pruners. She trudged back to the barn to get them, but stopped when her phone rang in her pocket. She checked the display and answered, then started walking again.

"Ruth, what's up?"

"We have results for that bone you found," Ruth said.

"Oh?"

"It was a human bone. Likely from a female."

Cam stopped in her tracks. A human bone. A female. A bracelet. An accident. She shot her gaze to the compost bins a few yards away, the ground around them still trampled by the teams who had been there only a few days earlier.

"Cam, are you there?"

"Sorry. Yes. What happens next?"

"We follow up about that bracelet. Did you ever ask Albert about it?" Ruth asked.

"He didn't think he'd ever seen it, but he couldn't say for sure that it had never been on the farm."

"And we try to identify the remains," Ruth said.

"Um . . ."

"Um?"

"I think you should talk to Pete. We've, I mean, he's learned of an accident from a long time ago that wasn't reported. That bone might be from an Irish girl named Fionnoula Leary."

"How do you know that? And how did it get onto your farm?"

Cam didn't know how deeply to go into it with Ruth, especially on the phone. Ruth must have forgotten what Cam had told her about the load of lobster shells. She gazed up at a red-tailed hawk drawing big loops in the cerulean sky. "Ask Pete. And thanks for letting me know."

* * *

Stepping back a couple of yards from the blueberries, Cam stretched her arms to the near midday sky as she surveyed the row. It had taken a couple of hours, but the pruning was finished, for this year, anyway. The garden cart sat full of pruned-out dead and broken wood, and the bushes looked clean and open. As she'd worked, she'd thought about the bone and the bracelet. They had to have come in with the lobster shells, which meant they'd been in or near the ocean all this time. With any luck, Pete would have extracted the details of the accident from either Catriona or Paul by now. How sad that none of the three teenage survivors had felt they needed to inform the family or the authorities about what happened. She couldn't imagine having that on her conscience for her entire adult life, and they had been living with exactly that weight. But then, what did they say about the teen brain? It wasn't fully developed in the area that could predict consequences.

She hefted the cart and wheeled it back to her brush pile, then upended it, raking the last bits of branch out with her hands along with a few fat earthworms that had hitched a ride. A nuthatch pecked head down at the bark of a nearby tree, and a newly hatched moth floated over the pile. The most pressing question was if that long-ago event was connected to Wayne's murder. Paul had said Wayne was ready to go public about the accident. Would Paul have killed him to prevent that exposure?

Cam walked the cart back to the barn, stopping to pick up the pruning tools on the way. She set the cart down at the chicken coop, which in this sunshine was smelling pretty ripe. All the girls were out, digging in the dirt, pecking at the dried feed she'd scattered for them, enjoying the near-spring warmth as much as Cam was. She'd planned all along to move the coop around the farm, since her volunteers had built it on a wheeled trailer bed and the fence was portable, too. She'd make time in the next couple of days to hitch the system to the truck and set it out in one of the fallow fields, so the hens could dig up weeds and fertilize the soil at the same time. Maybe she ought to rig a chicken cam, too. She'd seen a site like that on the Internet when she worked in a cubicle and it had seemed charming and entertaining to watch chickens poke around a yard. Her use of a camera now would be much more practical.

As she watched the chickens, Cam pictured Katie at the pizza house last night. Something was clearly still bothering her. She could ask Alexandra if she knew what was up. She pictured Katie sitting next to Tam and not acting particularly friendly toward this dude who was ostensibly her friend, and then leaving with him, after all. There was something odd about Tam. He was too smiley. Too polite. Too sincere. So sincere it didn't quite ring true. Even his posture was too good to be true, as was showing up out of the blue to volunteer.

She lifted the cart's handles again to wheel it into the barn and put the tools away. When it balked, she stopped and checked the wheels. Something black was tangled in the spokes of the left wheel and had gotten onto the axle. She squatted to examine the thing, which was a piece of fabric. She upended the cart to unweave it, tugging and turning the wheels. After it was loose she stood and shook it out. It was a scarf. A black fleece scarf.

Cam brought her hand to her mouth. Tam. He had been wearing a black scarf when he came to volunteer. A scarf very much like this one. He had been interested in her barn. He wasn't wearing the scarf at the House of Pizza. Of course, there could be plenty of young men wearing black scarves out there. Maybe he'd simply lost it. But with his connection to

Katie, and maybe to the animal rights folks, she had to report this to the police. It was their job to check it out.

She drew out her phone, pressed the number for the West-bury station, and asked for either of the officers who had come to check out the vandalism. When the female came on the line, Cam told her about finding the scarf, about seeing Tam wearing it or one like it on Wednesday and then not last evening.

"I don't know if it's his, but it looks like the same one," Cam said. "His full name is Tamlin Haskell."

"How do you spell Tamlin?"

"I don't know. I've never seen it written. That's how he pronounced it."

"Do you have an address for him?"

"No. But I think he's a student at Northern Essex Commu-nity College. He's a friend of Katie Magnusson's, you know—"

"The woman who was at the Laitinen vandalism. Yes. Thank you, we'll look into this. Please secure the scarf in a paper bag and touch it as little as possible. We'll send someone out to pick it up."

Cam thanked her and disconnected. She stared at the phone for a moment. Should she also let Pete know? First she had to secure the scarf. She held it by one corner and walked into the barn to where she kept a supply of paper bags for her customers. She'd just slid it in and folded over the top when she heard a car crunching the gravel in her driveway. She wasn't ex-pecting anyone, but her customers knew they were always wel-come to drop by.

Dasha began to bark from where she'd left him tied to a long line near the big old maple in the backyard. Cam walked out of the barn and stopped. Speak of the devil.

Tam Haskell stood next to a boxy, beat-up Volvo sedan. He

held up both hands to fend off Dasha. The dog strained at the rope, which didn't quite reach to where Tam stood.

"Dasha," Cam called. "Stop barking, now." She walked to the dog and pulled him back a few feet. Dasha quieted but didn't take his eyes off Tam.

"Hey, Tam," Cam said. "You here to volunteer again?"

Staring at Dasha with narrowed eyes and a grim set to his mouth, Tam shook his head with a quick move. "Don't have time today."

"That's good, because I'm almost caught up on chores." Where had his previous good nature gone? "So what's up?"

"I left my scarf here the other day when I was working. Wondered if you'd found it." He glanced at her, then back at the dog.

Aha. "What does it look like?"

"Black. Fleece."

"No, I haven't seen it. Did you leave it by the hens?"

"I guess so." He kept his gaze on Dasha. "You know, it's bad for dogs to tie them up."

"Thanks." Cam smiled, keeping her tone light. "He's not mine. I simply do what his owner asks me to do."

"His *owner*. Right. See you, then." He looked over at the barn. "I see you have a new lock. Good idea. You never know who's out there."

"That's for sure. Did you hear that vandals attacked my farm? My little defenseless chicks were put out in the cold. They're only a week old." She watched him.

He lifted a shoulder and let it drop.

"And a fox came in and ate several of them. The group seems to think that's giving animals their rights. Their right to die, I guess."

Tam didn't respond as he turned away. Before he climbed into the car and started it, Cam memorized the license plate number. The engine made a knocking sound as he backed onto the street. So that's who her prowler had been. She turned her head toward the barn. She couldn't even see the flat lock from here.

"Good dog, Dasha." She patted his head. He'd definitely recognized Tam from the night before. "Good boy." She pulled out her phone and dialed the Westbury Police Department once again.

Chapter 23

Cam took the last bite of her tuna sandwich and swiped an errant piece of celery off the plate. Tam must have suspected he dropped his scarf during the vandalism and had come back last night to what he thought would be an unlocked barn. Or maybe he was hoping to continue letting her chicks out. Good thing for good locks.

She bit off an inch of a deliciously sour and crunchy dill pickle and chewed, glancing idly at the wall calendar titled A Year in Tuscany. This month's photograph featured rolling hills covered in lines of grapevines with a sun-splashed sprawling farmhouse and winery nestled in the middle. Definitely not New England. But the calendar also pointed out that today was Friday, the day Pete had to produce results.

She was about to call him when someone knocked on the back door. Cam pulled the curtain aside on the window to see Megan standing there with a cloth bag in her hand. Cam opened the door. Megan's thigh-length jacket was misbuttoned and strands of her fine dark-blond hair had escaped from the clip that pulled it back off her face.

"Megan, come in."

"I can't, really. I'm on my lunch break from school." Megan extended the bag. "But I brought back your dish. Thank you for the lasagna."

"I was glad I could do something." Cam drew out the rectangular glass pan, setting it on the table behind her, and handed the bag back. "Are you sure you won't come in for a minute?"

Megan shook her head and stepped down one stair. "Have you gotten any closer, Cam? To finding out who killed my father?" Her eyes pleaded.

Cam cleared her throat. "I'm afraid not. I've been trying to follow up on a couple of things, but—"

"Like what?" Megan's eyebrows lifted in hope.

"Oh, it's something that happened a long, long time ago. With your dad and a couple of his friends when they were in high school."

"In high school?" Megan frowned.

"Yes. But I don't think it has anything to do with his death. I'm sorry."

Megan's shoulders sagged. She turned and made her way down the rest of the steps and turned to face Cam. "The detective won't tell me a thing. My mom's shut me out emotionally, and my brother already went back to Florida to rejoin his family on their vacation. I feel completely alone." She climbed in her car, shutting the door with barely a click.

"I'm sorry," Cam said softly, watching her drive away. A cloud gusted over the sun, casting somber shadows that matched Megan's mood. Cam blew out a breath and shut the door.

She picked up her phone and pressed Pete's number, tapping her foot as she waited for him to answer.

"Hey," she said, after he picked up on the tenth ring. "Just checking in. Got a minute?"

"Not really. I'll call you back in a little while." He disconnected.

"Okay, then," she said to the phone. She set it down and cleared her lunch plate, then stood uncertain in the kitchen. There must be other work she should be doing outdoors, but she thought she was pretty caught up. Poor Megan, feeling bereft and abandoned. And Cam no help to her what whatsoever.

Cam wandered over to her computer and sat. In her former life as a software engineer, puzzling out problems was so much more straightforward. If a piece of a program didn't work, she could always figure out the reason by testing smaller and smaller parts until she isolated the problem. But figuring out her fellow humans' motivations, secrets, feelings—that was another realm of problem solving entirely, one for which she possessed few talents.

Her fingers poised above the keyboard, she tried to think of an avenue she could follow that might further the case. She pictured Judith's whispered message to Greta at the wake. Remembered the exchange between Greta and Judith at Town Meeting. Heard again Wayne and Greta's argument about selling the land.

And then there was the vaping connecting Judith to the means of death. What if she could dig up information about Judith? She ran a consulting business; it couldn't be that hard to delve further into her life, even though Cam hadn't been able to find much the first time she looked. She searched for Judith's name and stared at the top result on the screen: "Judith Patterson in custody in the Laitinen murder case."

When had that happened? It must have been only this morning. No wonder Pete didn't have time to talk. Judith had said she'd been called in for questioning earlier in the week. But "in custody" had a much more serious ring to it, although Cam thought it stopped short of arrest.

She clicked the link and read the story, in which Pete was

quoted as saying evidence had come to light that linked Ms. Patterson to the crime, although the investigation continued. The article, only a few paragraphs long, didn't describe the evidence or go into any other details.

That would surely be a relief to Megan if the police succeeded in putting the killer behind bars. But, while Judith was a woman with an overly developed sense of self-worth, Cam was surprised that she would stoop to something as sordid as murder. Cam was sure Judith usually was able to get her way along much more conventional channels. And to kill a man over a piece of land? These puzzle pieces weren't fitting together for Cam. On the other hand, Pete had always been good at his job. He must have his reasons. And Judith's arrest meant it wasn't Paul or Greta who killed Wayne. Or Katie, but Cam had never thought it could have been her.

While she was on the Internet, Cam decided to see if she could learn anything else about Greta. Maybe she could discover some past experience, other than her thwarted ambitions, which might explain her grouchy attitude, dissatisfaction with her husband, and now distance from her own daughter, who, in Cam's experience seemed sweet and easy to like. Cam thought back to the times she'd talked with Greta before last Saturday, but she could think of only one or two over the last six months. Cam's dealings with the couple had been mainly with Wayne, as farmer to farmer, rather than socializing with them as friends, even though she'd always liked Wayne and how forthcoming he'd been with information about raising poultry.

Cam uncovered a scholarly article Greta had written as Greta Carlson while still an undergraduate at Wellesley College. The article was about naturally occurring toxins in the plant world. Things like the trumpet flower, whose dried leaves made into a tea could kill someone with an already weak immune system. Rosary peas, the bright red legume used in rosaries, were poisonous when pierced. Morning glories, poison hemlock, castor beans, deadly nightshade—all got a mention. How ironic that her husband was killed with another one, nicotine, although not in its plant form.

Next to Greta's picture on the Newburyport Library Web site was a link to something called Potter World. Cam clicked that, then smiled to see that Greta offered all kinds of activities for young Harry Potter fans. Costume construction, short fan-fiction writing workshops—"Write your own adventure for Harry ten years older"—plus in-depth discussions of every part of every book. The site also included the spell-casting session like the one Greta had been offering when Cam walked by on Tuesday afternoon.

How could someone so enchanted with a beloved children's fiction series be so difficult with adults? Cam wasn't all that good with adults, herself. What else could she find on Greta? She checked the years right after Greta graduated from Wellesley, but her presence in the academic world vanished. There were a few mentions in connection with the farm, including a blue ribbon for a Finnish pastry in a bake-off at the county fair, and a story about a Girl Scout trip when she was leader of Megan's troop fifteen years earlier. Her life had become very much that of a small-town wife, mother, and Hogwarts fan. And now widow. Perhaps she was simply in the anger phase of grief.

With Dasha lying asleep right inside the hoop house door, Cam stood spraying water onto the flats of maturing seedlings an hour later. The newly sprouted ones she continued to water from underneath so as not to disturb their still delicate roots and leaves. She ought to feel satisfied at Pete having Judith in custody, but it still didn't feel right. Ruth had dropped by and picked up the bag with the scarf in it, but she'd said she had to rush right back to the station, so they hadn't chatted.

When Cam felt her phone ring in her pocket, she switched off the watering wand at the handle and answered the call.

"Sorry I couldn't take your call, and I can't talk long now," Pete said in a soft voice. "I'm out in the hall. We have a suspect in custody, though."

"I saw it online, that you have Judith. Is she under arrest?"

"It's already online? That was quick. She's not under arrest, but we're hoping she will be."

"That should make your commander happy, right? Since it's the end of the week?"

Pete uttered a low whistle. "Maybe, maybe not. Ivan jumped in and took the lead bringing Judith in. Unfortunately, she has lawyered up and isn't talking. And I'm not sure we actually have the right person, despite the evidence."

"I had the same feeling when I read the news article. The puzzle doesn't quite seem to fit. Can you tell me what missing piece made you take her into custody?"

"We learned that she got an e-mail from Wayne asking her to come to breakfast," Pete said. "She says she didn't go. But we got a rush DNA analysis and it's her DNA on the nicotine canisters that we found. The murder weapon. Her fingerprints, too."

"How did Wayne ingest the nicotine, though? Doesn't it have a flavor?"

"It was in his coffee."

"That makes sense." Cam frowned. "He drank really strong, awful coffee. It would hide anything."

"So I understand. Hang on a minute."

Cam heard voices in the background. Dasha propped his head on his front paws and blinked at her.

"Gotta go," Pete said when he came back on the line. "Give Dasha a big noogie for me."

"Will do. Call when you can." After Cam listened to the call become the empty air that signaled he'd disconnected, she slid the phone back into her jeans pocket. Judith was the only person Cam had ever seen around town smoking e-cigarettes. The liquid nicotine was certainly for sale in the public domain, but if that was her DNA on the containers, it didn't bode well for her.

Cam walked over to Dasha. Squatting, she stroked the smooth short fur on his head. His pale eyes, the color of the Arctic sky, regarded her with the same calm gaze Preston gave.

"What do you think, doggie? Did Judith kill Wayne?"

When he didn't answer, she stood and stretched, her hands on her lower back. She had shed her work coat and her sweater in the humid warm air of the hoop house. What to do now? The plants were watered, the chicks were fine, and it was only two o'clock in the afternoon. Dasha would appreciate another long walk, and at least today they wouldn't be accosted by Judith on a horse.

At the sound of a knock, Cam glanced up to see a person's shape through the plastic. A chill rippled through her. If Ivan had made a mistake and Judith wasn't Wayne's killer, whoever it was still roamed at large in the community. She couldn't make out who it was, and wished she'd inserted a piece of clear plastic in the door frame instead of the semiopaque material the rest of the hoop house was covered in.

"Who is it?" she called out, standing, her heart thudding.

"Ken Wallace." The *Globe* reporter pushed open the door.

She blew out a breath of relief. "Hey, Ken."

"Hope you don't mind my coming back." He smiled. "I had a couple of follow-up questions for the article. Which is due in two hours for tomorrow's edition."

"I don't mind. Pull up a milk crate." She gestured to the all-purpose thick plastic crates that served as chairs, as makeshift table supports, as containers for carrying supplies and bags of produce. She lowered herself onto a red crate, while Ken took a green one.

He pulled out his notebook and pen again.

"You're not much older than me. Why the Luddite tools?" Cam grinned as she pointed to his scribing supplies. "You could use a digital tablet and get a head start on typing the story."

Ken cocked his head. "I think differently with a pen in my hand. And I'm a little hard on stuff." He held up the notebook bound with a spiral wire on the top. "If I drop this in a puddle or forget it somewhere, I haven't lost hundreds of dollars of equipment."

"Gotcha."

"I don't know if you've heard that a Judith—" He broke off to consult his notes. "A Judith Patterson is in custody for the murder. Can I get your opinion on that? Do you think the police have the right person?"

Cam picked a piece of dirt off the knee of her pants. "I have every confidence in the state police." She pressed her lips together into a smile and folded her hands on her knees.

"Did you know Ms. Patterson?"

"Not well. I spoke with her a few times."

"Did she strike you as a killer? Did you feel safe around her?"

Cam laughed. "Are you serious? The most ordinary of people can feel compelled to kill. I don't understand it, but I've seen it happen." As he opened his mouth to speak, she held up a hand. "No, she didn't strike me as a killer, and yes, I felt safe around her." *Except alone with her on a trail at Maudslay.*

"Okay. Back to farming for a moment. Do you know what the widow's plans are for Laitinen Poultry Farm? She was unwilling to let me interview her for this story."

"I don't know. It's a lot of work. I only have forty hens and they keep me busy a couple times a day. Greta hasn't told me what she's going to do with four hundred layers."

"I understand she's something of an expert on Harry Potter and the Hogwarts books. Has a small business offering activities for children."

"That's right. She does some of it at the Newburyport Library."

He glanced up at Cam. "I'll bet she wishes she could cast a spell to make Wayne come back to life."

"Her daughter would love that."

"Megan?"

"Yes. She's having a hard time with Wayne's death."

"But not the wife?"

"I didn't mean that. Of course, I'm sure she would love to have him back, too." *Maybe.*

"I also learned that Greta Laitinen was quite the brilliant scientist in college. She was offered a full ride to go to Yale for a PhD degree program in biology, but never accepted it."

"That's interesting. Did you also learn why she didn't go?"

"I can guess." He tapped his pen on the notebook as he continued. "She and Wayne were married four months before their son was born. You have to be awfully motivated, and have a lot of family support, to be a successful grad student while raising children."

Talk about thwarted ambitions. "And maybe she didn't have that," Cam agreed. "I think Wayne was fairly traditional, despite how much he seemed to love her. But you sound like you know something about being a graduate student."

He tilted his head. "Actually, I do. My wife is finishing her PhD at MIT. And we have a three-year-old son. When I'm not out chasing a story, I'm Mr. Mom at home." He checked his notes again. "Well, I think that's it. Thanks for your time. I appreciate it." He stood.

Cam stood, too. "Not a problem. I'm not exactly interested in being famous, but I believe in print journalism. I guess I'm old fashioned in my own way, too. There's something about curling up on the couch with a real newspaper that I like."

"Once again, you're preaching to the choir." He stuck out his hand.

Cam shook it. "Take care. Have fun with your little boy."

He rolled his eyes. "It's not always fun, but it's always interesting. Taking care of him is the hardest thing I've ever done, and the most meaningful, too. He's a great kid and he never stops moving." He stopped at the door. "On the off chance this Patterson woman is not the right person in custody, I'll be back."

Cam nodded, watching him go. Despite the fecund warmth and light of her hoop house, she shivered, wondering, *What if Judith wasn't the right person in custody . . . ?*

Chapter 24

Dasha trotted ahead on the leash as Cam moved at a brisk pace along Middle Road. A wind had picked up, and she was glad she'd donned a windbreaker before setting out for a walk after Ken Wallace left. Attic Hill Road, where her farm was situated, fed into Middle, which coursed up and down gentle hills the full length of town a couple of miles behind and parallel to Main Street. Houses dotted the road between swathes of woods, with the occasional open field running right down to the road. From deeper into the woods a northern flicker tapped out its *wik-wik-wik* call as busy chickadees buzzed next to the road. A few yards into the woods Cam spied maidenhair ferns popping up from the leaf litter, their green furled tops looking like the heads of stringed instruments.

As she walked, she mused on what Ken had said about Greta's PhD program. So Cam had been correct about child rearing interfering with Greta's pursuit of her studies. Would Greta return to her passion of science now that Wayne was gone?

After a mile or so, Cam came to the lane where the Laitinen farm was. On a whim, she steered Dasha down the narrow road and onto the long drive into the farm. When she neared the buildings, Pluto loped up and Cam pulled Dasha to a halt.

"Hey, Pluto," she said, holding out her hand for him to sniff. After he and Dasha checked each other out on both ends, Pluto barked once, then began to trot toward the barn. Cam followed and Dasha strained to run with Pluto, but she kept hold of his leash for now.

Greta appeared in the doorway of the chicken house, a bucket of eggs in one hand. She raised the other to shield her eyes from the sun.

"Is that you, Cam?" she called.

Cam waved her free arm. "It is. Dasha and I were out for a walk and I thought I'd stop by. Is there anything I can help you with?"

Greta glanced down at the eggs, her frizzy hair sticking out from under a faded Red Sox baseball hat. "Sure, if you want to wash eggs with me." She pointed at Dasha. "You can let him off leash if you want. Pluto's a friendly old guy."

Cam unclipped the leash from Dasha's collar and watched as the dogs raced away and then enacted a play fight in the middle of the front yard. She stuffed the leash in her windbreaker pocket as she followed Greta, who was dressed in old jeans and a baggy gray sweatshirt, into the barn.

"Did Megan return your dish?" Greta asked, running water into the bucket she had set in the industrial sink. The skin on her forearms was an angry red and bore scratches.

"She did, thanks. She seems pretty broken up about Wayne's death." Cam watched Greta work. Cam didn't think Greta needed to know that Megan had asked for Cam's help. Or that Cam hadn't been able to offer any. "Hey, are your arms okay?"

"Poison sumac. I'm terribly allergic to it, poison ivy, too, and I didn't see some in the woods the other day."

"Looks painful."

"Itches like crazy. Grab a few of those flats, would you?" Greta pointed to the stack of egg flats. "But yes, Megan runs to the emotional. She'll be okay." Flecks of shavings floated to the top of the water as she took a small, soft brush to one egg after another.

Cam set a flat next to the towel where Greta was placing the clean eggs and began to transfer them to the cells in the flat. "Have you decided what you'll do with the business, Greta?"

Greta shook her head. "No, I haven't. I'm not interested in all this work. Well, this kind of work, anyway. Scrubbing crap off eggs isn't my idea of a good time, but I can't bring myself to throw them away, especially when the Food Mart is buying them. I'm not in any hurry to make a decision."

"Sounds wise."

"I used to do much more interesting things. When I was young." Her voice held a wistful note.

Cam cleared her throat. "So did you hear the police have Judith Patterson in custody for Wayne's murder?"

Greta's hands stilled. She turned slowly to face Cam. "Yes. They called me. How do you know about it?"

"I read it online. Custody. Does that mean she's been arrested?" Cam asked.

Greta focused on the eggs again. "I don't know."

"It must be a relief for you, to know they found out who did it," Cam said.

"Oh, it's a relief, all right. Rich lady thinks she can boss poor farmers around. Serves her right. Glad the cops figured it out."

"Did you suspect Judith?"

"I'm not in the business of suspecting anyone, Cam." She shot Cam a sharp glance. "I've been busy trying to hold my life together, and that of my daughter and all the damn livestock around here."

"Something about the arrest seems off to me," Cam said. "Judith is, as you say, rich. I don't understand why she felt she had to kill Wayne."

"There's lots about folks that's hard to understand." Greta shook her head. "Lots. You're young yet. You'll learn."

"I'm sure I will." True, Cam was at least twenty years younger than Greta, but the comment seemed like it came out of left field. She sure didn't feel young, not after running her own business, being associated with more than one murder, and having her own life endangered.

Cam filled one flat and set another one on top. "Megan will be happy to hear the news, I'm sure."

"And Henry, too," Greta said.

"I wanted to ask you about something that happened a long time ago, Greta."

"Shoot."

"Well, it's not related to the murder, but it does involve Wayne." Cam told her about finding the bracelet and the bone. "And apparently the girl whose bracelet it was was named Fionnoula Leary." She watched Greta, but all Greta did was lift a shoulder and drop it.

"Never heard of her."

"There was some kind of accident and she died."

"What does this have to do with me?" Greta asked.

"Paul Underwood was with her and another girl named Catriona Brennan. And Wayne was with them, too."

"Really?" She looked at Cam, her hands still in the bucket. "He never told me. We were never that kind of couple, though. You know, the ones who have to share everything with their darling spouse." She snorted. "After his great-aunt died, she left him a nice inheritance. He didn't share that with me, either, even though we could have used the money to help support this losing enterprise. Seems like his business hemorrhaged money." She fell silent for a moment, gazing at the eggs. "But . . ."

Cam waited.

"I never really understood what was up between Paul and Wayne," Greta continued. "Wayne didn't care to spend time with him. But last Saturday, after Paul came to see him, Wayne seemed excited about something. Or nervous, more so."

What had Paul said? *Wayne was ready to go public.* "You don't know what it was about?"

Greta shook her head. "They went outside to talk."

Pluto ambled into the barn, with Dasha right behind. They both settled in near where Cam and Greta worked, Dasha striking a Sphinx pose, Pluto watching from an upright sitting position, tongue lolling.

Greta looked at them and laughed. "New best buddies, looks like."

"Did you guys have fun?" Cam asked the dogs.

Dasha gave a little bark before returning to inscrutable. The two women worked without speaking for a few minutes, until the last flat was filled with glistening tan eggs.

Greta dried her hands and used her left hand to pick up the pencil hanging from a string above a piece of paper taped to the fridge. "Wayne always said we have to keep track of the yield." She wrote the date and a number.

"So what were the interesting things you did when you were young?" Cam asked as she slid the flat onto the bottom rack in the refrigerator. She straightened to see Greta staring at her.

"Did you come over here to help me or to grill me?" Greta asked in a near whisper. "Why are you so damn interested in my life?"

Chapter 25

Cam strode back along the left edge of Middle Road. She always walked facing traffic, harboring a possibly irrational belief that if she made eye contact with an oncoming car, she'd be safer than if a car approached her from behind. Dasha trotted ahead of her on the leash, occasionally slowing to investigate something at the side of the road, but mostly heading straight home for his dinner. Cam carried a plastic grocery bag in the hand not holding the leash. Greta had insisted she take a dozen eggs home, even when Cam protested that she had her own hens' eggs and that she lived alone.

Greta was an odd mix of kind and caustic, smart and suspicious, grieving and yet not seeming particularly sad. Cam was surprised at what she'd said about Wayne not sharing either secrets or his great-aunt's money with Greta. Cam would have pegged him as more of a share-all sort, and if anybody would be the withholding type, it would be Greta. Which only confirmed what Cam already knew—that one can never truly understand what goes on in other people's relationships.

Greta hadn't wanted to talk about her earlier life as a scientist. Cam could understand that. She was a private person, too.

She hadn't felt she could come out and say what Ken had told her about Greta's scholarship to graduate school. Cam had thought, since Greta had opened the door to the "interesting things" she'd done when she was young, that she'd be willing to keep talking about it. Clearly wrong.

Also curious was why Wayne had chosen last weekend to tell Paul he was going to go public. Why now? Why not a decade earlier, or next year? She shook her head. She'd likely never know. Having to keep a secret like that for all those years had to be corrosive to the soul, though.

Dasha slowed to sniff out the trunk of a swamp oak at the junction of Attic Hill Road with Middle. A black sedan crested the hill just ahead on Middle and came speeding toward them. Cam pulled Dasha in close to her at the edge of the shoulder and slid the bag over her wrist so she'd have that hand free if she needed it. Surely the driver saw them, but she wasn't about to get over in case he or she didn't. As the car sped by, Cam glimpsed Paul Underwood at the wheel, and what looked like a backseat full of boys. Paul braked suddenly, pulling over behind her with a spray of gravel.

Cam turned to see him climb out. He leaned in and said something to the children, then stalked toward her with storm clouds on his face. Dasha barked at him and took an alert stance.

"What do you think you're doing, meddling in other people's business?" Paul stopped two feet in front of her. He folded his arms and stared.

"What do you mean?" Cam kept a firm grip on Dasha's leash.

"I mean I had to spend all morning talking to the police about an accident that happened when I was seventeen. I was a kid."

"Hold on, now." Cam held up a hand. "I'm not meddling. I

found a human bone on my farm and the bracelet that it had worn. I reported it. Wouldn't you have done the same?"

"Maybe. Maybe not." He pursed his lips, his eyes smolder-ing. "Who cares what happened? It was a long, long time ago."

"Anyway, didn't Catriona already tell them what happened?"

"I don't know what she told them and what she didn't. She's not picking up her phone. And the cops weren't about to reveal that information to me."

"What did happen?" It didn't hurt to ask.

He gazed into the woods for a moment and then back at her, his anger morphing into lines of sorrow around his eyes. "Oh, what the hell. I'm screwed now, anyway."

"Telling the truth can free you." Where had she come up with that piece of drivel? Did it sound as trite as Cam thought it did?

"We were young. Not that much older than my own kids." Paul rubbed his forehead as he glanced at his car. "We were drinking and getting high. We went to the cliffs over the ocean up near Hampton one night."

Cam waited as a stiff breeze rustled through the woods. Under her windbreaker the sweat from her vigorous walk started to cool and she shivered.

"Wayne had borrowed his father's car. We were playing a tape of Irish music and horsing around in the park up on the bluff pretending to do traditional dance. You know, like River-dance, but it was before that, and we were all lousy at it, ex-cept for Fionnoula. Wayne was going to back up the car so the headlights would shine on us, like we were on a stage. But he put it in drive, instead. It hit Fionnoula."

Cam gasped, bringing her hand to her mouth.

"He knocked her over the cliff. She landed on the rocks down below." He hung his head and folded his hands, as if in prayer.

"Did you try to save her? To get help?"

He lifted his head. "No. There was no way to get down there." Now the look in his eyes was haunted. "She never moved. We knew she was dead. As we watched, a wave crashed over her and she was gone. We panicked. We knew our lives would be ruined, too, if we said what had happened. We made a pact never to tell."

Chapter 26

Cam and Dasha made it home without further incident, although Cam barely saw where she was walking, her mind filled instead with the horrific image of a car knocking a girl over a cliff. She had left Paul leaning on the trunk of his car staring at the road ahead.

Dasha barked as he trotted up the back steps of the farmhouse. When Cam pulled open the outer door, a large manila envelope fell onto her feet. Picking it up, she read the message written in a neat hand on the outside.

"Please see if you can make sense of these. I found them going through Daddy's papers. Megan."

Cam juggled the fat envelope, the eggs, and her keys to unlock the door. Preston was in the kitchen sitting on the mat in front of the stove, waiting for his dinner. She gave him a few strokes, and then fed both animals before pouring a glass of water for herself and sinking into a chair at the table. Inside the envelope was a sheaf of papers. Bank statements with Wayne's name at the top. And only Wayne's name. Could it be the great-aunt account? It was odd that Megan would leave them for Cam instead of simply asking her mother about them.

But maybe Megan had a sense that that would only make trouble. Or maybe Wayne had mentioned something about the private account to Megan.

Pressing Megan's number on her phone, Cam waited, but she didn't pick up. Cam left a message asking Megan to call back, and then studied the statements. It looked like there had been monthly automatic transfers of a hundred dollars to an account at the same local bank going back almost twenty years. Next to the account number were two letters, *PU*. She flipped through the pages. The last one was from January, only two months ago. And the final balance was zero. She whistled.

Cam brought a half glass of wine from the kitchen and sat again. Wayne had been paying *PU* a hundred dollars a month— *PU* who had to be Paul Underwood. It wasn't a huge sum, but had been steady over the years. If Paul had blackmailed Wayne, threatening to tell about him being behind the wheel at the accident, that would explain why Wayne never shared the account with Greta, and why he couldn't plow the extra money into the farm. What had Greta said the day before he died? That their money vanished into thin air. So maybe Wayne was also paying Paul cash out of the house account. But now that the great-aunt's funds were exhausted, no wonder Wayne would want to tell the truth and refuse to pay Paul any longer. Especially if the alternative was selling off a piece of the cherished Laitinen farmland. Cherished by Wayne, at least.

She needed to share this information with Megan. And with Pete. Unless Paul had already told him about the blackmail, but she doubted that. Why would Paul be so desperate for money, though? He worked in sales for a big company. Surely they paid him enough to raise a family on. Although with his wife in a mental hospital, he must have expenses associated with that, and, of course, no second income in the family to help support three growing boys. But he wouldn't risk his children's well-being by killing Wayne to prevent him talking. Would he?

Cam's stomach growled. She hadn't eaten since her tuna sandwich hours ago, and it had been a full afternoon of work and walking. She perused her refrigerator, which didn't yield any likely dinner unless she fixed an omelet. She desperately needed to go grocery shopping tomorrow. If Judith was arrested and this case was a wrap, Pete should be free for a nice Saturday night home-cooked meal. She found her phone and pressed his number.

"Any chance of meeting me for a quick dinner out?" she asked, after greeting him.

"Hang on a minute."

Cam heard voices in the background, then Pete came back on.

"Sure. I can get away for an hour. How about the Japanese place in Port Plaza?"

"Perfect. See you in fifteen?"

"Perfect."

"Wait, make that twenty. I need to get the hens closed in before I leave."

"Twenty it is."

Pete popped the last piece of sushi into his mouth and chewed with a dreamy expression on his face. Many of the tables in the small restaurant were occupied and most of the counter stools, too. Behind a counter, a chef never stopped slicing and arranging planks full of sushi. A waitress wearing a kimonolike top scurried back and forth from the kitchen. The air was warm and smelled deliciously of seaweed, sizzling meat, and something sweet.

"You really like that stuff, don't you?" Cam asked. She finagled a piece of tempura sweet potato almost into her own mouth, and then lost control of the chopsticks and dropped the morsel on her plate.

Pete laughed at her. "You can use a fork, you know."

Cam stabbed the batter-fried slice with the point of the chopstick. "I never got the hang of chopsticks, but I feel like I should. Especially if we're going to be coming to places like this." This time the sweet potato made it into her mouth.

"I do love sushi. Even though my father was from Greece, he served in Japan in the US Navy after he immigrated here. He taught me to use chopsticks when I was five."

"Well, you can have raw fish." Cam shuddered a little. "Give me a nice cooked meal any day." She sipped her green tea.

Pete drained his own cup of tea and set it down. They'd agreed to not talk about murder until they finished their dinner, but that time had come.

"Is the Judith thing going to stick?" Cam asked. "Are you going to be able to make an arrest?"

"No." Pete shook his head. "She's already out. That woman brought a high-powered lawyer up from Boston."

"That's too bad. Do you think she did it?" Cam glanced around, glad the adjacent tables were unoccupied, but she lowered her voice, anyway. "Killed Wayne?"

"I'm not sure. The evidence is looking like it. But she's quite adamant that she never went over there that morning."

"And your commander—is he still on your back about solving it this week?"

"Of course he wants to have it all wrapped up. Who wouldn't? I think he was bluffing about demoting me, though. Just wanted to make sure I stayed on top of the investigation." He pressed his lips together as he shook his head. "As if I wouldn't, anyway."

"Did you get the truth out of Catriona or Paul about the accident?"

Pete cocked his head. "No, but how do you know we talked to Paul?"

"He told me. Dasha and I were walking home from Greta's—"

"You were at the Laitinen farm again?" Pete frowned.

"We were out for a walk and stopped by. I helped Greta with the eggs. And I learned a few interesting things."

Pete set his jaw in his hand, elbow on the table. "I clearly can't stop you. So you might as well fill me in."

A couple with two children in tow walked in, to the waitress's high-pitched voice calling, *"Irashai!* Welcome!" She bustled in from the kitchen and seated them at a table in the far corner.

Cam told Pete that Greta didn't seem to know about the accident. "She said Wayne had gotten an inheritance from a great-aunt but that he hadn't shared it with her," Cam continued. "Then, when Dasha and I were walking home, Paul drove by with his sons. He stopped and was angry with me about telling you he was involved in the accident. But get this, Pete."

"Yes?"

"He told me exactly what happened on that night." Cam gave Pete the details about the drinking and pot, the dancing in the park on the bluffs, the headlights, and Wayne losing control of the car, knocking Fionnoula onto the rocks, and then her being swept into the ocean. "The three made a pact never to tell what had happened. They were teenagers and terrified of the consequences."

"I gathered that from Catriona's interview, even though neither she nor Paul would say exactly what went down that night. He should have told me. They both should have." He drummed the table with his fingers, frowning again.

"Here's something else." Cam reached across the table for

Pete's hand. "I think Paul was blackmailing Wayne all this time, because Wayne was the driver who hit Fionnoula. Megan dropped off an envelope full of Wayne's bank statements at my house today. She asked me to look at them. I think it was the account holding the money from his great-aunt, and he was paying someone with initials *PU* a hundred dollars a month for the last twenty years. And maybe cash, too. Greta said she didn't know where their money went, that they never had enough."

Pete sat up straight. "That is interesting, all right." He squeezed Cam's hand and let it go. "Why did she want you to look at the statements?"

"I don't know. Maybe she doesn't trust Greta? I wasn't there when she left them, so I didn't get a chance to ask her."

"I'll check it out," Pete said.

"Paul told me Wayne was going to go public. I think the money ran out, and he wasn't about to sell his land to Judith so he could keep paying Paul. Do you think Paul could have killed Wayne?"

"He had an alibi for the time of death. That's why we didn't suspect him all along. But maybe . . ." He stared over Cam's shoulder.

"Maybe what?"

The waitress hustled by, laying their check on the table.

Pete examined it and left cash in the folder. He gazed at Cam. "His alibi is his oldest son. He said his dad was home making pancakes for them. Paul could have coerced him to lie, though." Pete nodded slowly. "We've already been digging deeper into that story."

Chapter 27

Cam sank onto her couch and drew her knees up. It had been a day full of talking. To Sim, to Tam, to Megan. Ken Wallace, Greta, Paul, Pete. Way too much interaction for a native introvert. She picked up the *New Yorker* magazine and flipped through, scanning for the cartoons, smiling at one that depicted every person in Times Square walking around texting while using red-tipped white canes to avoid obstacles.

The magazine rustled in her hand. Why had she ordered green tea with dinner? Its caffeine always made her jittery. She turned to an article about the increased use of drones in a number of areas of life, from police surveillance to news gathering to observing how crops were growing on megafarms. The article also described how owning a drone had turned into an expensive hobby. Certain customers who bought one of the remote-controlled hovercraft to play with didn't fully read the instructions, and often crashed it into a building on its maiden flight. The software aspect of the systems interested Cam, but the article didn't go into any depth about how the devices were controlled.

She tossed the magazine on the coffee table and headed to

the kitchen, bringing a glass of chilled Chardonnay back to her desk. Maybe doing farm-related desk work would calm her down, that and the wine. She shrugged on the thick sweater she'd left on the back of the chair. The sunny day had turned into a cold, clear, windy night by the time she'd driven home from the restaurant, and the last time she'd filled her heating oil tanks the amount on the bill had made her choke. Soon enough the furnace wouldn't be kicking on, but for now, she'd rather bundle up than turn the thermostat any higher than the sixty-five degrees she usually set it to during the evenings.

Staring at her spreadsheet of farm tasks for the next couple of months, Cam narrowed her eyes. She'd set up an ambitious plan for spring planting. She should be able to till at least one of the fields if it didn't rain or snow again. Working wet soil destroyed its natural structure of air pockets and turned the earth into a brick. If she got the side field tilled up tomorrow, she could get the early peas direct seeded into the ground. Seed potatoes would go in next, since they also tolerated cool soil and even light frosts.

Sipping the wine, she checked her expenditures and income file. If the summer CSA filled up, and if she got that greens contract with Phat Cats, she might be able to hire someone as regular help, at least part time. She'd already landed a contract with the Food Mart to supply them with tomatoes and other produce for the summer, and so far the farm-share program was about half spoken for. It looked like a few hours of publicity work was in her near future, not something she cared for in the least, although Alexandra had been a big help in the past with setting up the Web site and even designing the farm logo.

Cam pushed back her chair and stretched out her legs. The back of her brain was consumed by all the unanswered questions about Wayne's death. If in fact Judith hadn't gone to Wayne's for breakfast that morning, if she hadn't slipped the nicotine in his coffee, who had? Paul was there. He could have, especially if his alibi fell through. Greta, of course, had said she'd fixed Wayne's breakfast. Katie conceivably could have poisoned Wayne, too, but Cam couldn't believe she would do something like that. Anyone could buy liquid nicotine these days. But how did Judith's prints and DNA get on the vial if she didn't do it?

Cam's phone rang from the kitchen counter where she'd plugged it in to charge. She checked the ID and saw Ruth's name.

"Ruthie, what's up?" Cam said.

"Thought you'd like to know we made an arrest in your vandalism case."

"Really?"

"You were right, it was that Tam Haskell. He was part of the Laitinen incident, too. Seems he's a young mastermind of sorts in this extremist group."

"I'm glad he'll be off the streets. He seemed to have two sides to him. When I first met him, he was all polite smiles and helpful. But when he came back looking for his scarf, he almost snarled at me about having Pete's dog on a leash. I guess in his world all animals would be wild and running free."

"Yeah, he mentioned something like that. I'll tell you, he wasn't very polite when we apprehended him."

"Is Katie Magnusson going to be arrested, too?" Cam asked.

"We struck a deal with her in exchange for information. She was pretty frightened of Haskell, as it turns out. He'd threatened to hurt her if she identified him."

"No wonder she was walking around looking haunted, scared." The image of Tam's insincere smile floated in front of Cam's eyes. "Do you think it's possible he came back and killed Wayne?"

"I don't believe he's being considered for that. The murder is Pete's bailiwick, though, as you know."

"Of course."

"I expect he's checked Haskell out. I know he was notified of the arrest."

"Well, thanks for letting me know about Tam being caught. Hey, remember you were going to bring the girls over this weekend sometime. And maybe we can have a glass of wine and not talk about crime of any kind."

Ruth laughed. "Sounds like a plan. How about Sunday?"

After they disconnected, Cam took another sip of wine. She'd be just as happy if she never saw Tam's fake smile again.

After sipping wine while reading a short story in the *New Yorker*, Cam watched the local news, which included a story of an aggressive coyote attacking people in the next town.

"The coyote should be considered rabid and dangerous, and anyone who comes into contact with the animal will require medical attention," the reporter warned in a dire tone. "Groveland residents are advised to keep children and pets indoors."

Cam shuddered at the thought of a rabid coyote approaching her in broad daylight and taking a chunk out of her leg, as apparently had happened to a man only a few miles down the road. Maybe she should keep Dasha and Preston indoors tomorrow, too, although she had no idea how far coyotes ranged.

She swore as she glanced at the table where she'd left the bank statements. She should have called Megan again, but now it was too late. What would Cam tell her, though? That regular payments were going out of the account to a *PU*? She didn't know what Megan could do with that information, and Cam didn't particularly want to be the person delivering it. She would wait until tomorrow, at any rate.

Cam watched television a little longer, and finally went up to bed at eleven-thirty. Surely the green tea would have worn off by now. She set her phone on the bedside table, changed into her night wear, a long T-shirt worn smooth and thin by years of wear, and slid under the comforter. She was slipping into dreamland, that state where she knew she was still awake but also saw random dream scenes inside her eyelids, when her phone beeped twice in quick succession.

Her eyes flew open. What was that? It wasn't her ring tone indicating a call, or the text signal, either. The phone beeped again, two short bursts. She sat up and grabbed it. The new round icon with an eye in it blinked at her. Something had triggered the barn cam. She pressed the icon to bring up the app and stared at it, her palms cold and clammy. Despite Tam having been apprehended, it could be a different intruder. It could even be Wayne's murderer if the police were wrong about Judith.

In the picture, the floodlight had come on. It illuminated the area around the door, but the camera didn't show anyone. The video wasn't the best she'd ever seen, likely a direct consequence of how little she'd paid for the device. Cam groaned. Should she get dressed and go out there? According to Ruth, it shouldn't be more chicken vandals, if Tam was indeed the ringleader. And sure, Wayne's killer might still roam at large, but why would he or she be coming after Cam? She rolled over to the far side of the double bed and sat up, gazing out the window that overlooked her back door. That motion-triggered light wasn't on, although the waning moon shone yellow and still presented a fat profile as it rose over the maple in the yard.

The wind must have picked up since she came home. The sound of it in the trees roared like an armada of tractors rumbling over her fields. But there were no trees in front of the door to the barn. That wouldn't have triggered the light and the camera. The pulse in her neck beat double time. She looked at the phone again.

As she watched, a small shadowy figure crept across the screen. A four-legged figure. Cam let out a breath. And a moment later, over the noise of the wind, a high mournful cry pierced the night. A coyote was her culprit. It howled again, and then uttered short barks, raising goose bumps on her scalp. Coyotes, most of whom weren't rabid, were even fiercer hunters than foxes. At least all her hens were safe inside, as were the chicks. She set her bare feet on the cold floor and lifted the sash for a moment.

Answering barks called out from the woods as well as another far-off howl, triggering one more ululation from the animal outside her barn, the cry fluttering and then rising to a sharp finish. She slammed the window closed and locked it, then dove back under the covers, pulling the fluffy comforter over her head. She didn't want that terrifying sound to disturb her sleep. Although, a coyote lurking was certainly better than a malicious human up to no good.

Chapter 28

Saturday dawned sunny. When Cam checked the outdoor thermometer, it was still cold, and a brisk wind blew the trees toward the south. Cam yawned, then popped the last bite of her peanut butter toast into her mouth, washing it down with the last gulp of French roast. Between the coyote cam and the green tea, it had been a short night. But the life of a farmer didn't allow indulgences like sleeping in.

Instead of tilling this morning she'd resolved to move the coop and the fencing out onto part of a field where she'd planted winter rye. The cover crop was green and vigorous, and if she didn't deal with it now, it would grow tall and thick and be harder to till under later. But if she let the hens roam over it, they would turn the organic material back into the soil for her, and add their own fertilizer, as well. Moving the coop would mean a longer trek twice a day to let them in and out and to feed and water them. At least the weather was on its sure path to eventual warming.

After she'd sent Alexandra a text asking for help this morning, Alexandra had texted right back that she'd be over shortly.

Sure enough, as soon as Cam stepped outside, Alexandra rode up on her bicycle.

"No loaner car today?" Cam asked, trotting down the back steps as she pulled on her gloves. Preston ambled out of the house while Dasha ran down ahead of Cam and headed straight to the barn door.

"Nope, the 'rents are coming back today and Katie's going to pick them up at the Manchester airport." Alexandra's cheeks were pink from her exertion in the cold. Cam's farm sat at the apex of Attic Hill and it was a steep uphill ride.

"How's Katie doing?"

"Eh. She's my sister." She set the bicycle on its kickstand and hung her helmet from the handlebars. She glanced toward the back of the property. "Let's get this job done."

"Sure." Cam knew what it was like not to want to talk for long about a difficult topic. "I'll move the truck around to the coop. Can you start dismantling the fencing? We'll throw it in the back and set it up again once the coop is situated."

Dasha was sniffing all around the barn door. He looked up and barked.

"Smell that coyote, do you, Dash?" Cam said.

"You had a coyote? Was it that rabid one from Groveland?"

"I don't know if it was rabid or not." Cam pointed upward. "See that little thing? It's a camera. I installed it yesterday."

"Wise move." Alexandra grinned. "With all the trouble you seem to attract."

"Yeah. What can I do?" Cam frowned. "I was going to keep the animals inside today, I just remembered. Dasha, come here, boy." She patted her leg.

Dasha trotted over to the bushes at the side of the yard and took a leak, then came to Cam's side.

"Good boy. Preston," she called as she slipped her fingers

under Dasha's collar. "Be right out," she said to Alexandra, then headed for the house, Preston following at his usual amble. On the back porch, she persuaded Dasha to go in and held the door open for Preston.

He hesitated on the bottom step, glancing around.

"Preston, come on," Cam urged.

When an old blue Civic pulled into the drive, he dashed into the house. Cam gave a wave to Lucinda as she climbed out of the car, then went into the house to make sure the cat door was closed. It didn't do much good to shut Preston in the house if he could go right back out at will. She locked the back door and clattered down the stairs. Lucinda stood talking with Alexandra. A warm feeling rose up in Cam. How lucky was she to have these women as friends? They were fun, hard-working, and generous with their time.

"We working today or what?" Lucinda called with a smile.

"Sure," Cam said. "Glad you showed up. What do they say, many hands make work light?"

"I think it's many hands make light work. Same difference." Alexandra's blue eyes twinkled.

"Speaking of trouble, Ruth called me last night. She said Tam was arrested for leading the vandalism here and on Wayne's farm."

Alexandra wrinkled her nose. "Good riddance. Maybe now Katie can get her act together. That guy had too much influence over her."

Lucinda looked from one to the other. "Who's Tam?" Her curly black shoulder-length hair was particularly wild today, forming a mane that rose up from her head, with tendrils tangled every which way.

"He's the animal rights radical who vandalized Wayne's farm. And mine."

"Glad they got him," Lucinda said.

"Ruth said they're not going to arrest Katie," Cam said.

"No, thank goodness." Alexandra shook her head. "She told them everything she knew. She finally got hold of my dad's lawyer, and it looks like she'll only get probation or something." Alexandra pointed to the camera. "So is that wireless, with an app that controls it?"

"Exactly. And it works, too. The motion light came on last night and I got an alert from the camera. I was worried, but it turned out to be a coyote, not a human. And boy, was it howling. Barking, too, sort of."

"Dude, I've heard them." Alexandra shuddered. "Creepy, isn't it? They're wicked bad carnivores."

"So what's on the schedule today?" Lucinda asked, rubbing her gloved hands together.

"We're going to move the coop and the fence back to a field where the hens can work for me turning under a cover crop. I'll move the truck. You both can start pulling up the fencing."

At their agreement, Cam climbed into the truck, driving it around the back of the barn and backing it up near the coop's trailer hitch. Twenty minutes later the three women had the wire fencing detached from its posts and rolled into the back of the truck, and all but one of the metal posts pulled out, too. Cam grabbed the last post and worked it back and forth until she could pull it out of the ground. She had kept the hens latched inside the coop even though she knew they'd rather be out in the daylight.

"Now, I've never attached the trailer before, but I looked at a video online. Should be easy. Direct me when I get there, okay?" She climbed back into the cab and shoved it into reverse.

Alexandra directed her back until the ball sticking out behind the license plate was under the half-hemisphere ball cup of the trailer hitch. Cam climbed out and cranked down the vertical support the trailer hitch rested on until the ball nestled in the cup, then folded down the lever that locked it in place.

"Just like in industry." Cam straightened. "As Uncle Albert used to say." A blue jay perched on top of the coop and emitted its metallic seesawing cry.

"What are those chains for?" Lucinda asked, pointing to two heavy chains attached to the hitch. The chains ended in big S hooks.

"Oh, yeah. Those are supposed to cross over underneath and hook to those holes next to the trailer ball. In case the whole thing detaches on the highway."

"Highway? I thought we were going out back to a field."

Cam laughed. "We are. Know what? I'm going to attach them, anyway." She leaned over and hooked each chain through its hole. "If we were going on the highway we'd need brake lights and such, too, but I don't need those here." She headed back to the cab. "Give me a shout if it turns over or anything. And follow me out. Alexandra, can you grab a couple of hammers from the barn?"

Cam started the truck and gradually let the clutch out, feeling the pull of the heavy wagon behind as she accelerated. She glanced in the rearview mirror to see Alexandra holding up two thumbs, so she steered for the wide central path leading back to the field where she wanted to situate the coop. As long as she stayed on this beaten-down path, which she mowed in the summer, she didn't think the truck would get stuck in the thawing soil. In the mirror she saw Lucinda following along with one hand on the coop to steady it. The Ford bumped along until she neared the band of woods at the back. She shoved the gearshift into reverse and turned the wheel, maneuvering the trailer onto the greening field. Alexandra strode up.

"Uh, barn's locked."

"Right." At Alexandra's questioning look, Cam went on. "Bobby came by and installed locks for me after the vandalism." She pulled the keys out of the truck. "Catch," she said, tossing them to Alexandra.

A moment later Alexandra was back with two heavy hammers. "Fencing, anyone?"

Working together, it didn't take more than an hour before they had attached the five-foot-high fencing to the hooks on the posts and reattached the simple gate into the area. Cam grabbed a roll of fishing line out of the truck.

"Now that the hens are out here, I'm going to run fishing line across the top. Apparently it keeps the hawks from picking them off. Help me? If you're on opposite sides outside, I can walk it back and forth inside."

Lucinda and Alexandra positioned themselves as Cam brought the line across, looped it around a fence post, and then walked it to the other side, zigzagging back and forth until the top was covered. At the end she had to stoop to move around.

"Maybe I should have made the fence taller than I am. Too late now." She laughed as she opened the coop door, then pulled the ramp down to the ground.

"Come on, girls. I know it was a bumpy ride, but you're going to love it out here." She stepped back, hunching her shoulders and head to avoid the line.

Hillary's head appeared in the opening, after which the lead hen hopped down the ramp. It wasn't long before all the rest were shoving their beaks into the soil holding the rye, scratching at it with their feet, and generally looking like they were enjoying finally being sprung into the cool but sunny spring air.

Cam made her way out the gate, then held up her palms and high-fived Alexandra and Lucinda. At least something was going right.

* * *

Megan climbed out of her car in the Maudslay parking lot a little after eleven. She waved at Cam and walked toward her.

"Megan, thanks for your call," Cam said. "Dasha and I could use a good walk." After Lucinda and Alexandra had left, Megan had returned Cam's call and suggested a walk at Maudslay, to which Cam readily agreed.

"Thought we ought to talk in person." Megan stuck her hands in her pockets. Her face looked less ravaged by grief, but there still wasn't much light in her eyes.

"Fine with me. As long as you don't mind me in my work clothes." Cam gestured to her worn jeans and work jacket.

"Of course not."

The two women and Dasha headed down the path toward the road and then crossed to follow the wide former carriage trail that led toward the Merrimack River. They walked in silence for a few minutes until they reached the stretch lined with tall antique rhododendron bushes.

"Did you learn anything from those bank statements?" Megan asked.

Cam glanced over at her, but Megan's eyes focused straight ahead. "You must have seen that it was your father's personal account. It didn't have your mom's name on it."

"I know."

"Did you look closely at the papers? Or show them to Greta?"

Megan shook her head. "I'd heard them argue about the money my dad's great-aunt left him. And one time, not that long ago, Daddy looked really upset when he got home when I was over there. Mom was out, and he shoved a stack of papers in his desk drawer. He saw me watching him and asked me not to tell Mom about it."

"And you didn't."

"No, of course not. But after he died, I went looking for them. And then I was afraid to study them, so I brought them to you, even though I didn't want to keep a secret from my mother. That sounds confused, doesn't it?"

Yes. "It's okay. Do you want to know what I think?"

Megan nodded without speaking. She pointed to the left into the rose gardens, so Cam steered Dasha in that direction.

"Your father was making a payment of a hundred dollars to someone every month for the last twenty years."

Megan whipped her head toward Cam. "Every month for twenty years? Who was he paying?"

"Someone with the initials *PU*."

"Who's that?"

"I think it might be Paul Underwood."

Megan slowed to a stop. "The man who found Daddy dead," she whispered.

Cam pulled Dasha to a halt, as well. "That's right. I think he might have been blackmailing Wayne."

"Blackmail? You have to be kidding. My father isn't . . . I mean, wasn't a criminal. He would never have hurt anyone." Her gaze cast around the low rows of severely pruned shrubs arranged in geometrical shapes, which would be gorgeous, fragrant displays of roses in a few short months.

"Something terrible happened a long time ago. When your dad was a teenager. Paul was with him and two girls when one of the girls died in an accident."

Megan's face collapsed. "Oh, no. That's awful."

"Absolutely."

"But that's no reason to blackmail him." Megan started walking again, but slowly, like a sleepwalker.

"Wayne inadvertently caused the accident."

Megan's eyes went wide, then she shook her head, hard. "I don't believe it." She lifted her chin and picked up the pace until they'd reached the hedge at the end of the garden. She led the way through the passage and headed on the path across an open field to Curzon Mill Road, but instead of turning back to the parking lot, she continued toward the right.

Cam lengthened her stride to keep up. "Both Paul and the surviving girl, Catriona, have confessed to the accident. Paul told me himself only yesterday. Megan . . ." Cam reached out a hand to Megan's arm to try to slow her down. "Your mother never mentioned knowing anything about what happened?"

Megan did slow, shaking her head. "No, nothing."

"Well, it was before she met Wayne, so that makes sense. And all three of them—I mean, Paul, Wayne, and Catriona—apparently made a pact not to ever tell the story."

"Which resulted in my father paying off some guy for years and my mother complaining about us never having any money for most of my life. Brilliant."

They reached the small footbridge that spanned the Artichoke River before it ran out to the Merrimack. Dasha's toenails clicked over the thick wooden boards.

"Well, anyway, it's over now," Cam said. "I brought the statements back for you. They're in my truck."

"Maybe it's over, maybe it's not. Blackmail is a crime. Paul Underwood is going to have to pay that money back. He owes it to my mom. To the whole family."

For the first time, Cam caught a glimpse of Greta's spirited side in Megan, instead of Wayne's sweetness. They kept walking along the road, Dasha alert and trotting with his tongue out. Suddenly he stopped and barked. From around the bend ahead of them came two men in long black robes, walking slowly and talking in quiet voices.

"We must be on the Emery House grounds," Cam said softly. "Maybe we should turn around."

"Oh, no. I know those guys." Megan smiled, her face bright-

ening. "They come and volunteer at Sunday school sometimes."

"The monks do?"

"Yeah. Brother William, Brother Matt," she called, waving.

The men looked up as if startled, and then the taller one
waved. They continued toward them until they reached Megan.
The taller monk towered a good eight inches above Cam and
was built like a grizzly. He leaned down and enveloped Megan
in a huge hug.

"Our poor dear Megan," he said, releasing her. "I'm Brother
Matt," he said to Cam, sliding his hands into the opposite
sleeves and lowering his head for a moment.

"Cam Flaherty. Nice to meet you."

"Brother William." The other one, light-haired and thin,
copied the same movement toward Cam, then it was his turn
to hold out his arms to Megan.

Brother Matt squatted and petted Dasha for a moment,
which Dasha seemed to enjoy, despite it coming from a total
stranger.

After another hearty embrace, Megan surfaced, sniffling
and wiping her eyes. "You guys are the best," she said with a
wan smile. "You really are." She looked at Cam. "They come
in and teach Bible stories to the primary class, sitting on the
rug with a bunch of five-year-olds."

"Don't be silly, my dear," Matt said. "We care for all our
brothers and sisters, young and old. How is your mother faring?"

"Not great. I think. She isn't really talking about her feelings."

The monks exchanged a look. "We will pay her a visit soon,"
Brother William said.

They both did their sleeve bows again, reminding Cam, except for the outfit, of the Buddhist monks she'd once met in

Cambridge. After they said good-bye, the monks headed back the way they'd come.

"I should get back," Cam said. "I have an afternoon of tilling ahead of me."

"And I have to get back for lunch with Mom."

Cam turned and made her way back to the bridge. At the edge, Dasha stopped and barked. As Cam turned, she realized Megan had lagged behind, so she waited.

"Something funny happened when I went over to my parents' farm this morning." Megan frowned. "That Judith woman drove over in a big huff and accused my mom of going through her trash. Why would Mom do something like that? We're not that poor."

"What did your mom say?"

"She denied it, of course."

"Did Judith say she'd seen Greta do it?" Cam glanced at Megan.

"I don't know. Mom told her to leave and then followed her outside, so I couldn't hear what else they said. Can't the world just leave my family alone?"

Chapter 29

Cam lingered over a cheese sandwich and a glass of milk when she got home, reading the paper and practicing work avoidance. She indulged in two pieces of dark chocolate and checked her e-mail and Facebook. Finally she glanced at the clock.

"Two o'clock, Preston. Time to get serious."

From where he lay on his back in a patch of sunshine, he opened one eye and closed it again. Dasha gave a little doggie-mare twitch from his bed.

The day had warmed by the time she'd come home from the walk, so Cam slipped on her dark khaki work vest instead of a jacket. It had big patch pockets on the front, perfect for her keys, phone, and a pair of pruners or a few seed packets.

She locked up and headed out to the barn, once again leaving the animals inside. It was time to till. After checking the oil in the tiller and topping up the gas, and after several pulls of the starter rope, Cam finally got Red started. She wanted to call the rusty, formerly red rototiller Old Rustbucket. But she didn't dare offend the heavy machine she'd inherited from

Uncle Albert, along with all the other farm tools and supplies, even though parts of the tiller were nearly rusted out. One of its back-mounted circular tines was almost worn through, and a piece that kept the handles upright was about gone, too. She guessed she ought to be grateful that the tiller ever started, and that it ran, too. She needed it for the heavier work of turning the beds in the spring, and once it got running, it didn't quit until the gas tank ran empty. She'd taught herself the rudiments of small engine maintenance and rescue last summer, which had kept the tiller in operation more than once.

She shoved the engine in gear and walked behind it out of the barn, then let it die by releasing the lever on the right handle. She took a moment to lock the barn before firing up the tiller again and heading out back. She walked slowly behind the big machine, her hands vibrating with the engine even though the tines weren't engaged. The sunshine had heated up the day into the fifties, but it felt warmer than that. Cam realized with a start that today was the equinox, signaling the shift to longer days and shorter nights, so it was a day farmers all over the northern hemisphere traditionally rejoiced in. Should she go find a flagon of mead to drink and splash on the ground or something?

Nah. She had fields to turn. The hens would be able to clear only so much, and each fenced-in area would take them several weeks. Cam had crops to get in the ground before that. But the equinox was a major turning point in the season, even if there was still the danger of freezing temperatures well into May. She could understand why rural people everywhere celebrated it. Maybe next year she'd hold an equinox potluck on the farm to drum up customers for the summer. One more missed opportunity for this year, which just showed that she was a geek farmer, not a brilliant marketer. Good at code and cucumbers instead of knowing how to make the news of her farm go viral.

Arriving at the area she wanted to till, this one planted with hairy vetch, she engaged the tines and pressed down on the tiller handles so the curved blades dug into the soil as they turned. DJ would advise her to just use a no-till method and plant right into the small leaves and curly tendrils of the nitrogen-fixing vetch. But since he was off on his retreat, she couldn't ask him how she was supposed to get earth loose enough to plant in if she didn't loosen it. At least she was adding organic material to the soil, one of the main purposes of planting winter-hardy crops in the fall.

As she worked, she considered what Megan had said about Judith accusing Greta of going through her trash. Could Judith have meant Greta did it this week? But why?

The tiller encountered a more compacted bit of ground and bucked. Cam focused on pressing the back down again as a counterweight against the heavy engine in the front. She came to the end of the row and pressed down on the handles as she swung the tiller around to go back the way she came. She tried to walk to the left so she didn't compress the newly tilled soil, but it was awkward, and she was almost too tall for the machine, so her back already ached from the effort of bending over and controlling the weight of the machine, the pressure downward, and the forward motion.

She reached the end and turned again. Maybe Megan was wrong. Maybe Judith hadn't said trash. Why would Greta be going through Judith's trash, anyway?

Cam swore and let go of both levers on the handles. The blades stopped rotating and the engine cut out. Greta could have been stealing Judith's vaping supplies to make it look like Judith had killed Wayne. Cam stared at the dark soil she'd brought to the surface, at earthworms wriggling to the surface, at stray vetch tendrils reaching for the sky. She didn't see any of it.

Greta would have framed Judith for only one reason: if Greta had killed Wayne herself.

Chapter 30

Pulling off her gloves, Cam grabbed her phone out of her vest pocket and stabbed Pete's speed dial. "Pick up, pick up, you have to pick up," she whispered.

When his voice mail answered, she blew out a breath and swore again. Maybe he was in a meeting. Maybe he'd call back in a minute. Should she leave a message or wait for him to call? The beep sounded.

"Pete. You have to find Greta. Judith says Greta stole her trash. It must have been the vaping stuff that she planted to frame Judith. Judith has a security cam by her front door. Maybe she has another one—"

Her message was cut off with another beep. Cam stabbed at the phone again, this time disconnecting. Damn it, Greta might have killed her own husband. How could she do such a thing? A shiver rippled through Cam despite the bright, mild, happy-looking day. She'd had enough experience with murder over the last year to know logic didn't always prevail, and that one person's difficult situation became another's intolerable one. But why hadn't Greta simply filed for divorce if she was so unhappy with Wayne and her life with him?

Cam didn't know what to do next. She wasn't about to go over to Greta's and confront her. That was a job for the police, not for an unarmed farmer. *Uh-oh.* What about an armed one? Cam had seen Greta's ammunition for a small gun. She must also own the gun. That must have been what she was hiding in that bag. For sure it wasn't medicine for Pluto. Double reason for Cam to stay right here on her own farm, do her tilling, and listen for the phone. She made sure it was set to both full volume and vibrate before sticking it back in her pocket.

Starting up the tiller, she made her way down the row again, and back up. And back down. And back up one more time, finishing that small field. She let the tiller die to check her phone, just in case she'd missed Pete's call from the noise and vibration of the machine, but there was no indication of a new call. He had to call her back. Or maybe he was already following up on her tip.

Cam had her hand on the starter rope when she realized how thirsty she was. She let it go and trudged to the barn. It was a pain to have to unlock it every time, but a nuisance was better than vandalism or, worse, an assault. She drank down a cup of water and then reversed her actions. She locked up and was turning toward the rear of the property when a rattling car slowed near her driveway. Cam whirled. It wasn't a vehicle or driver she recognized and it sped up again, driving off down the hill. It wouldn't be Tam's rattling car, anyway. He was in custody.

Drawing on her work gloves again, Cam walked back out to the far field where she passed the hens' new location. She slowed at the sight of forty multicolored hens delighting in their new luxury vegetative digs, quite literally.

"Hey, girls, how's the salad? Hey, Mama Dot. You like?"

The Silver Laced Wyandotte ran right up to the fence and chirped at Cam, the chicken's feathers forming a gorgeous scalloped pattern of black edging a silvery white. Cam reached down and through the fence to pet her, but the hen slid out from under Cam's hand, as she always did.

Her phone emitted two short bursts. Her eyes widened. It was the barn camera. She hadn't heard a car drive up, but she could be too far back on the land for that. It could be any one of her volunteers. It could be someone wanting to sign up for the CSA. But she had a bad feeling about this. The phone repeated the beeps, two quick ones in a row.

She grabbed at her pocket but the glove was too bulky. She ripped it off and pulled the phone out with too much force. It dropped to the ground in front of the chicken fencing. Her hand shaking, she retrieved it and pressed the camera icon.

The picture showed Greta standing in front of the barn, banging on the door with one hand. In her other was a gun.

Chapter 31

Cam stared at the screen. Greta must think Cam knew she was the murderer. But why? And now what? All Greta had to do was come around to the back of the barn and she'd see Cam out here. Cam's heart raced as she swiped back to the home screen, hit the phone icon, and stabbed 911. She rushed around to the far side of the coop and crouched as the dispatcher asked her what her name and emergency was.

"Cam Flaherty, Eight Attic Hill Road," she whispered. "Greta Laitinen is here with a gun and she looks angry. Please help me."

"Where is she?"

"She's in front of my barn. I'm out back in the field. I need help." Cam heard keys tapping.

"We'll send help. Please stay on the line. Have you been hurt?"

"Not yet." Cam peeked around the side of the coop. She couldn't see Greta, but now she couldn't see her camera display, either. She squatted again, afraid if she swiped back to the display, she'd end the call.

"Should I run into the woods at the back of my farm?" Cam asked. "They're twenty yards behind me."

"I can't say, ma'am. Do you feel unsafe where you are?"

"Damn right I do."

"Help is on the way, ma'am."

Cam peeked around the side again. She swore as she ducked back behind the coop. Greta moved directly toward her. Cam couldn't see the gun. A siren started up somewhere in the distance. Was it getting closer? She couldn't hide behind the coop forever, and she'd be a sitting target out here, even if she tried to escape over Tully's field. At least in the woods she might be able to hide and then get away, especially if she could find the trail that ran through them.

"She's coming. I'm going into the woods." Cam could barely swallow, her throat was so thick with fear. She slid the phone back into the vest pocket. Staying at a crouch, she dashed for the line of trees. She tried to keep the coop between her and Greta. She could barely run bent over like this.

"I see you," Greta called out in a steely voice.

Cam straightened and ran with all the speed her long legs could muster. Her lungs ached. The woods had never seemed so far away. She'd almost reached the first row of trees when a sharp sting hit the left side of her back. A crack split the air. The pain was sharp, insistent. She kept going, crashing through the underbrush. Ten yards in stood a thick old oak, with hairy poison sumac vines clinging to its trunk. Cam ducked behind it. Her side hurt. She looked down. Blood seeped out through her vest. *Oh, no.* A woozy feeling came over her. She took a deep breath and tried to shake it off. She couldn't afford to faint.

"So now you want to play hide-and-seek?"

The woods made it hard to know where Greta was, but Cam didn't think she'd followed her into the woods. Yet.

Cam had to get deeper into the woods. Farther away from

Greta. Ruffles must have felt this terrified the moment before the fox caught him. She glanced ahead of her. A trail ran through here somewhere. But Cam only saw more underbrush. Saplings and tangled deadfall. She turned and lifted her foot carefully, picking her way toward the next big tree back. She tried to stay in the cover of the one behind her. A branch cracked under her foot right before she reached the wide trunk. She slid behind it.

"You're not going to get out of here alive, you know." Greta's voice now sounded closer.

Where was she and how had she approached so quietly? Cam was sure Greta would be able to hear the thundering sound of her heart. She tried to breathe without making noise. Her wound burned. She felt light headed.

"You've been messing in my business, Cam Flaherty." Greta's words came out strained, like she was barely containing her fury. "Who do you think you are, grilling my daughter about my husband's accounts?"

Cam didn't dare speak. She changed her mind about getting deeper into the trees. It was a stupid idea. Greta could kill her back there and her body would never be found. She crept past a thick stand of saplings to her left and crouched behind them. At least she wore a dark green shirt and dirt-stained jeans with her vest, the most camouflage she could hope for.

"Asking questions about Wayne's past, and about mine, too." Greta now sounded breathless. "Snooping around my barn. Talking to that witch, Judith. She's one person you won't be talking to ever again."

No. She must have killed Judith. Cam couldn't think about that now. She listened for where Greta's voice came from. It seemed like she was directing it farther into the woods, that she thought that's where Cam was heading. *Good.*

"Judith's rotting in hell right next to Wayne now," Greta

spat out. "Nothing made me happier than to end his life. Everybody thought he was such a sweet pushover, but he wasn't. I never got to have my own life."

Cam eyed another big tree closer to the fields, a craggy dead maple. She felt her side and her hand came up smeared with blood. She pressed the back of her left hand against the wound, wincing at the pain, suppressing a cry. She had to get out of here before she lost any more blood. She took a careful step. One more. And one more. She made it to the safety of the big tree and glanced around before hiding. She couldn't see Greta anywhere and now she'd stopped talking. Cam let herself take a breath as a hawk screamed its high scratchy call from the sky. From where she stood it looked about thirty feet to the end of the trees. She could make a dash for it except for the underbrush. It would have to be a careful dash.

She counted silently as she inhaled deeply. One, two, three. Go! She walked as quickly and as quietly as she could. She lifted her feet above the dead branches littering the ground, onto a mound of moss, over an unfurling fern. Thorns grabbed at her pants leg. She ripped her leg loose and took another step. The scent of the freshly turned soil of the field reached her nostrils, called to her. Almost there.

A puff of smoke surrounded a hole in the tree right in front of her and another crack resounded. Chips of bark flew out.

"Freeze!" Greta demanded, the word a cold steel dagger.

Cam froze. *I don't want to die.*

With a quick rustle, Greta strode toward her. She gripped the gun in both hands. A gun pointed at Cam's chest.

"Put that thing down!" Cam held a hand up, barely able to speak. "You don't have to point it at me." Her hands numbed and her breath came fast and shallow.

"Wanna bet? Turn around. Now." Greta's breath smelled sour. The pale skin around her eyes was strained and a tic beat below her right eye. Her hair frizzed loose in all directions above a worn denim jacket. She reached for Cam's shoulder with her right hand, keeping the gun steady with her left.

Cam turned. The movement sliced her with pain. The gun pressed hard and angry between her shoulder blades. It hurt, but not as much as her side. Her insides turned to ice. Would the police get here in time? They had to.

"Walk." Greta prodded Cam with the gun. She gripped Cam's right shoulder with her hand.

"Where are we going?" Cam tried to keep her words from wobbling. Her throat was dry. She could barely swallow.

"You'll find out." She pushed Cam back into the woods.

Cam moved as slowly as she could. "Put the gun down, Greta." Cam croaked as loudly as she could. "You're not going to shoot me, are you?" *Let them hear, let them hear.*

"I'm finally going to do exactly and only what I want to do, after all these years," Greta snarled. "And yeah, it might just include shooting you." The acrid scent of nerves and desperation exuded from her.

No. Cam's legs felt like a baby calf's up on its feet for the first time. "Why did you kill Wayne?" She fervently hoped the phone could pick up their conversation from her pocket. Should she tell Greta she'd called the police? No, Greta would probably kill her on the spot.

"I was going to be a world-class scientist, but he trapped me." Greta wove through the trees like she didn't know what her plan was, trudging mostly parallel to the border with the fields. "He kept money from me, he stuck us in this godforsaken village, he made me deal with chicken shit, of all things." Greta pushed Cam to change direction, heading deeper into the woods again. She fell silent.

"Where are we going?" Cam asked.

"Just shut up and walk."

They trod, cracking branches underfoot, brushing past young maples still bare of leaves and a young pine straining for the canopy.

"What about Megan?" Every time Cam tried to slow the pace, Greta nudged her with the barrel of the gun.

"What about her?" Greta asked.

"What's going to happen to her when you're arrested for murder?"

"For one thing, I'm not going to be arrested. I have a plan. And Megan's fine. She's an adult, she has a job."

The smell of evergreen needles dredged up an incongruous memory of Christmas. What if Cam never saw another Noel? The trees opened up onto the trail. *Damn.* Greta had found the path, narrow though it was. Now she could easily force Cam to walk far into the woods. Cam needed her own plan, and soon.

"Why didn't you get a divorce? Or tell him you needed to work in your own area? Why kill Wayne?" She saw a flash of something on her right. She didn't dare turn her head. *Please let it be rescue.*

"You make it sound so easy. What do you know?" Greta barked. "You're single. You don't have kids. I'll bet you've been handed privilege your whole life."

Cam forced herself to keep moving, but no police appeared. Apparently the flash hadn't been her rescue angels. Cam was on her own. She slowed to a halt and planted her feet. She tensed her leg muscles.

"Hey, I didn't tell you to stop." Greta's hand pushed Cam's back and the pressure from the gun let up.

Cam whipped her head to the left. "Watch that poison ivy," she cried.

Greta looked. Cam spun to the left. She smashed her elbow into Greta's face. The gun fired. Cam's ears rang and another sharp sting hit her right arm. Greta cried out and staggered. She cupped her right hand over her nose, her eyes streaming. Cam grabbed Greta's left forearm and twisted it until she screamed and dropped the gun. Cam put both hands on Greta's chest and pushed, ignoring her own pain.

Greta yelled and fell to the ground, landing on her rear with a thud. She reached for the gun, but Cam kicked her hand away. She bent down to pick up the weapon, never taking her gaze away from Greta, and pointed it at her. Cam's side and arm were on fire, but at least she was alive.

"Don't move." Cam willed her hand to be steady on the handgun's grip, still warm from Greta's grasp. Cam hadn't fired a gun since Albert had taught her as a teenager. But if she had to, she would.

"I wasn't going to hurt you," Greta said thickly. "I was only trying to scare you, get you to quit sticking your nose where it didn't belong. And now you broke mine."

"Right." Cam kept the gun pointed at Greta but made sure she stayed out of reach of Greta's hands and feet. If the police weren't on their way, if that flash had been only sunlight on a puddle or a piece of metal, she had no idea how she was going to get Greta out of here and into the hands of the authorities. She assumed the call to dispatch was still live in her pocket. But if that flash was the police, wouldn't they have appeared by now?

Cam's right arm started to shake and the upper part where she'd been shot ached something fierce. She brought her left hand up to support the gun. Greta pushed up on her elbows and made a quick scoot toward Cam. She nearly grabbed Cam's ankle. Just in time, Cam lashed a kick, landing her work boot toe squarely on Greta's upper arm.

Over Greta's yell of pain, Cam said, "I told you not to move."

Greta grabbed her arm with her other hand and turned her face away. Cam heard a soft rustle. She didn't dare take her eyes off Greta.

With a rush of noise, three officers burst out of the woods onto the trail to Cam's right. Led by Ruth, they had weapons drawn and wore thick vests over their uniform shirts. They arrived at Cam's side in seconds. Greta scrabbled backward with elbows and knees, her eyes wide.

"Don't move," Ruth commanded Greta as she pointed her weapon at her.

Greta stopped. Blood ran in rivulets from her nose and dripped off her chin.

"I already told her that," Cam said, lowering Greta's gun. She tried to laugh but it came out half sob.

Another officer trained his weapon on Greta while a third rolled her over and cuffed her hands behind her back. Ruth reached out a gloved hand and took the weapon from Cam.

"You're hurt," Ruth said to Cam. Worry lines creased her face as she looked at Cam's arm.

"She hurt *me*, you know," Greta said, struggling against the restraints. "She broke my nose. She lured me out here and was going to kill me. I think she killed my husband, too. She's the one with the gun."

Cam turned her back.

The cuffing officer squatted next to Greta. "Keep quiet. We've been listening to you our whole way over here." He read Greta her rights as she glared at Cam with narrowed eyes and flared nostrils. The other office spoke into the mike on his shoulder, saying something about the woods and about gunshot wounds.

"You were great," Ruth said to Cam, holstering her own gun. "Let's get you out of here." She ushered Cam a little ways down the trail until they could see the fields. "I need you to sit down. The paramedics can get to us just fine."

"She shot me in the side, and then my arm got hit when I attacked her. She fell for 'made ya look,' the oldest trick in the book." Cam made the smallest of smiles as she started to sway. Ruth extended her hand and helped Cam sink to sitting on the mowed path between the woods and the last field. The ground was cold but at least it was solid. And safe.

"Hang on, Cammie." Ruth squatted next to her. "Medical is on its way." A siren confirmed her words as it keened ever louder.

"You could have stepped in a minute or two earlier." Cam's words came out so slowly it was like talking underwater.

"Believe me, we got here as soon as we could."

Two EMTs carrying bags appeared at the opening to the fields. Ruth stood and waved them toward Cam. "She's been shot," Ruth called.

They hurried toward Cam. "Ma'am, can you tell us what happened?"

"I got shot in a couple of places." Cam glanced up at a concerned-looking EMT. "I just need to rest a little." Drawing her knees up, she folded her arms on them. Blood dripped from her upper arm onto her leg. She lowered her head, closing her eyes.

And then everything went black.

Chapter 32

Cam opened her eyes. To her right, sunlight filtered into the room through half-closed blinds. She sniffed a sweet smell, then spied a bowl of blooming narcissus on the windowsill. Next to which sat Pete, engrossed in his phone.

She was in a hospital room. The sheets and blankets were white. The wall across from her was fake wood paneling and the other walls were painted a pale green. A tray on a stand next to the bed held a plastic cup, a pink plastic pitcher, and a matching basin. Her right arm hung in a sling over a blue-print plainly styled nightgown. The memory of the attack flooded over her. Greta, a murderer of her own husband. And of Judith, and almost of Cam, herself.

When she shifted in bed, a sharp pain stabbed her side, making her moan. Pete looked up. He strode around the bed and picked up her left hand.

"Oh, Cam," he said. His eyes filled and he blinked hard.

"Hey, I'm alive, aren't I?"

He nodded, smiling.

"But my side and my arm hurt like hell."

"You took a round, but it really only scraped through the top layer of flesh. A slightly different angle and it would have nicked a rib, or worse. Same for your arm. You're going to be fine."

"Good," she said slowly. She stared at the blanket on her lap. She had rescued herself. She could still feel the gun poking her in the back. She remembered her desperation to stay out of the deep woods. Greta saying she'd killed Wayne and shot Judith. And . . .

Her stomach roiled. "Oh, no. Give me that." Cam clapped one hand over her mouth as she pointed at the pink kidney-shaped basin next to the pitcher.

Pete handed it to her. Cam bent over it, despite the pain, and retched up the remnants of her long-ago lunch, her heaves making the injury in her side burn.

Pete stroked her hair off her forehead and murmured, "It's okay. You're going to be all right." When she was done, he took the basin to the bathroom and came back with a damp washcloth.

She wiped her eyes and mouth, and gazed at him. "I'm sorry. That was gross."

"You have nothing to be sorry about. You were tough and brave today, and you overcame a murderer." He took the washcloth and tossed it into the bathroom, then poured her a little water before taking her hand again.

"Are they giving me pain meds?"

"I imagine so, but we can ask the nurse."

"Those things never agree with me," Cam said after she sipped the water, grateful that her stomach now felt settled again. "Any idea why I'm wearing this sling if the shot only nicked my arm?"

"I'd say it's to immobilize it so you don't irritate the wound as it heals. But you can ask the nurse when he comes back in."

"Sit down, will you? I still have questions."

Pete obliged, hiking up a hip to perch on the edge of the bed facing her. "Hit me."

"You got my message about Judith's trash?"

"I did. I tried to call you back but you never picked up. It must have been when you were on with dispatch. Anyway, Judith had called us, too. She found a little wand under her trash barrel. Like a miniature magic wand."

"I've seen that." Cam narrowed her eyes. "It was on Greta's key chain. You know what a big Harry Potter buff she was."

"Yes. And Judith knew it wasn't her daughter's."

"Right, she'd said her daughter hated Harry Potter," Cam said.

"Then Judith went and checked her security camera footage. You were right. Greta had stolen Judith's nicotine canisters and planted them near Wayne and on the property. We knew Greta had made Wayne's breakfast. Looks like she poisoned it, too." He blew out a breath. "Our cyber-crimes guy found something else. Wayne never invited Judith over for breakfast. Greta used his account to send the e-mail, but she sent it from the library's computer when she was logged in as herself."

"To make it look like Judith could have poisoned his breakfast."

Pete nodded. "If she'd sent it from their house, we wouldn't have known. I don't know if you've heard that Greta shot Judith?"

"She implied that she killed Judith. Is she—"

"Judith will live," Pete said. "Greta only wounded her, as it turns out, but Judith was smart enough to lie still and make Greta think she'd succeeded with another murder. I was over there when you called. Judith's only mistake was to go to the Laitinens' this morning and confront Greta about the theft."

"Megan told me about that." Cam stroked the back of Pete's

hand. "You know, I'm glad it wasn't Paul. He's a single dad of three little boys. Can you imagine?"

"People driven to murder are all types. You know that by now."

"I guess. But I'm glad he wasn't the one. And I never did think Katie could have killed anybody."

"You were right about that," Pete agreed.

"Judith, maybe. But it seemed kind of extreme for somebody like her, with all her money." Cam pushed down with her left hand to shift position. "Ow." She squeezed her eyes shut at the sudden stab in her side. When she opened them, Pete was looking at her with his own eyes full of pain.

"Hey," Cam said. "I'm going to be all right. You said so, remember?"

"I know. And you will." He smiled. "I hate to see you hurting."

"Now you know how I felt when you got your own arm shot up not that long ago."

"Fair trade." He gazed at her. "You know, you were amazing today. Speaking up for the dispatcher even as Greta had you at gunpoint. And then disabling an armed murderer. Where'd you learn that elbow jab?"

She laughed. "Just made it up. I'm taller than Greta, and I'm pretty strong from all the farm work. It was the only tool I had at hand. But I also used to read a lot of female superhero comic books. They're always elbowing somebody or other in the face. Or worse."

"It was very effective. I think from now on your middle name is Courage."

"Nah." She batted down the suggestion with her good hand. "What else was I going to do? I was just glad Ruth and the others showed up when they did."

"Do I hear my name?" Ruth peeked in around the door. "Permission to enter?"

Cam smiled at her. "Granted."

Ruth walked in holding a huge bunch of yellow tulips in one hand and a vase in the other. She went around the other side of Pete and bent down to give Cam a kiss on the cheek. Pete glanced at her.

"No, you don't get one, too, Detective." Ruth lifted her eyebrows but her eyes were smiling. She wore black jeans with a red sweater instead of her uniform.

He laughed. "That actually wasn't my primary concern, Officer Dodge."

Ruth focused on Cam. "I'm sorry we didn't get there sooner. Based on what you very intelligently let the dispatcher hear, we had to detour around to the road behind your neighbor's place and come in through there so Greta wouldn't see our vehicle. We knew we couldn't charge in from the direction of the barn or you might have been dead before we got there. Luckily the neighbor has an access way to the other road or it would have taken us a lot longer."

"It all worked out," Cam said. "Thanks for the flowers."

"Thought they might brighten things up."

Cam fell silent for a moment, her gaze on the foot of the bed. She couldn't shake the images of the past week that circled in her brain. The bracelet and the bone from that poor Irish girl in her compost. Greta pretending to grieve when all along she was the one who had killed Wayne. Paul talking about the accident.

"Earth to Cam?" Pete said.

"I was thinking about Paul. Have you talked with him? Was he really blackmailing Wayne all this time?"

"He confessed that he was. He's going to be charged," Pete said. "He could have blackmailed Catriona, too. Or she him, but that never happened. He targeted straight arrow Wayne."

"And he's going to owe Megan and her brother a lot of money," Ruth added.

"Poor Megan. Now she's lost both parents." Cam turned her mouth down. "At least she has those nice monks at the monastery to comfort her."

The phone on the bedside table rang and Pete picked it up. "Cam Flaherty's room." He listened, smiling, then handed it to Cam, extending the receiver attached to the base by a curly cord. "For you."

"Hello?" she said.

"Cammie, I heard you're going to get the medal of honor or something. Listen, my dear, I am so proud of you, and grateful you put away that killer."

"Aw, Uncle Albert. Thank you for calling. I really had no choice."

"Well, next time try to avoid the situation in the first place, would you? My heart doesn't need any more excitement."

"I promise."

"I love you, honey."

Cam tried to say, "I love you, too," but choked up on the last word. She handed the receiver back to Pete and gazed from him to Ruth and back. "How'd I get so lucky? To have both of you, and Albert, too?"

Pete stroked her hand. "We're the lucky ones."

Ruth cleared her throat and headed into the bathroom, emerging with the vase full of water.

"It's pretty much your own doing, Cam," Ruth said, arranging the flowers. She looked at Cam. "You may be a geek, but you're pretty good company. Right, Detective?"

"She is, at that. A bit too interested in investigations, though." He softened the comment with a smile. "We might have to hire her on as a consultant."

"As if." Cam snorted quietly. "So do I assume you still have your job?"

"As a matter of fact, I do. We'll be lucky if Judith doesn't sue our asses off for false accusations. But if she does, it'll be Ivan's head that will roll, not mine."

Cam cocked her head at the sound of a different ring tone. "That's my cell. But where is it?"

Pete opened the drawer in the bedside table and drew out Cam's cell phone, handing it to her. Holding it in her slinged hand, she didn't recognize the number but connected, anyway, and then managed to shift the phone to her free hand.

"Hello?"

"Cameron, honey."

"Dad?" Her eyes widened. She never heard from her parents. Like, ever.

"The one and only. Hey, thought we'd come for a visit. After the semester's out, middle of May or so? Wanted to check out that farm of yours, see Albert, et cetera."

"Um, all right." Her father was the only person she'd ever met who actually said, "et cetera," as if he were reading an academic paper.

"You sound great, honey. Okay, Mom sends love. Talk to you closer to the time. Bye, now."

The call disconnected. Cam swallowed.

"Your father?" Pete asked.

She nodded slowly. "They're coming to visit in May. And he didn't even ask how I was." She rolled her eyes. "Some things never change."

RECIPES

Irish Beef Stew with Stout

Makes 8 servings. Use as many local organic ingredients as possible.

Ingredients
- 2 tablespoons olive oil
- 3 tablespoons all-purpose flour
- 2 pounds beef chuck, cut into 1½-inch cubes
- 1 pound carrots, peeled and cut into 1-inch chunks
- 6 large potatoes, peeled and cut into large chunks
- 1 white onion, cut into large chunks
- 2 cloves garlic, minced
- 2 cups beef broth
- 1 (6-ounce) can tomato paste
- 1 tablespoon rosemary
- Black pepper
- Hot sauce
- 1 12-fluid-ounce bottle imperial stout beer
- ½ cup cold water
- 3 tablespoons cornstarch

Directions

Heat the oil in a large skillet over medium heat. Toss beef cubes with flour to coat, then fry in the hot oil until browned. Place the carrots, potatoes, onion, and garlic in a Dutch oven or large pot. Place the meat on top of the vegetables. Mix together the beef broth, tomato paste, rosemary, and a dash of hot sauce. Pour the broth mixture and the beer over the other ingredients in the pot.

Cover and cook until tender. During the last hour before serving, dissolve the cornstarch in cold water and then stir into the broth. Season with salt and pepper to taste. Simmer on high for a few minutes to thicken.

Alexandra's Carrot Muffins

Preheat oven to 400 degrees F. Makes one dozen.
Use as many locally produced ingredients as possible.

Ingredients
2 eggs
¼ cup honey
½ cup safflower or canola oil
¼ cup buttermilk
1 teaspoon vanilla
1½ cups whole wheat flour
1½ teaspoon baking powder
½ teaspoon baking soda
½ teaspoon salt
1 teaspoon cinnamon
½ teaspoon nutmeg
1½ cups grated carrots (about four medium)
½ cup chopped walnuts (may omit)

Directions
Beat eggs lightly, and then mix in honey, oil, buttermilk, and vanilla. In a large measuring cup, combine flour, baking powder and baking soda, salt, and spices. Add dry ingredients, carrots, and nuts to the egg mixture, and mix lightly with a fork until just combined.

Bake in greased muffin pan for 20 to 25 minutes or until golden brown on top.

Lamb Ragout

(Cam recreated the dish she tasted at
her dinner out with Pete)

Serves four. Make with as many local organic ingredients as
possible.

Ingredients
2 tablespoons olive oil
1½ to 2 pounds lamb stew meat (lamb shoulder), cubed
Salt and pepper
1 carrot, finely chopped
1 rib celery and leafy tops, finely chopped
1 onion, finely chopped
1 bulb roasted garlic
½ teaspoon or less dried chili flakes
1 teaspoon thyme, finely chopped
1 sprig rosemary, finely chopped
5 to 6 sage leaves, thinly sliced
1 cup white wine
2 cups lamb or chicken stock
3½ cups roasted tomato sauce or 1 28-ounce can San
    Marzano tomatoes and juice, crushed by hand
1 3- to 4-inch curl orange or lemon rind
¼ cup cilantro (or flat-leaf parsley), finely chopped

Directions

Heat a Dutch oven over medium-high to high heat with olive oil. Pat the meat dry and brown in small batches; season with salt and pepper. Remove from pot and reserve. Lower the heat to medium. To the drippings (add more oil if the meat was lean), add carrot, celery, onion, garlic, chili, thyme, rosemary, and sage. Season with salt and pepper. Cook to soften, 5 to 7 minutes, partially covered. Add white wine and reduce by half. Add stock and lamb, scrape down the sides with a rubber spatula, and cover the pan. Bake in 300 degree F oven for 1 to 1½ hours, until tender.

Shred the meat with tines of fork. Add tomatoes, cilantro, and citrus rind and partially cover. Bake another 1½ to 2 hours. Remove citrus rind.

Serve over baby roasted potatoes or rotini.

11